"I don't plan to marry for passion or love..."

Amelia said. "I plan to marry for companionship."

"Companionship?" George asked, his expression blank. "You don't want to be in love with your husband?"

"If our interests are compatible, I believe that love will follow. Eventually."

"You're talking about a business deal, not a marriage."

"That's what marriage is—a business deal."

"What about sex?"

"Don't be crass," she said with a lift of her debutante chin that made George grin. "If we truly respect each other and admire each other's intellect, I'm certain that the sex will be satisfactory."

He snorted in disbelief and leaned into the seat. "I don't know about you, Farrow, but I don't want my sex to be just 'satisfactory.' I like it sweaty and hard and loud. So good it makes your eyes roll to the back of your head."

He couldn't prevent his voice from lowering to a husky whisper as he asked, "Have you ever had that kind of sex, Amelia?"

Praise for Tamara Sneed and her novels

"Flowing smoothly from chapter to chapter, there are no lulls in Ms. Sneed's latest. The characters interact naturally and the use of humor is a huge bonus! Sean and Logan refer to themselves as Cinderella and Prince Charming; and I loved 'their' version! An excellent story!"

—Romantic Times on *When I Fall in Love*

"AWESOME is the only word needed to describe *A Royal Vow*! This charming, romantic story is every little girl's dream come true . . . to fall in love with a handsome prince and live happily ever after. This story even has an evil 'frog' prince and the mad palace guard to make things more interesting."

—Romantic Times on *A Royal Vow*

You've Got a Hold On Me

TAMARA SNEED

St. Martin's Paperbacks

YOU'VE GOT A HOLD ON ME

Copyright © 2004 by Tamara Sneed.

Excerpt from *All the Man I Need* copyright © 2004 by Tamara Sneed.

ISBN: 0-312-98729-3

Printed in the United States of America

St. Martin's Paperbacks edition / February 2004

St. Martin's Paperbacks are published by St. Martin's Press, 175 Fifth Avenue, New York, NY 10010.

10 9 8 7 6 5 4 3 2

To my mother, Pat, and my sister, Alyson—
my two biggest supporters before I learned how to write

Chapter 1

"I object, Your Honor!" Amelia Farrow passionately announced. She hadn't expected the judge's chambers to become so silent at her objection, but all activity in the room came to an abrupt stop as Judge Stants, the court reporter, and Amelia's opposing counsel, George Gibson, all stared at her.

Judge Stants glanced around chambers as if he had missed something incredibly important, then he carefully asked Amelia, "On what grounds?"

"I haven't said anything yet," George reminded the judge, then sent a pointed look in Amelia's direction.

She sent George one of her most sincere smiles, then apologetically said, "I object to what you're about to say."

From Judge Stants's sour expression, Amelia Farrow knew that he wasn't amused by her statement. No one in the judge's chambers made a sound except for the court reporter, who suspiciously coughed while her lips twitched with a hint of laughter, in the corner of the room. As the silence weighed in the room, Amelia vowed that she would not apologize. Her statement was on the record, it was unprofessional, and there was no doubt that her father would hear about it. The idea of being reprimanded by the most feared federal circuit court judge in Los Angeles, who happened to be her father, should have been enough of a reason for her to plead for the withdrawal of the statement. But she held her ground.

Amelia refused to even glance at the tall man standing next to her in front of the judge's desk. She had been looking at him for the past four days in the courtroom and dealing with his snide glances and abrasive questions, not to mention the borderline inappropriate looks he directed at the women jurors, who all flushed or gave their own looks in return. Besides, she had a feeling that if she did look at him, she would find him laughing. Whenever she thought she had finally done something to wipe that insufferable smirk off Gibson's face, she would find him smiling even wider.

"You are out of line, Ms. Farrow," Judge Stants announced, with no hint of censure in his voice. He just appeared tired.

"Your Honor—"

"Deirdre, take us off the record," the judge ordered. The court reporter immediately stopped typing. Amelia tried to speak, but the judge once more interrupted her. "Frankly, Ms. Farrow, I don't want to hear one word that you have to say."

George Gibson sent the judge one of his dazzling smiles, then tried to speak. "Your Honor—"

Judge Stants cut off George. "I don't want to hear from you, either. Over the last four days—actually, the last year, since I've had the displeasure of presiding over cases with you two as counsel—I've dealt with more than I want to hear from either one of you. You have turned this court into a mockery."

"Your Honor, I have not done anything that could be construed as an insult to this court," Amelia protested, even as her face warmed with embarrassment and shame. She worked hard to ensure her reputation. She didn't want Judge Stants to feel she was an incompetent attorney or, worse, an immature one.

"You've toed the line, Ms. Farrow. Too often. I expect that from Mr. Gibson." The judge actually paused to give George a look that would have made an average man hang his head in shame but only made George grin. Judge Stants shook his head in disgust at George's reaction, then turned once more to Amelia. "I expect more from an assistant district attorney. You represent the people of California in this courtroom. You are their eyes, their ears, their only way to achieve justice. You also have the responsibility to make certain that the defendants receive a fair shot from the criminal justice system. Normally, you do a wonderful job. I would point to you if I were District Attorney Grayson as a shining example of an ADA. But, whenever you come against Mr. Gibson in court, you sink to his level."

Amelia averted her eyes. A small part of her knew that the judge was right, and she felt the guilt that he obviously wanted her to feel. She was supposed to play fair. Not just because she was an ADA, but because she was a Farrow and that carried certain responsibilities in Los Angeles. Judges expected certain behavior from her, not to mention impeccable work, because she was a Farrow.

And she delivered, no matter how late she had to work the night before or how many times she had to turn her cheek to prove she was "better" than the antics opposing counsel threw at her. She was accustomed to the expectations and to meeting them. She had been doing it her whole life. But not where George Gibson was concerned. Where he was concerned all bets were off.

She couldn't place her finger on the exact moment when George Gibson became her Public Enemy Number One. He didn't treat her with any less respect than he treated any other prosecutor from the DA's office. He didn't ignore her any more than he ignored any other prosecutor from the DA's office. And maybe a small part of her admitted that was the problem. She was often ignored—before people recognized her last name and what that meant—but she didn't like being ignored by a man who haunted her dreams. Or more like her nightmares, because George Gibson was certainly not her type. She had never even thought she had a type until she ran across George Gibson.

He was arrogant, sarcastic, rude, and . . . and loyal to his clients—almost to his own detriment. He was also the most intelligent defense attorney she argued against . . . and George Gibson was just plain *fine*. More than attractive, he could have posed for his own swimsuit calendar and sold it in the lobby of the courthouse. His lean figure easily stretched over six feet, with brown skin the color of warm Caribbean sand flowing over the muscles emphasized even in the modest suits he wore. His lips were plump and always curled either in a seductive smile that drove women wild or a teasing smirk that drove women wild. His chocolate brown almond-shaped eyes had the ability to mock Amelia one minute, then turn sympathetic and warm for a client on the stand the next. The black curls on his head were a tad too long to be respectable for a courtroom and silky enough to remind Amelia of a baby's head.

Regardless of his looks and the fact that every woman in the courthouse and in her office would have paid for him to smile at her, Amelia saw his looks as only another aspect about him that irritated her. Besides, she told herself that she would never date a man who wore a wrinkled suit and shoes with rubber soles to court. Shoes with rubber soles. Her father would have banned George from his courtroom. And beside the fashion problems, George was a defense attorney. The Farrow family would have disowned her for even thinking of dating him.

Amelia also constantly reminded herself that she was twenty-nine years old. Pretty faces did nothing for her anymore. She had spent her entire life being tricked by pretty faces who only wanted her for her money. She, at least, could admit that George knew who she was, what she represented, and didn't care. He still thought she was a worthless prosecutor. He was scared of no attorney, no judge, no defendant. When she wasn't annoyed by George's complete lack of concern for social dictates inside and outside the courtroom, she probably admired him. Maybe that explained why she was attracted to him. That and because he had a voice that could melt ice cream in the Arctic and the sexiest smile she had ever seen on a man.

When Amelia realized, to her horror, that she had been openly staring at George, she instantly turned to Judge Stants and tried to apologize for her statement once more. "Your Honor—"

"As you both are well aware, I feel that courtroom decorum has absolutely disappeared."

Amelia barely resisted rolling her eyes in exasperation, although she noticed that George openly glanced at his watch. Judge Stants's view on the lack of courtroom decorum and civility was well known throughout Los Angeles County. When he wasn't lecturing the attorneys in his courtroom, he was holding court at cocktail parties and boring people at Bar dinners.

"Your Honor, I mean no disrespect, but—"

Judge Stants interrupted George, saying simply, "I've come to a decision. You two have this weekend to hammer out a deal in the O'Connor case."

"Your Honor, that's impossible!" George croaked, the smile for once disappearing from his face. "My client has refused to even consider serving one day in jail and Ms. Farrow wants to bury him under the jailhouse."

"That is not true," Amelia protested, feeling like she was back in elementary school standing in front of the principal when Billy Collins blamed her for throwing the cherry bomb during assembly. She would never have done anything like that, although she had been tempted.

The judge ignored both of their protests and calmly continued. "Daniel O'Connor is a first-time offender who arguably was provoked into the attack on the victim. I believe the only reason this matter came to trial is because of counsels' mutual personal animosity toward each other. If I look up from the bench Monday morning and see either one of you, I will not be happy. You don't want to see me not happy."

"You can't force us to settle. Such course of action

plainly violates my client's constitutional rights," George said.

"I'm not forcing you two to settle. I'm just stating that if I see *People versus O'Connor* on my trial calendar Monday morning, if either of you breathes wrong, I'll find a way to hold you in contempt. Do you both understand? Don't speak; just nod."

Amelia gave a curt nod. She noticed from the corner of her eye that George stuffed his hands into his pants pockets and returned the judge's expectant gaze.

"Is that all, Your Honor?" Amelia asked through clenched teeth, feeling the humiliation and anger flush her walnut brown skin.

In her four years of practicing law, she had never been reprimanded by a judge. Not in the courtroom or in chambers. She didn't know whether to be angry or embarrassed. She settled on anger. Directed at George Gibson. If he hadn't baited her in the courtroom by winking at her when his back was to the jury and the judge, she never would have "accidentally" tripped him by dropping a book in his path when he returned from the lectern to his seat at the defense table.

Judge Stants nodded, then stared down at the papers in front of him, effectively dismissing Amelia and George. She grabbed her briefcase out of the chair and hurried out of his chambers as quickly as she could in a skirt and high heels. Unfortunately, that meant George Gibson easily could match her stride. The two emerged from the judge's chambers directly into the now empty courtroom, where thirty minutes ago the judge had ordered the two to follow him into his chambers in front of the jurors and the court spectators as if they were children sent to the principal's office.

"We should report him to the Bar," Amelia said to George, although she didn't care if he responded. Her anger increased as she thought of the arrogant expression in Stants's eyes. "He can't control our case. He can't run roughshod over O'Connor's rights, over the prosecutor's office. I had heard that Judge Stants was having personal problems, but I never thought that he would allow it to affect his work like this. This is absolutely preposterous—"

"Maybe Stants has a point," George said casually.

Amelia stopped in her tracks in the middle of the now empty, dimly lit courtroom to glare at George. He took another three steps before he realized that she had stopped; then he turned to her.

He shrugged under her gaze and then had the nerve to smile. She ignored the rush of heat that ran throughout her body and fought the urge to smile back at him. There was something about George's grin that made her want to see if there was anything more to him than arrogance and a dislike for her office.

"We should have settled this case weeks ago," George continued. "Maybe we've allowed *our* personal feelings to affect our work."

She coughed in disbelief, then straightened her headband, mostly to avoid his gaze. She composed her rampaging emotions, then met his expectant gaze again.

"I have no personal feelings toward you," she said clearly and firmly.

"Right," he said, nodding, but openly giving her a look of disbelief.

Instead of attempting to convince him and herself that there was nothing between them, Amelia ignored him, then stalked across the room toward the exit. She didn't bother to hold the swinging door that separated the public seats from the rest of the court. She heard his grunt as he ran into the still-swinging door behind her, which made her smile even though she knew it was childish.

She continued through the double doors of the court-room and into the empty hallway. It was six o'clock on a Friday evening. The shadows lengthened across the hall, creating an almost romantic effect. She abruptly stopped her strange thoughts. Romantic? What made her think that anything about a courthouse could be romantic? Then she smelled George's soapy scent as he came to a stop next to her at the elevator.

"I have to admit, Farrow, you have some balls. Objecting before your opposing counsel has a chance to say something worth objecting to? Saves everyone a lot of time, doesn't it? You may want to submit that one to the Judicial Council for review. Another great contribution by a Farrow to the law."

She ignored his sarcasm and viciously jabbed the elevator call button. A long moment of silence followed as she felt his eyes boring a hole into her. She kept her eyes trained on the numbers above the elevators doors that told of the nonexistent progress of the elevator cars that remained ten floors below.

"Let's not ruin each other's weekend over this case. I don't want to spend next week arguing with you any more than you want to be arguing with me," George said, actually sounding serious enough for her to be either insulted or hurt. "Give me aggravated assault, probation, and this case is over."

She laughed in disbelief and looked at him. "Your client intentionally ran a Ford truck into the Tanner household. Children could have been inside—"

"Barry Tanner slept with Danny's wife and told everyone at their job. He had adequate provocation."

"And that's perfect justification for you, isn't it?" Amelia snapped, even though she had vowed that she wouldn't allow George to make her lose her temper. Again. Farrows did not lose their tempers, because—as her father always told her—"it just isn't done."

Farrows laughed and talked with their colleagues but never became too close with them. Farrows went to afterwork drinks with their colleagues but never had more than one-half of a drink or stayed for more than an hour. And, most important, Farrows did not express their dislike for people who made it a point to get under their skin as George Gibson was apparently attempting to do with her. Farrows were perfect and Amelia was perfect . . . when she wasn't around George Gibson.

She told herself that it didn't matter, especially since he acted as if spending the weekend around her was a fate worse than death. She forced a smile. She would be nice to George Gibson if it killed her.

"Here's a news flash from the twenty-first century," she said through a tight, forced smile that hurt her jaw. "A woman is not a piece of property. Just because O'Connor's wife slept with someone else does not give O'Connor the right to act like an enraged fool. Did it ever occur to you or him that he's the problem and not

Barry Tanner? If Mrs. O'Connor felt loved in her own home she wouldn't have to . . . Why am I even explaining this to you?"

She once more punched the button. The courthouse elevators were notoriously slow. Since no one should have been in the building, except a few judges working late, Amelia prayed the elevator would not take the usual eternity to reach the tenth floor.

"If I didn't know better, I would think that you're taking this case personally," George said in his usual nothing-upsets-me-because-I'm-so-cool manner that drove Amelia insane.

"Don't be ridiculous, Mr. Gibson," she snapped. "I apply the law equally to every case I prosecute."

"What's the saying? Something about a scorned woman making a man's life hell."

She rolled her eyes in irritation, then stopped herself from making the rude gesture. She smoothed down the front of her suit, then said calmly, "I believe you're referring to *'Hell hath no fury like a woman scorned,'* which has absolutely nothing to do with the conversation at hand."

"Unless you're the woman scorned."

"Now you're insulting me," she said, too amazed by his audacity to be truly angry.

George shrugged. "I call it like I see it."

She grunted in disbelief, then abruptly whirled around and stalked toward the door that led to the courthouse stairwell. She threw open the door and proceeded into the dimly lit metal staircase. She suppressed her groan when she heard his footsteps on the stairwell behind her.

"Are you actually storming out on me?" he asked, sounding amused. "I don't think I've ever had that happen to me."

She ignored his last remark and abruptly turned to face him and said through clenched teeth, "For the record, the complete quote is: *'Hell hath no fury like a woman scorned, but a scorned woman's triumph is heaven indeed.'*"

"Let's lay our cards on the table," George said, obviously planning to ignore her last statement. "We both know the reason you can't settle this case is because Tanner is a second cousin twice removed from the mayor."

Amelia kept her shock off her face. George Gibson's contacts went deeper than she imagined. "I told you once before that I prosecute my cases equally, no matter who the defendant or victim is related to."

George actually grinned before he said, "Don't bullshit a bullshitter."

She suppressed her need to laugh at his statement. "I don't have time for this."

"Big plans?" At her silence, he grinned. "Do you have a date, Farrow?"

She rolled her eyes in indignation, then whirled around and continued down the stairs, the click of her heels on the concrete steps echoing throughout the stairwell.

"Just when things are getting good, you clam up on me," he said, a laugh apparent in his voice. "I would pay money to see Amelia Farrow on a date."

Instead of telling him that he would probably be as bored as she inevitably was, she said, "Another clue that I didn't need as to how absolutely sad your life is."

At his silence, she paused on the step and stared at

him. It once more took him a few steps to realize she had stopped. He abruptly turned, then moved to stand in front of her. Even though he didn't deserve it, she felt slightly guilty, because she didn't treat anyone liked she treated him. Then again, no one treated her like he did.

She reined in her anger, then took a deep breath and tried to be mature. "I apologize, Mr. Gibson. No matter how horrible and rude you are to me, it gives me no right to pass superficial judgments on your life. Even though I'm sure you have a joyless bitterness-filled existence that drives you to represent the people you do, it does not mean that I have the right to insult that existence."

He stared at her for a few seconds before he actually smiled and said, "I wasn't insulted before, but I think I am now."

She sighed in disappointment and tried to think of another way to apologize. Before she could respond, George abruptly grabbed her arm and drew her to him, pressing her back against his chest at the same time that he clamped his hand over her mouth. She was initially too confused by his sudden movements to be angry, until the smell of soap and fresh laundry began to invade her senses. Electric currents once more flashed through her body and jump-started her heart, forcing her to struggle against his iron hold. She had never thought of George as muscular until she felt him press his body up against hers. She wondered if there was an ounce of fat on him. In response, he tightened his arm around her waist and silently shook his head.

Then Amelia heard the voices. There were two men a few floors below arguing. Their quiet voices traveled in the empty, narrow confines of the stairwell. It could have been two men having a conversation, but it wasn't. There was more. There was something that made Amelia's blood turn cold and that made George become as still as a statue.

"You aren't going to do anything . . ." a harsh voice spat out, then abruptly lowered to a whisper that Amelia could not hear.

A different, more nervous voice replied, "You can't. . . . Last month things got out of control . . . too dangerous. . . ."

George's arms moved from her when he realized that she understood the situation. Amelia grabbed his arm for balance and peered over the railing as the voices fell in and out of range.

"I can't see anything," George whispered in her ear, his warm breath fanning her cheek.

One of the voices said, "You've been warned . . . last time . . . sorry."

The nervous voice firmly said, "I want out. This is completely out of control. No one ever said anything to me about killing jurors and bribing judges and cops. Do you know what would happen to me if I was linked to any of this?"

Amelia gasped at the mention of jurors. George sent her a silencing glare as he squeezed her arm. She waved his arm off and concentrated on the two voices.

"You won't be linked to this," the other man calmly assured. "We have people in all the right places. Nothing will ever be linked to you."

"Whether that's true or not, I don't believe it. I'm getting out and if your boss is smart, he'll let me go."

If possible, the man's deep voice grew deadlier. "Are you threatening us?"

The other man sounded close to a heart attack as he breathlessly answered, "I just want out."

"You were always too weak," the other man replied, sounding almost resigned.

George grabbed Amelia's hand and tugged her toward the door, but she shook her head and whispered, "We have to see who it is."

"It's none of our business. Let's just go," George said, shaking his head.

"Bribing judges and killing jurors? As officers of the court, we have a duty—" Amelia was interrupted by a high-pitched sound that echoed throughout the stairwell. She didn't know what the sound meant, but it scared her. She looked at George, and from his expression she suddenly knew what the sound meant. A gun with a silencer attached. Someone was dead. She covered her mouth with her own hand before the scream she barely contained escaped her throat.

George grabbed her arm and pulled her toward the door at the same time that she tried to move down the stairs toward the sound. She glared at George.

"You find the police while I take a quick look. I'll be right behind you," he ordered in a tone that made her back automatically straighten. She blamed it on being a Farrow, but she was not accustomed to receiving orders.

"I'm not going anywhere."

"You can't stay here." He cast a frantic look down the stairs as his whisper carried obviously louder than he meant.

"But you can?" she demanded.

He sighed in agitation and tried to once more forcibly push her toward the door, but she evaded his grip.

He threw up his hands in frustration and appeared on the verge of screaming before he hissed, "We don't have time for these games, Amelia; they could still be down there."

"George—"

Suddenly she heard footsteps on the metal stairs, headed toward them. They froze, staring at each other in horror. In a flurry of abrupt activity, George ripped open the door and grabbed a stunned Amelia around the waist, pulling her once more into the hallway of the courthouse.

With her briefcase slapping one thigh and her purse bouncing against the other, Amelia ran after George toward the closest courtroom door. He pulled the handle and cursed when the door wouldn't budge. He immediately ran to the next courtroom door, pulling her behind him. Amelia glanced over her shoulder toward the stairwell door, expecting any moment to see a monster with a gun headed toward them. She had led a sheltered life. She was the first one to admit it. In her life, guns only existed as facts in a police report she read while preparing for a case. Now she was in danger of being shot if she and George couldn't find some place to hide.

The fourth door George tried opened and the two ran into the dark courtroom just as Amelia saw the door to the stairwell slowly open. She knew that she should have waited to catch a glimpse of the murderer, but a stronger force in her body that she cursed as cowardice made her sprint into the courtroom.

As George frantically scanned the courtroom for a

hiding place, Amelia wordlessly tugged his wrinkled suit sleeve and pointed to the elevated judge's bench. The two ran across the courtroom and scrambled into the cramped opening beneath the high desk. She found herself crushed between one side of the desk and George. She tried to move closer to the desk and control her ragged breathing.

George pulled the chair back into position just as the courtroom door opened with a loud creak. She unconsciously held her breath and hoped that the frantic loud thump of her heart against her chest didn't carry across the courtroom. Instead of attempting to move farther from George, when she heard the deliberate and cautious footsteps in the empty courtroom where no one else should have been, she moved even closer to him.

The footsteps sounded closer and she glanced at George. There was a restless energy in his coiled body. He seemed ready to spring from beneath the desk at any moment. She placed her hands on his arm to keep him in place. He didn't look at her but squeezed her knee in response. She squeezed her eyes shut as a tidal wave of fear washed over her. She couldn't die today. She had on an old pair of underwear that would make her mother cringe in embarrassment.

Amelia heard the tinkling sound of a cellular telephone, sounding like a screeching wild animal in the silence of the abandoned courtroom. For one horrified second she froze, thinking that the ringing telephone belonged to her or George. Then she heard the familiar deep voice from the stairwell answer, "What?"

There was a long pause; then the man said, "I'll be right there."

She heard his rapidly retreating footsteps, then the sound of the courtroom door closing. She released the breath she didn't know she had been holding, then turned and stared straight into George's dark eyes and lost her breath all over again. Her gaze dropped to his mouth. She didn't know what she feared more—the man from the stairs or the dark expression in George's eyes.

Chapter 2

George crouched lower as he listened for a sound that meant the killer was still in the courtroom. He had seen one too many horror movies where the unsuspecting and stupid characters crawled from their hiding spot, thinking the killer was gone, just in time to be slashed or shot or bludgeoned. George didn't have to watch a scary movie to know curious or brave people died. He had discovered that depressing but true fact of life on his own by the time he was twelve years old. George was a black man from Los Angeles' "South Central," as the news dubbed it. He grew up knowing when to run and when to hide. And it didn't surprise him that he now had to do both with Amelia Farrow, since she had that special knack of placing him in uncomfortable positions.

When Amelia's knee brushed against his thigh he suddenly remembered that she was next to him, close to him, and he didn't want to move. He wanted to remain close to her, to smell the sweet scent of her shampoo. It was a strange feeling for him, a strange feeling that was becoming too familiar around Amelia. It was strange because she was not his type, with her perfectly coiffed chin-length hair, tailored suits, and ridiculously matching headbands. She had light brown skin that shone like gold honey under the dim courtroom lights and large brown eyes that could flash with anger, irritation, and compassion in rapid succession. And she was too perfect, too ADA-ish, for him to be attracted to. She probably left notes on the windshields of the cars she tapped in the parking lot. Or, at least, that's what he always told himself whenever he was in the courtroom with her for too long and noticed that her legs were just his type.

Slashers, shooters be damned, George crawled from under the desk and smoothed down his hopelessly wrinkled suit.

Amelia followed and he watched her smooth the wrinkles from her immaculate suit. She missed a spot of dirt on the front of her skirt and he wiped it. At her glare, he instantly stuck his hand into his pants pocket before she bit if off. He quickly walked to the door and slowly and carefully opened it a crack. He stared from one end of the empty hallway to the other, then sighed in relief.

He was just congratulating himself on another near-miss when he heard an electronic beep. Amelia had a cell phone in her hand and her finger was poised to dial. He raced across the room and snatched the phone from her hands.

"What are you doing?" he sputtered.

"Calling the police," she answered, then grabbed for her phone. He moved his hand over his head. She crossed her arms over her chest and glared at him. She was close to five-ten with her usual sensible two-inch heels on. She towered over most people, and he knew it irked her to have to crane her neck to glare up at him.

Her tone was cold as she said, "A man has been shot. We have to call an ambulance and the police. Then I have to contact my supervisors in the DA's office, since there's obvious corruption—"

"Let's take this one step at a time," George said, shaking his head at the whirlwind of activity she instantly had become. "We don't know what happened on the stairs. All we heard was a conversation—"

"We heard a gunshot."

"We heard a noise that sounded like a gunshot. We don't know for certain what it was."

"A man chased us into this room," she said, then took a deep breath. She cleared her voice and firmly continued. "The same man who argued with and then shot someone on the stairs chased us into this room. We have to call the police. They mentioned bribery and murders. We have to tell someone."

"Amelia—"

"What is the problem, George? Are you worried that one of your clients may be involved?"

He didn't find himself speechless very often, but he was when he saw the open accusation painted in her expression. George knew that most of the prosecutors in the DA's office would never be his friends. They thought he and most of the other defense attorneys were bottom feeders—no better than insects on the sidewalk. But he liked to think they at least respected him. Or he had thought that until he started appearing against Amelia. She had a way of looking at him that made him feel like he was only a play lawyer, who shouldn't waste her time.

Instead of becoming angry at her statement, like he wanted to, he shrugged nonchalantly and said, "Maybe."

She shook her head in disgust. He liked to think that he had been insulted by bigger and badder people than Amelia. He didn't care what she thought of him. If she wanted to think that he was a horrible lawyer, then he didn't care. He had never cared.

"Keep the phone," she said, the irritation plain in her expression. "I'll walk to the security office downstairs. You can stay here and wait for your next client that I'll be certain to send to you."

"Wait, Amelia!" he called while rubbing his hand tiredly down his face. She turned and stared at him expectantly. This woman gave him a constant headache—notwithstanding his momentary lapse of sanity when he actually thought he wanted to be near her. "Can we at least check the stairwell first and see if someone was shot or not? For all we know, that sound could have been some new cell phone ring or pager."

"Do you really believe that, George?" she asked doubtfully.

He flashed her a smile, then said, "Unlike the district attorney's office, I only believe in hard facts, not wild hunches or guesses."

"After you, counselor," she said with a dramatic gesture toward the door.

He glared at her for a second, then motioned for her to walk. She sent him an obviously fake smile, then walked toward the door.

There was nothing. No body. No blood. Not even the scent of gunpowder on the stairwell. And, best of all, there was no man with a gun waiting for them. George barely withheld his sigh of relief. He was not a coward, but he wasn't stupid, either. A man with a gun never ranked high on George's list of people to encounter on dark empty stairwells.

"I don't understand," Amelia whispered, shaking her head in amazement. "You heard it; I heard it. Someone was shot here."

"You're jumping to conclusions again. We don't know what happened."

She ignored him as she scanned the stairwell. George could see her mind running in a million directions, and he had a feeling that each one would give him a huge headache. She suddenly snapped her fingers and said, "There are cameras in the main lobby of each floor. Whoever the men were, they entered the stairs only minutes before we did. The camera must have captured their entrance and, hopefully, their exit. We can—"

"Slow down," he muttered irritably. "Can we think about this for a few seconds before we start making accusations?"

"You're counseling me to go slow?" She actually looked disappointed in him as she said, "If there is the hint of corruption in the judicial system, don't you think that it's our duty to do everything possible to expose it?"

"You're joking, right?" he asked blankly, amazed that such truth-justice-and-the-American-way would come out of her mouth. When he was a kid, he thought people like her only existed on television.

Her chin lifted as it always did when she felt she and all that was good and right in the world had been insulted. "I would not joke about something this serious. Someone may have been murdered or hurt in our courthouse.

Someone may be buying verdicts in our courthouse. I take that very seriously. You should, too."

He couldn't deal with her accusations and opinions about him. Normally, he wouldn't have cared. Normally, he would have gone with her to the security office, but tonight he was tired. Tired of wanting things he could and would never have—like respect from Amelia Farrow, if he'd ever wanted such a thing.

He purposely tried to sound annoyed as he said, "There is no body, no blood, no sign that there was a murder or struggle on the stairwell. As my old law professor said, 'If it looks like a duck and quacks like a duck, then nine times out of ten, it's a duck.' I'm going home."

She frowned at him, as if she didn't know how to respond; then she demanded, "Why?"

He sighed once more. "Because it's been a long day— a long week—and I'm tired. For the next two days, I want to forget I'm a lawyer, forget the guilty verdicts against my clients, forget my clients who should have gotten guilty verdicts, and forget that there will be more of the same facing me next week. Since I'm the heartless money-grubbing lawyer type, I'm going to go home and forget about all of this for a weekend."

"What?"

He hesitated before he added, "And I have plans tonight."

She looked too shocked to speak for a moment before she repeated dumbly, "You have plans?"

"It is Friday night. I have a date."

"A date?"

"O'Connor has aggravated assault." Confusion crossed

her features as she stared at him. He shrugged. "Since you're repeating everything I say, I thought I'd throw that one in there."

He laughed while she crossed her arms over her chest and just glared at him. He stopped laughing when he realized that she continued to stare at him.

"Everything is a joke to you, isn't it? Fifteen minutes ago, you weren't laughing. You were running for your life. That means nothing to you."

"What do you want from me, Amelia?" he asked while throwing up his hands in surrender. She continued to stare silently at him. He groaned, then relented. "Monday morning I'll go with you to the security office and ask for the videotapes, but it's Friday night. . . . They only come once a week. Give me this weekend. It won't hurt anyone. That's a reasonable deal, right?"

She gave him a look that rightfully should have frozen his innards; then she said coolly, "I hope that a possible murder didn't ruin your evening. Have a good night, George."

"Now you're trying to guilt me into going with you."

He cringed at the false smile that suddenly covered her face. "I'm not trying to make you do anything you don't want to. I shouldn't have attempted to control your actions in the first place. It was rude of me. I can't expect everyone to care about the judicial system as much as I do."

He was surprised and insulted by her obviously rehearsed speech. "I care, Amelia."

"Of course you do," she murmured with a slight nod. "Enjoy your weekend, George."

Without another word, she swung open the nearby

door and walked out the stairwell. He did smell something now. The lingering scent of her soap hung in the air. And he barely stamped out the urge to run after her. Run after Amelia Farrow? He laughed in disbelief, because George Gibson ran for no woman. And George Gibson did not become involved.

He hadn't actually lied to Amelia about the "date." He did have a date . . . with Wayne Phillips, his best friend since he was six years old and entered McPherson Family Home, his first of ten orphanages or foster homes where he spent the majority of his childhood and teenage years. Wayne had been the first boy George couldn't beat up, so of course they became instant friends—from first grade until the two were officially adults and no longer wards of the state at eighteen years old. The friendship had lasted through the good, the bad, and the ugly—which George marked as the day that Wayne became a Los Angeles police officer. George had grumbled the whole day even as he took pictures at the police academy graduation and clapped louder than anyone in the auditorium.

Now, thanks to Wayne, he stood in Pool Shark—a dark, small bar in one of the forgotten corners of Echo Park—staring grimly at the pool table and trying not to admit to himself that he was in a no-win situation. He would once more lose a game to the biggest "pool shark" in Los Angeles County. One of the LAPD's finest, Wayne Phillips. He should have known. Wayne had been beating him at pool since they were children, when the pool sticks had been taller than they were.

Even after a few beers and watching Wayne's pathetic

lines get shot down by various women, George still was in a bad mood. He couldn't pinpoint exactly why he was in such a funk. Sure, he had possibly heard a murder earlier that evening, but there was more.

Then the truth had hit him around the third beer. George felt guilty. It was a new emotion for him. It had taken him three beers and four hours to recognize it. All because of Amelia and her opinion of him. He had never allowed anyone's negative opinion of him to affect him before, but for some reason what she thought did matter. Too much. And he should have stayed at the courthouse with her, regardless of the weak evidence and faulty story.

And even after telling himself that there was nothing he could ever do to win her approval, including corroborating her story with the security office, George still couldn't get the picture of Amelia out of his mind. Not her anger or sarcasm but the disappointment he had seen briefly flash across her face when he told her that he wouldn't help her report to security. For a man who never had anyone to disappoint, it was strange to realize that he could do it.

George glanced at his surroundings and blamed Amelia for sending him to this new low. Normally, George would have avoided a place like this with a ten-foot pole. Country music wailed in the background, there were enough pickup trucks in the parking lot outside to tow a small island, and every man in the bar except him probably owned those reflective aviator sunglasses that only cops seemed to buy.

But here he was. On a Friday night, playing pool with Wayne when George should have been at one of the bars in town that did not have a four-to-one male-to-female ratio. Especially when the only women at this bar looked capable of beating his ass with one hand tied behind their backs.

"Staring at the pool table won't change the fact that you're going to lose," Wayne practically sang from his perch on a stool near the table.

George shot him a look, then muttered, "I'm weighing my options."

"Your options are to lose on this shot or the next shot."

George stared at Wayne's smug grin. "Some people should not win."

Wayne laughed. "I heard an interesting story about your girlfriend at the end of my patrol earlier tonight."

"My girlfriend?" George repeated, confused, as he leaned over a potential shot.

He wracked his brain over the numerous women he had told Wayne about over the last six months. George knew that he would never use that label "girlfriend." He never dated a woman long enough to even call her a friend, except for Babette. She had been a lot of fun for those three weeks.

"Amelia Farrow."

George turned to glare at his friend. "That's not funny."

Apparently Wayne thought it was funny, because he laughed and said, "She's not bad, George."

George took his shot, then winced as the ball narrowly missed the pocket. Wayne sent him a smug grin and jumped off the stool. "Step aside and watch a master work."

He sat on his stool and watched Wayne chalk his stick.

George rolled his eyes at the obvious intensity on Wayne's face, then said, "By the way, my qualifications for a woman involve more than 'not bad.'"

"Like what?" Wayne asked blankly, glancing at him.

"Sexy, gorgeous, a great ass—"

Wayne grinned. "Amelia could probably be sexy . . . maybe. And she could be gorgeous . . . maybe. She does have nice legs, probably better than nice, and then there's that mouth. I could think of a few things I'd want her to do with that mouth, besides talk, because then she just ruins the whole picture. And she does have a great—"

For some reason, George became irritated with Wayne's listing of Amelia's assets and impatiently demanded, "What did you hear about Amelia, Wayne? Did she win another Perfect Lawyer of the Year or something equally as nauseating?"

Wayne bent over the pool table and lined up his first shot. It sank like an arrow to the target and he moved to his last two balls. "Word's going around that she finally cracked. One of the guys from the station was in the security office talking to a friend who works there and told me the whole thing. She barged into the office after-hours, forced the night crew to search the stairwell . . . all because she thought that she heard an argument and a gunshot. As if anyone could sneak a gun into that court-house or a dead body out with metal detectors and cameras everywhere."

George silently cursed, then ran a hand over his hair, which badly needed a cut. He had heard the gun on the stairwell. There was no doubt in his mind that's what it was. He had heard the sound every week when he was a child. For a debutante like Amelia, he realized it was probably a shock to hear a live gunshot and not just read about it in the news. And once more George felt that strange twisting in his stomach—guilt.

Wayne continued, oblivious to George's silence. "A gun in the courthouse, murder in the staircase . . . has she lost her mind?"

"It's not impossible, Wayne," George muttered. "Cops make mistakes, too. The only people who apparently don't know that are cops."

Wayne looked up from the pool table and asked, "Are you feeling all right? You've been irritable all night. You're only like that when you're sick."

George cleared his throat to eliminate the somber tone and forced a laugh and said, "Obviously not. I'm defending Farrow."

Wayne hesitated, then asked, "You don't think there's any truth to Amelia's allegations, do you?"

"I don't know. . . ." George's voice trailed off as he felt a strange emotion clog his throat. It almost felt like shame. Amelia had put herself on the line—no doubt bullying and ordering people around like she did in the courtroom—and he couldn't even tell his almost-family what he'd heard. First guilt, then shame. She was already rubbing off on him.

"She ordered all these tests," Wayne continued, sinking his next two shots before chalking again. "She wanted samples taken from the stairwell, security tapes, the whole nine yards. She ordered a full crime scene team to the stairwell. A lot of cops on overtime were not happy with her."

"Have the test results come back yet?"

"By Monday. Although I spoke with one of the guys

in the crime scene department and they all think it's a wild-goose chase. A Farrow throwing around her weight to prove something. Who knows? I do know it'll take her a long time to live this down. A kid pops a balloon in the stairwell and the taxpayers pay thousands of dollars to calm the nerves of a jumpy ADA."

"Amelia is not the jumpy kind."

Wayne once more looked up from the pool table before he asked, "Are you sure you're all right?"

"I'm not her biggest fan, but she's not jumpy. She's very calm. Too cool. A defendant jumped at her from the witness stand during trial. She was still questioning him as the deputies wrestled him to the ground."

Wayne sank the last shot and grinned at George in triumph. George grimaced, then motioned to a waitress circulating nearby for two more beers. Wayne racked the balls for another game.

"I wonder what makes her tick?" Wayne mused.

"Who?" George asked as he jumped off the stool to pull balls out of the pockets of the table.

"Amelia Farrow. She has enough money to never work a day in her life, but she works at the DA's office, where she comes across some of the worst that LA County has to offer. If she wants to practice law, she could be at some big corporate firm making six figures, drinking champagne, and laughing at the little people. Why doesn't she?"

"Rich people guilt," George said with a careless shrug, although he had asked himself that question numerous times over the year and a half since he first walked into the courtroom and saw Amelia standing across from him. He had found himself unable to stop staring at her. She had asked him if he had a problem before she instantly apologized for her "rudeness." He smiled at the memory.

"I think it's more than rich people guilt," Wayne said. "It can't be the people. She seems uncomfortable around most people, unless there's a judge and jury present. I've never seen her with the other ADAs at social events. She always seems separate, apart."

"Maybe she's a crusader, defending everything good and just in the world," George muttered while rolling his eyes.

"Those are good qualities, George," Wayne reminded him with a wry smile.

"If you say so."

Wayne shrugged, then said, "Well, if she's right about this one, you should thank her for pursuing it. It could mean big bucks for you. For once, you could pay a bill on time, maybe a few bills on time."

George's money, or lack thereof, was a sore subject between the two men. George had once made the mistake of telling Wayne about the numerous clients who still owed him money. Wayne had made it his personal duty to collect the money from every client within twenty-four hours—every last cent.

George had felt so guilty about taking money from people who needed it desperately more than he did that he had returned half of it to most of the clients—a fact he never told Wayne. But no matter how apathetic George pretended to feel, he had been hungry and cold for most of his life when he was a child. He would never forget what it felt like, and he would never subject a child to that just because that child's parents couldn't afford to pay his bill.

"How could a murder in the courthouse mean 'big bucks' for me?"

"You're the lawyer. Do I have to spell it out for you?"

"Yeah. Pretend I'm a cop and talk real slow."

Wayne rolled his eyes in response as George grinned. "Amelia said that she heard the supposed victim and murderer talking about corruption—bribery and jury tampering. If there's evidence of jury tampering, or bribery, no one can be certain when and where the bribery started. Every prisoner has an instant appeal—"

"And if his or her conviction is overturned, the state pays attorney fees," George excitedly finished. "I could get some of my clients out of jail or, at least, have their sentences reduced."

"And you'd get paid for your work." George wisely didn't comment. Wayne sighed, then said, "She's your only hope, George. You need the respectability of the Farrow name and her office to make anyone take any charges of corruption seriously. And from what the guys were telling me, Amelia is not going to let this drop. You may actually owe her a favor once this is all resolved."

George kept his doubts to himself that Amelia would continue her crusade if she knew it would benefit him.

"Are you ready to lose again?" Wayne asked, motioning toward the table.

"Sure," he muttered with a shrug. He flubbed the first shot, but he barely noticed Wayne's grin. He once more thought about Amelia staring at him in the stairwell. Guilt, shame, and a strange twinge of lust, all at once. He shook his head in disbelief.

Chapter 3

Amelia stared at the dark ceiling of her bedroom with her arms crossed over her chest and her jaw clenched. It was almost three o'clock in the morning and she could not sleep. She wasn't tired. In fact, her body hummed with energy, like the time she drank two cappuccinos in the span of half an hour. Her mind raced in a million different directions, from old cases to the sounds on the courthouse stairwell. To George.

She abruptly ripped off the covers and stood from the bed, abandoning any notions of sleep. If she couldn't sleep, she could at least continue her research into potential judge corruption and jury tampering. Even though the police and courthouse personnel had not hidden their disbelief that evening when she reported what she'd heard, Amelia was not going to give up. She vowed that by Monday morning she would have a definitive answer when District Attorney Grayson asked her, "Why in the hell did you call a crime scene unit to an empty staircase on a Friday?"

She grabbed her trusty cotton robe thrown across the window seat and stuck her arms into the sleeves, then viciously tied the sash. She partially knew her drive to discover the truth was not merely about the potential victims but also about proving George Gibson wrong. He wanted to dismiss the entire incident because he didn't want to be bothered. She wanted to bother him. She wanted him to look at her and not just see her as opposing counsel who occasionally irritated him. Then she would send him packing. It was her constant fantasy, although she didn't always send him packing. It was silly and immature, but Amelia figured that if good came out of it—getting rid of corrupt judges and wrongful convictions—then the fact that she derived personal satisfaction from it meant nothing.

Proving George wrong had become a major motivator in her life lately, she realized. He was too arrogant for her to allow him to dismiss her that easily. It was one thing for a man to ignore her because of her looks—she was used to that—but she could not allow him to ignore her as a lawyer.

She had met many people who resented her money throughout her life. She was the great-granddaughter of Tyndale Farrow, who had established one of the most prominent and wealthiest black-led law practices in Los Angeles. Two of Tyndale's three children had entered the law and thrived despite the racist obstacles in their way. Amelia's grandfather had become a federal judge, and her father had followed him.

Besides the fact that she was from the DA's office, she had a feeling that her entire background was insulting to George. From her lineage to her Stanford and UCLA

education to her home address. And it bothered her that it
bothered him. She had never apologized for who she was
and she wouldn't start now, but she often wondered if
George would have been friendlier if she were just
Amelia Jones from Los Angeles.

Amelia flipped the hallway light switch as she
turned toward the study. The switch flipped, but no light
chased away the shadows throughout the house. She
frowned and flipped the switch several more times. She
groaned and made a mental note to once more remind
her housekeeper to replace the old lightbulbs when necessary. Amelia sighed and groped her way along the wall
toward the study. She turned the lamp switch on the desk
and again nothing happened.

Frowning, she groaned, then walked down the stairs
and headed for the linen closet where she kept the spare
lightbulbs. Even though George Gibson had nothing to
do with her lights, she cursed him. She had a feeling that
if she thought long and hard enough, she could find a
way to blame George Gibson for most things, no matter
how ungracious it was.

She stopped at the entrance to the living room, surprised at how dark the room was. She noticed that the
curtains were closed, which blocked out even the faint
glow of the moon that had spilled into her upstairs bedroom. She smiled to herself because she couldn't
remember closing them. She was getting old. The big
three-oh was right around the corner, and most of her
friends had husbands or, at least, a man who *could* be a
husband in a weak moment.

A second too late Amelia realized that she was
not alone in the living room. A large, broad-shouldered

figure emerged from the shadows of the room. It seemed like an eternity, but was more like a few seconds as she stared at the black mask that hid his face, and noticed the black gloves on his hands before her mind made the connection that she should run and not simply stand and stare. She opened her mouth to scream at the same time that she tried to turn and run. The man lunged at her.

In a tangle of legs and arms the two crashed to the ground, her arms slamming into the glass coffee table in the middle of the living room. The two bounced onto the hard floor as pieces of glass rained around them. Amelia shook her head and tried to catch the air that had been knocked from her body from the fall. White spots partially blinded her as her body began to sting from pain at the points of contact where her body had slammed into the floor. Before she could regain her thoughts, the large man straddled her body, his weight imprisoning her on the floor. For one fearful moment she thought his hands would reach for the hem of her gown. Then she realized as his gloved hands wrapped around her neck and began to squeeze that it was worse.

He was strangling her. She stared into the dark circles of the black mask where his eyes were camouflaged as she gasped for the air that his hands around her throat would not allow her to breathe. Her head felt like it would explode from the blood caught in the cinch as his grip tightened even more. She tried to scream and when she heard her helpless gasp—the loudest sound she could make—it galvanized her into action. She began to struggle. She tried to kick her legs, but he was too heavy and his weight prevented any movement on her part. She

tried to pry his fingers from around her neck. He only
squeezed tighter.

She was losing consciousness. She would pass out
first and then the man would continue to squeeze until
she died. Tears blurred the shadows in her vision at the
thought that she would die tonight.

It galvanized Amelia into one last attempt to save herself. Her hands groped the floor and one finger brushed
against a large shard of glass. She gripped the piece in her
right hand, feeling it slice into her flesh and blood trickle
down her palm. She raised her arm and plunged the glass
into the visible expanse of brown skin on the man's neck.
Blood squirted onto her face and hands. The man howled
in pain. His grip loosened as he fell onto the floor and
tried to tear the piece of glass out of his neck.

She rolled away from him and onto her knees to draw
air into her deprived lungs as the man sputtered and
hacked on the floor. She tried to rise to her feet, but her
weak knees refused to cooperate. She crawled across the
floor, struggling against the vicious pain in her throat.
Her right hand was practically useless. She grabbed the
edge of the sofa, pulled herself to her feet, and rushed
toward the telephone on the table on the other side. As
the tips of her fingers touched the phone she heard a loud
roar. She turned to see the man swaying on his feet as he
lumbered toward her like a cheap small-screen version of
the *Terminator*.

She tried to scream, but no sound came out of her
abused throat. Adrenaline and a sudden anger that she
hadn't known she could possess surged through her body.
She grabbed the solid, wide lamp on the table near the
telephone and swung. The lamp shattered in her hands as

it connected with the man's head. He staggered again, then collapsed to the floor in an unmoving heap as more of his blood flowed across her floor. She grabbed the telephone and punched out 911.

"What's your emergency?" came the operator's droning voice.

"Help," Amelia gasped, her voice merely a hoarse whisper.

"Hello." The operator sounded annoyed. "Is anyone there?"

The man on the floor groaned and slowly shook his head. Amelia frantically tried to speak into the telephone again, but no sound came out. Her throat was swollen shut.

She clutched the phone in her uninjured hand, then half-stumbled and half-ran toward the kitchen while the operator repeated, "Hello." Amelia scanned the dark kitchen for any signs of a way to communicate with the operator. She stared at the cabinet filled with wineglasses and ran toward the cabinet and threw it open. She grabbed several glasses and threw them on the ground, causing them to splatter in numerous pieces on the floor.

"Hello." The operator sounded confused. The operator spoke to someone else, saying, "I think someone's on the line. Should I send a unit out?"

The operator said into the telephone, "The police will be there in a few minutes. Hang in there. I can hear you breathing. I'll stay on the line until the police arrive."

Amelia threw more glasses on the ground as answer, and tears of relief rolled down her cheeks. She heard another crash from the living room and fear momentarily paralyzed her. She ran out the wide-open kitchen door and into the damp night air, toward the sound of the police sirens in the distance.

"And that's all you can tell us about the attacker?" Detective Boris Thorndyke asked suspiciously as he stood over Amelia's hospital bed several hours later. Behind him stood the uniformed police officer whom Amelia had waved down in the street.

Amelia nodded, then glanced at her father, who stood on the other side of her bed. He looked irritated. That was nothing new. Kenneth Farrow was always irritated, whether with his only daughter or one of his employees or his tailor. Amelia could count on one hand the number of times she had seen her father smile, and none of those smiles had been directed at her. She had thought she was too old to care about her father's opinion of her, but when he walked into the hospital room and he looked more irritated than worried that his daughter had been attacked, Amelia's disappointment had surprised her.

"My daughter has already answered all of your questions to the best of her ability," Kenneth said, his deep voice booming through the room. "She's had a trying night. It's time for her to rest."

"We're just trying to get all of the facts while they're fresh in her head, sir," the detective answered with a wavering smile.

Amelia rolled her eyes, because obviously Thorndyke had heard of her father. Judge Farrow was feared and probably despised by most cops and lawyers in Los

Angeles County. Amelia almost felt sorry for Thorndyke. Kenneth was an intimidating man. He stood close to six-four, had the same muscular build as in his days as a competitive tennis player, and had the same golden-brown skin and brown eyes as Amelia.

"Amie can barely speak. What good is grilling her tonight going to do?" Alice Farrow chimed in from a chair in the corner of the room.

Instead of looking afraid, the detective directed a worshipful gaze at Alice. At fifty-four years old, Alice Farrow still looked as beautiful and sensual as when she became the first black woman to grace the covers of major fashion magazines during the 1960s. Her beauty caused stares and whispers wherever she went, and the most traitorous part to Amelia was that her mother enjoyed the attention.

Her chocolate brown skin still shone as it did in her thirty-year-old pictures that were framed throughout the family mansion in Bel Air. Her ear-length raven black hair was no longer the trademark waist length from her model days but now fell to her ears in loose curls. Amelia lay in a hospital bed with bruises from a man's hands around her neck, she could barely speak, but Alice had been the one the doctor expressed concern for when he first walked into the room. Amelia had also noticed that while the doctor ran to Alice, Kenneth had glared at her and moved farther across the room. Amelia didn't think that her father and mother could be farther apart without leaving the room.

Amelia had always wondered why her parents—who had probably spoken less than ten nice words to each other in the last five years—didn't divorce. She finally discovered the reason when she went to law school: California's community property laws. Upon divorce, each would have been entitled to one-half of their combined property, and Amelia knew that each of her parents would rather be miserable with the other than allow him or her to have half of anything and lead a perfectly happy life. So Alice occupied the Beverly Hills mansion and Kenneth took the Bel Air mansion and the two never saw each other except when their only daughter unfortunately brought them together.

"You're right, Mrs. Farrow," the detective conceded. "When Ms. Farrow feels better, tell her to come to the station. We'll continue her questioning there."

"What about that man?" Amelia croaked, her voice barely able to rise above a whisper.

"He was gone by the time we got there," Detective Thorndyke answered, looking at Kenneth and Alice.

"How difficult can it be to find a man with a piece of glass sticking out of his neck?" Kenneth snapped, the irritation evident on his face.

"We believe the suspect had a car parked in the area," Thorndyke answered, the nerves apparent in his voice.

"Sounds like a guess to me. I hope, for your sake, this investigation will be based on more than your hunches," Kenneth demanded.

"Of course not, sir," Thorndyke said quickly. "We searched the area and sent a forensic team into the house to find evidence of the attacker's identity. There was blood on the living room floor that we believe . . . that *definitely* belonged to the attacker. So far, there's been no word on the test results, but I'll contact you as soon as I hear anything."

"Do that," Kenneth said, then added in a warning tone, "If I don't hear from you, then I'll ask Chief Edmunds when I see him at our weekly golf game."

At the mention of the chief of police, Thorndyke's eyes grew wide; then he cleared his throat and nodded. He motioned to the uniformed police officer and the two walked out of the room. Before the door closed, Amelia noticed another uniformed officer sitting outside her door.

"Did you request a guard, Dad?" she accused, glaring at him.

"I didn't request anything; I demanded one," Kenneth snapped. "I told you to start using that alarm. What's the use of having one if you never activate it?"

"Here, darling, use my comb. We never know who could be in the halls. Reporters, cute doctors," Alice said while brandishing a comb at Amelia, who moved away as quick as she could, considering her entire body throbbed from pain.

"Damn it, Alice, she doesn't need a comb," Kenneth sniped irritably. "She needs to have this maniac caught before he tries to finish what he started tonight."

Alice directed a gaze at Kenneth that could have burnt bread. Amelia quickly decided to intervene and tried to sound firm and forceful, even though her voice was hoarse and weak. "I don't care about reporters or cute doctors and I don't need a guard. I especially don't need the police reporting to my father about my case. I don't want any special treatment."

"This attitude of yours is getting on my nerves, Amelia," Kenneth said as he picked imaginary lint from the lapel of his dark, expensive suit.

Years ago that tone would have scared Amelia. If she were honest, it still did. She rarely talked back to her parents, but then, she rarely spoke to them. They talked at her, told her what they wanted her to do—and she listened most times—but they rarely talked *to* her. She knew that it was partially her fault for not demanding more from them, but Amelia wasn't certain if she wanted more. Anything more would mean her involvement in her parents' relationship, and even though her job was based on it, Amelia could not stand confrontation. She was the peacemaker, the mediator, whenever she was around her parents, and she didn't like the role. After a full day of listening to ugliness in court, the last thing Amelia wanted was to hear ugliness at home. Seeing her parents together, dealing with their reactions to her, always brought home how completely dysfunctional her family was.

But now she forced herself to sound indignant as she said, "I didn't realize that my wishes would be considered an attitude."

He continued, ignoring her. "You wanted to work in the district attorney's office. You wanted to live in that godforsaken neighborhood. And this is exactly what happens as a result—you're lying in a hospital bed with a swollen throat and a cut as deep as the Grand Canyon in your hand. Who knows what could have happened if you hadn't gotten lucky? And that's all it was, Amelia. Luck."

"Hollywood Hills is not a slum, Father," she said

simply, then thickly swallowed due to the strain on her voice. She winced as she tried to find a more comfortable position on the bed. There was none, considering the sheets felt about a shade softer than paper.

"Don't talk, darling; you're just hurting yourself," Alice softly commanded, a frown crossing her face for the first time since she swept into the room. She glared at her husband and ordered, "Stop talking to her."

"You have never been able to handle the fact that I have my own life that doesn't include a large corporate firm and Brian," Amelia whispered defiantly to her father.

Maybe it was the painkillers or her gladiator battle earlier that evening, but Amelia suddenly felt tired of defending herself. She sagged against the pillows and tried like hell not to cry. It would have ruined the image she was trying to sell her father. The image of a strong, independent woman.

"That's not true, Amie," her mother soothed. All tenderness left her face as she glared at Kenneth and demanded, "Tell her that's not true."

"Of course that's not true," he retorted. Amelia watched her father struggle for calm before he quietly said, "I know the type of people you prosecute, Amelia. I know how dangerous they are and I know that sometimes they hold grudges. Did it ever occur to you that this attack was in response to your job? That I don't just hate your job because we both know you shouldn't be wasting your time there, but because it's dangerous for a young woman to put herself in a position to be hated by dangerous criminals?"

She clenched the sheets in her hands in anger, then

said calmly, "This is not about my job. Like I told the detective, this is obviously about the conversation that I heard on the stairs. Whoever was on the stairs and killed that man knows that I know—"

"I don't want to hear another word about that nonsense, Amelia," Kenneth snapped while shaking his head in disbelief. "Judges and cops being bribed . . . I would expect some liberal activist clamoring for attention to scream about things like this, but you're . . . Are you trying to embarrass me?"

"I'm telling the truth."

"I've been hearing good things about you from the courthouse. Don't ruin it with this ridiculous conspiracy talk. Whatever you thought you heard is not what you think. If in fact someone was killed, there's no body; there are no visible signs that anyone was killed. You may have heard an argument, but it's a courthouse—it's a requirement to argue when you step through the door. There's no proof, no evidence, and you're embarrassing yourself and this family by continuing with this line of discussion."

Amelia shook her head and tried to speak, but Kenneth continued to speak over her: "I don't believe in coincidences, and if you're smart, you won't, either. You have a job that the county rightfully should give you hazard pay for, and you live in a neighborhood that hasn't had a robbery in five years. Someone broke into your house and tried to kill you, not your neighbor the neurosurgeon or your other neighbor, the movie producer, but you, the assistant district attorney. That leads me to one conclusion. This attack was because of your job."

Amelia refused to answer and instead stared at the

ceiling. She briefly shut her eyes as she tried to swallow over the pain in her throat. Talking had been too much for her. Being with her parents for more than ten minutes had been too much for her.

"She's tired, Kenneth. We should leave," Alice said, getting to her feet. Amelia was surprised when her mother actually walked to stand next to Kenneth at her bedside. Alice's voice was soft as she leaned over the bed rail and asked, "Unless you want me to stay? I can have them roll in a bed—"

"I'll be fine," Amelia whispered, surprised by the concern on her mother's face. Alice Lyle Farrow normally didn't handle tender moments very well. She had never gotten the nurturing part down. Her answer had always been to take Amelia shopping, as if the concerns of the world could be resolved after a day at Bloomingdale's.

Kenneth grunted at his wife, then looked at Amelia and said, "You'll be released tomorrow morning. I'll send the car. You'll stay at the house with us until this whole matter is resolved and that lunatic is caught."

"I'm staying in my house," she said firmly, holding her father's gaze.

"It's too dangerous. The police have no idea who the man is or where he is. He could come back or—"

"I'll turn on the alarm, but I'm staying in my house."

"Won't you be frightened?" Alice asked, a hand at her throat as if in sympathy.

"No one is running me out of my house."

"You were almost killed, Amelia," Kenneth said, as if he had to remind her.

"I know; I was there," she retorted.

Her father didn't laugh, but his eyes narrowed as he

glared at her. Kenneth didn't speak for a moment; then he abruptly turned and walked out of the room.

Amelia released the breath she didn't know she was holding, then placed a hand on her sore neck. When she opened her eyes, she realized that her mother still watched her. She was once more surprised by the concern in Alice's eyes. Amelia knew that Alice loved her, in her own Alice Lyle international-cover-model way, but Amelia often wondered if her mother liked her. They were so different. Alice had spent the majority of her life selling her beauty, and Amelia wondered if her mother felt like a failure because her only child couldn't buy her way onto the cover of a fashion magazine, let alone have a career at it.

"Don't say no just because you want to spite your father," Alice said softly. "I know what it's like to want to prove Kenneth wrong, but your situation is too serious for those games now—"

"This has nothing to do with Dad."

Alice didn't look convinced, but she nodded, then visibly hesitated before she placed an air-soft kiss on Amelia's forehead. "I have meetings all day tomorrow for the benefit for the children's hospital, but I'll have Natalie swing by and make certain that you have everything you need. I already have Lupe scheduled to come in before you arrive from the hospital, and clean the house."

"Thank you, Mom."

"Everything will be fine, darling."

Amelia nodded, then watched her mother sail out of the room. She turned on her side to face the window and the view of the large concrete buildings next to the hospital. Of course, her father had made certain she had the most luxurious suite in the hospital. She tried to close her eyes and sleep, but the now dull pain in her body made it too difficult. She stared out the window and, before she could stop herself, she thought of George Gibson. She didn't want to think of him when she was at her lowest, but she did and, for some reason, it made her feel better.

Chapter 4

"Hey, man," Wayne said as he sat across the table from George in the same diner, at the same table, where they had met for the last ten years. George signaled their waitress. The older woman nodded in recognition, obviously annoyed that her conversation with one of the other waitresses had been interrupted by someone actually wanting her to work.

One Saturday morning a month, the two men met for breakfast in a cheap diner where each could afford to buy the other breakfast. No matter their schedules or how busy their lives were, they always carved out one Saturday morning to have breakfast—no one else allowed. George didn't know if it was a testament to each man's failure to find a woman who would keep him in her bed on a Saturday morning or if it was a testament to their friendship.

"Sorry I'm late," Wayne said as he took off his jacket and laid it on the chair next to him.

"No problem," George said as he folded the newspaper

he had been reading. "I already ordered for us."

"You did? I wanted scrambled eggs and—"

"Two pancakes, one piece of French toast, and hash browns," George finished with a theatrical sigh. "How else could you eat ketchup if you didn't have your hash browns?"

"I'm that predictable?" Wayne asked, perplexed. When George only laughed in response, Wayne shook his head.

The waitress slammed their plates of food on the table in front of them, then snarled, "Anything else?"

George would have liked another cup of coffee, but he decided not to risk the woman's wrath and said, "No thanks."

Wayne had always been braver, and he said, "A cup of orange juice for me, and my friend needs a refill on his coffee."

As if Wayne had asked the woman to fly to the orange groves in central California herself and pick the oranges, then hop the next flight to Colombia for the coffee beans, she loudly sighed, then turned and walked toward the kitchen.

"Don't be surprised if your orange juice tastes funny," George warned.

Wayne laughed, then began to dump ketchup on his hash browns until it flowed over the contents of the plate. "Don't you have a date tonight? Big move, G. Interacting with a woman outside the courtroom."

"I canceled," George murmured.

"Why does that not surprise me?"

"I have work."

"Of course," Wayne said, disbelief dripping from his

voice. "Wasn't this the architect you met in the bookstore? If I remember your exact words, she could have been Vivica Fox's twin. Why would you cancel on that?"

"It's been a long week, lots of court time, lots of late nights. With a woman like Debbie, I need to be at one hundred percent."

"I thought her name was Danielle."

George paused, then repeated uncertainly, "Danielle? Maybe that's why she got so snippy when I called her to cancel."

"Women tend to get annoyed with that whole name thing," Wayne said with a laugh. George shrugged and stuffed his forkful of pancakes into his mouth. "I knew you would cancel. You always find a way to get rid of women you could have something in common with. The one-night stands . . . you would never think of canceling on them, but a decent woman with something going for herself, you flake every time."

"What are you . . . my date doctor now? I do just fine in the female department, unlike you. You haven't had a date since Kennedy was in office."

"We weren't alive when Kennedy was in office."

"I rest my case," George said, which caused Wayne to grin.

"We're both losers then," Wayne finally said while raising his water glass for a toast. George laughed and obligingly clinked his coffee cup against the glass.

Wayne laughed just as his cell phone rang. George dug into his pancakes and tuned out Wayne's conversation. He didn't know why he'd canceled his date with Debbie/Danielle. He just knew that he couldn't sit across from her at dinner when he would spend the whole time seeing Amelia's face. Hearing the disappointment in her voice.

He cursed himself. It was over. Amelia didn't know anything about him that he hadn't told her and a million other people before. He didn't like expectations, and a woman such as Amelia would have a million of them. George stopped himself. Why should he care what Amelia Farrow thought? She was nothing to him but opposing counsel, the woman who wanted to send his client to jail. She had a great pair of legs and a mouth that could make a grown man beg, but that was it.

He noticed Wayne's grave expression when he replaced the cell phone in his pocket.

"That was McKrie. He asked me to take his shift again tonight. His wife just had a baby and she needs some rest before she drops from exhaustion." Wayne stopped rambling and visibly hesitated before he blurted out, "He told me that his shift included patrols around Amelia Farrow's house every half hour. Any suspicious signs warrant an immediate call for backup."

George felt a surprising lump in his throat at the mention of Amelia's name. He swallowed thickly before he said, "Why?"

"She was attacked last night in her house. She spent the night in the hospital, and she's home this morning."

George coughed when he realized that he had been holding his breath while Wayne answered. He cleared his throat and tried to sound calm as he said, "Attacked? What does that mean?"

"Some man broke into her house and tried to kill her. He attempted to strangle her. Somehow, she got away. She's not hurt too bad—a few bruises and cuts. We're going to patrol her house for the next few days, though, to make certain there are no repeat attacks."

"I'll be the first to admit that the woman can work your nerves until you want to scream, but . . . she wouldn't hurt a fly."

"She works for the DA's office, George. Those attorneys have tough jobs. They receive death threats and other threats of violence on a regular basis. I'm not surprised that someone would go so far as to attack an ADA in her house."

George's heart sank and that guilty feeling he was becoming too familiar with slammed down on him. He hesitantly asked, "You don't think it's a random attack?"

"If it was anyone other than an ADA, I'd think so, but there were no signs of an attempted robbery that she interrupted or an attempted rape. It was an attempted murder, plain and simple. I'm sure the case detectives will cull her caseload to see who she's prosecuted in the last few months that would be capable of something like this, but this was not random."

George was silent as he stared at his plate of food. He suddenly wasn't hungry. Once more the instincts that had never failed him told him that the attack had nothing to do with any of Amelia's cases. Damn it, he should have been the one to report the incident to security, to deal with whatever consequences followed. But, as usual, his first instinct had been to not become involved, to not show any sign that he cared, because caring gave people the ability to feel hurt or to hurt. Except that George was beginning to realize that maybe he already cared about

Amelia and it was too late for him to do anything about it now.

He had been beaten up and had beaten up people. He didn't like it, but he could handle the repercussions, but not Amelia. A woman who wore headbands should not have been fighting off attackers and spending the night in a hospital. It made him sick to think of someone hurting her. Not because he knew her or because she was a woman, but because she was her.

"You have that look again, like the time when you were nine years old and saw those three high school boys kicking that puppy," Wayne said. "They almost beat you a new face when you tried to stop them."

"You know that I was trying to walk away and I just tripped into that one guy and then the other guy swung—"

"Yeah, right," Wayne muttered sarcastically.

"You know me better than anyone, Wayne. It was an accident."

"Was it also an accident when you returned half of the money I got for you from your clients a few months ago? You accidentally gave back each check, twenty-dollar bill, and IOU I gave to you?"

"How'd you find out?"

Wayne grinned as he shook his head in amusement. "I know you. You can't stand the thought of actually being paid for your services. I don't know why you're still playing this don't-give-a-shit role, George. We're not eight years old anymore. Mr. Ashford is not going to lock you in the closet for the night because you gave your lunch money to a kid with no shoes."

George inwardly flinched at Wayne's reference to

Mr. Ashford. For a few years when George was a child and living with the Ashfords, he had wondered if there were any adults in the world who didn't scream or hate children like him. He could thank Mr. Ashford and a few other of his "guardians" for inspiring such thoughts in him that no child should have. George wanted to thank Mr. Ashford and some of his other guardians for a lot of things, and all of his gratitude ended with seeing them behind bars.

When Wayne initially became a police officer, he and George had looked up all of their foster parents—the good and the bad. George had still been in law school, but when he spouted his legal mumbo jumbo to Mr. Ashford, the older man's dark face had turned ashen. It could have been George's legal mumbo jumbo or the hand that Wayne had wrapped around the older man's pudgy neck. Whatever had happened, the next day Mr. Ashford told the county that he didn't want to be a foster parent anymore.

George did attribute one of his better traits to Mr. Ashford. Without the man, George never would have learned that showing concern and care meant showing weakness. The old man had been right about that.

"I'll get my money," George muttered, then set down his fork and reached for his wallet in his jacket pocket. He threw several dollar bills on the table and said, "I'll talk to you later this weekend. We should get together to shoot hoops tomorrow."

"Where are you going?" Wayne asked, surprised. "You barely touched your breakfast. Did you see our waitress do something to the food that I should know about?"

"I have this . . . thing I have to do."

"This *thing* wouldn't happen to be seeing Amelia Farrow, would it?" Wayne asked with a knowing smile.

"Why would I willingly torture myself on a weekend by dealing with Farrow? She's strictly a Monday-through-Friday, nine-to-five problem."

"It's not a crime if you're attracted to a woman like Amelia. I'm a cop. I know these things. Besides, after what she went through last night, she probably needs all the comfort she can get."

"I am not attracted to Amelia Farrow," George stated firmly. "I could never be attracted to a woman who has never asked for a continuance or stay in a case. How unnatural is that?"

Wayne's expression was blank. "You're doing that legal talk again."

George continued as if Wayne had never spoken. "Maybe I'll send an E-mail or leave a message on her phone because we're colleagues and I'd do that for anyone, but I'm definitely not going to her house."

George would have liked to walk out then. Maybe he could have saved some of his pride, because he *was* going to see Amelia—whether she wanted him there or not—but he remembered a vital piece of information. He had no idea where the woman lived, which meant he needed Wayne to give him her address.

"Fine, George. Whatever you say."

He stared at Wayne for a second, then said in one breath, "I need her address."

Like the good friend he was, Wayne didn't say one word as he pulled out his cell phone and dialed the police department.

• • •

George almost kept driving when he saw Amelia's house, or "the compound," as she probably called it. He gazed at the sprawling two-level house centered around imposing oversize double wooden doors and large bay windows on either side of the house, partially covered by sheer curtains. He could even see the outlines of large plants near the window.

He didn't want to be impressed, but he was. She lived in a remote, exclusive neighborhood in the hills above Hollywood, the hills that had almost been too difficult for his sedan to handle. Obviously, the city planners had thought only cars that could make it up the hills should be driving on the hill.

He had driven past her closest neighbor at the bottom of the hill five minutes ago before he even spotted the circular driveway that led to the front doors of her house. George could hear what his neighbor ate for dinner, but he couldn't see Amelia's neighbors through the trees and wild Amazon-like vegetation that edged the wide, smooth streets. Even the air in the hills seemed different from the congested smog in the city's just-this-side-of-respectable Miracle Mile section where George lived.

And then George noticed the several luxury cars neatly parked in the circular driveway. He didn't think that even Amelia would have that many cars, so obviously she had guests—very rich guests, who obviously would not be caught in any car that cost below $50,000. A perfect excuse for him to coast his car down the hill—to save on gas—and hightail it back to where he belonged.

Except he didn't leave. George got out of his car and resisted the urge to tuck his T-shirt into his khakis. It was Saturday morning. He didn't have to look neat. He took a deep breath, then walked up the stone-decorated walk toward the front door. He told himself that this was just Amelia. He wanted to see with his own eyes that she was all right; then he would leave. Maybe if he worked up enough nerve and remembered how to do it, he would apologize.

Before George could ring the doorbell, the door swung open. The woman who had been about to walk out the door stopped in her tracks when she saw him. Her latte-colored face expressed her shock, then curiosity, as she openly stared from George's slightly wrinkled clothes to his needed-a-new-pair canvas shoes. Since she stared at him, he returned the favor. She was probably in her late twenties and had lived her whole life accustomed to wealth. Neither her eyes nor her skin showed any sign of worry or hard work. She was beautiful in that Ice Princess way that George had never found attractive, not counting his momentary bout of insanity under the judge's desk with Amelia.

The woman didn't smile as she gripped her purse more tightly, then demanded, "Who are you?"

Before he could answer, more women like her came to the front door, each registering surprise, then suspicion, when she saw George. Four women stood in front of him, but as far as he was concerned they could have been the same person. They all had the same "fried-dyed-and-laid-to-the-side" hair of varying lengths, almost the same color homogeneous brown skin, the same amount of skin showing in their expensive clothes to make it just this side of respectable but sexy enough for their age, and the same level of beauty that George knew would cause men to stare wherever they went.

He did not see Amelia having anything in common with these women besides the fact that they all drove cars that could eat his sedan for breakfast.

"Who is this, Eileen?" one of the women asked while staring at George as if he had evolved from some lower form of life right in front of her eyes.

"I don't know. I don't think he can speak," Eileen, the woman who had opened the door, answered in the same cultured tones as Amelia.

"What do you want?" Eileen asked in a cool tone that George guessed sent lesser men scurrying. He didn't have the car to compete, but he had thawed out a few cold women in his time.

"I work with Amelia," George said, trying not to sound as annoyed as he felt and flashing a dazzling smile. With the Great Wall of Brown Beauty blocking the door, with no intention of moving, he knew he would never see Amelia if these women didn't want him to. "I heard about what happened last night. I just wanted to check and see if she's all right."

"How did you hear? Her father made certain it was kept out of the news," one of the women suspiciously demanded.

"I have a friend who's a cop."

Eileen's eyes narrowed as if she didn't believe that George would know a cop. He barely believed it himself, so he didn't take offense. She crossed her arms over her chest and said, "Amelia's fine. You can leave now."

"I would like to see her." He tried to sound as contrite

and apologetic as possible, which meant he just sounded annoyed.

"She's resting," Eileen told him. "As you know, she was attacked last night. She is not in the mood for visitors. We'll tell her that you stopped by."

"Who are you guys talking to? Another deliveryman? If Brian sends any more flowers . . ." George's palms instantly grew damp when he heard Amelia's voice. She broke through her friends' shoulders and came to an abrupt stop when she saw him. Her voice trailed off and her eyes momentarily grew wide.

He had spent a lot of time on his drive to her house trying to imagine her reaction. It ranged from her calling the police to her yelling at him that he was a coward. But she did neither. She simply stared at him. And he could only stare in return. His gaze traced her face for any sign of damage and he flinched as if he had been hit when he saw the faint bruise on the left side of her face. Then he noticed the red marks around her neck that the high collar of her sweater set barely hid.

George wanted to hit someone, preferably the asshole who had hurt her, but instead shoved his hands into his pockets. Then he noticed something else. Even after fighting down a maniac the night before, she still looked neater and more perfect than George did on his best day, including the matching headband. She wore a skirt and matching cardigan. He wondered if she owned pants. It would have been too unladylike, he supposed, for her to wear pants. He had only seen her business skirts and casual skirts. Not that he entirely minded, since he could ogle her legs when she wasn't looking.

If he didn't know better, he would think that damn

headband that held back her hair with an iron control that reminded him of a crazed Tipper Gore was turning him on. He knew that if Eileen and her Black Barbie posse had an inkling of what he was feeling for Amelia at that moment, they wouldn't think twice about using their expensive shoes to kick his ass.

"Should we call the police, Amie?" Eileen asked, breaking George out of his trance. He shook his head in confusion and tore his gaze from Amelia. He felt like he had been underwater for minutes and had just surfaced for air.

"No," Amelia said to Eileen in a hoarse voice before she asked George, "What are you doing here?"

He glanced at their audience, and when he realized that they were not going anywhere, he said, "I heard about what happened. Are you all right?"

She nodded; then he noticed that one of her hands flew to her neck, to cover her bruises. He dismissed the brief flash of hurt that raced through him that she felt the need to protect herself from him. He told himself he was not her friend and, judging from Eileen and the posse, he was not the type of friend Amelia would ever have.

"I'm fine, George," Amelia said through an obviously forced smile. "A few bruises, but that's all."

"We were just leaving, George, good timing," the until-then-silent friend said while looking from Amelia to George. She finally settled on George and said, "You'll make certain that Amie finishes the cake we brought her, right? We also rented a few videos and bought books and magazines. . . . There are a few casseroles in the refrigerator, too, if either one of you becomes hungry. And make certain that she locks the house tight. Understand?"

George nodded dumbly while Eileen shook her head and said to the drill sergeant, "I can stay a little longer, Heather. My massage isn't until one."

George's only ally in the group, Heather, shook her head and answered, "We're leaving, ladies. Amie's in good hands." She kissed Amelia on the cheek, then, with one last assessing look in George's direction, motioned for the other women to follow her.

Eileen glared at George one final time, then hugged Amelia while whispering in her ear. George didn't have to guess that she told Amelia to kick his ass to the curb. The final Barbie hugged Amelia, then followed the other two to their cars. With a sweep of their respective long hair, each got into her respective luxury car; then in a flash of purring engines they roared down the hill.

The sudden quiet settled on George as he turned to stare at Amelia once more. She met his gaze, then quickly looked away.

"Nice friends," he said, for lack of anything better.

Her gaze flew to meet his and she defensively said, "They are. I've known Eileen, Heather, and Vicki my entire life."

George held up his hands in surrender and said, "I just said they're nice. That's all, Amie."

She frowned at his use of her nickname, but then she abruptly turned and walked into the house. Since she didn't say he couldn't and since his one ally had practically forced him to break bread with Amelia, he followed her into the house and closed the door.

He looked around the house and realized that he was

sufficiently impressed. He could tell just from the colors of the pieces that the furniture was expensive. The dark colors and greenery were surprisingly comforting, he realized as he cautiously stepped into the living room. In fact, Amelia's home was very comforting, peaceful, like an oasis. It wasn't too feminine, so a man would feel uncomfortable and nervous about breaking furniture, but there was a definite female touch that made the room soft and inviting, like his apartment would never be. He had expected stuffed animals and pink, but he was in a home that even Martha Stewart would be proud to claim.

He also noticed that the room was immaculate, almost too clean. He then caught the unmistakable scent of new furniture. He briefly knew when he glanced at Amelia's expression as she stared at the brand-new rug on the hardwood floors that this was the room where the attack had taken place. There were no traces of it now, but the fear hung in the air.

He realized that she was watching him and he turned to her. For another strange moment, the two simply stared at each other. Then he realized with a shock that she was nervous. She hid it well, but he could tell from the way she glanced around the room and wrung her hands, then adjusted her headband more tightly. He finally realized that she used her headband to calm her nerves. Like Achilles' heel, there was Amelia's headband. He suddenly felt more relaxed. Almost comfortable. He never thought he would feel that way around Amelia Farrow.

"How about that cake Heather mentioned? I missed breakfast," George said, slapping his hands together.

She appeared relieved to have something to do and she quickly nodded, then said, "It's in the kitchen."

He followed her into the kitchen, trying hard not to notice that the tight skirt emphasized certain aspects of her body that he definitely should not have been thinking about.

Chapter 5

Amelia stared at the knife on the counter and wondered how she could hold it when there was a huge white bandage around her hand. She could have asked George for help, but she never was good with asking for help. Especially not from George Gibson . . . who stood in her kitchen, his overpowering alien presence forever altering her feelings about the room. He stood behind her at the counter, but she could feel his eyes on her.

It suddenly occurred to her that she never questioned the fact that he was at her house. It just seemed right. When she had seen him on the other side of her door, facing the wrath of her friends, she hadn't questioned the feeling of relief and joy that replaced the fear. She loved Eileen, Heather, and Vicki like sisters, but she had put on a brave front for her friends or she never would have gotten rid of them. She was closer to them than to her own family, but their constant mothering had been more than she could handle in one afternoon.

It never entered her mind that she wanted George

around her when she didn't want her own best friends. Now she thought about it. And she didn't like what she thought, how she felt.

She ignored the cake and the knife, then abruptly turned to face him and coolly said, "If you came in the hopes that after my brush with death I've seen the light, changed my ways, and decided to go easy on O'Connor, then you're wrong. Attempted voluntary manslaughter."

He actually grinned and if she hadn't felt weak before, she felt weak at that moment. He shrugged in response, then walked across the room to stand in front of her. She froze as his warmth wrapped around her, comforted her. He was too close. She should want him to move, but she didn't. She wanted him closer. He didn't look at her as he sliced two pieces from the large chocolate cake and set one on each plate.

He grinned at her, then ate a chunk of cake. His long pink tongue licked the edges of his fork, very slowly, and Amelia almost groaned. She found herself staring at his lips, wondering what they tasted like. When he suddenly smiled at her as if he could see her thoughts, she instantly turned her gaze to the cake.

He finally said, "With a comment like that . . . that answers my question. You're all right."

"I never said that I wasn't."

"Those bruises around your neck look pretty scary."

She didn't respond but stared at the bowl of apples in the middle of the island. She wanted to tell him that a large man in her house with his hands around her neck had been a lot scarier. Instead, she said nothing and clutched her trembling hands into fists. He set the plate on the counter, walked to the kitchen door, and squatted to the floor to examine the newly replaced lock. "He came in through this door?"

"The lock was smashed. The police believe that . . . he did it."

He stared at her for a moment, then asked, "In a fancy place like this, you don't have an alarm?"

She ignored the question because if she had to answer it one more time she would scream. She had lived here for two years and had never set the alarm at night. She had felt safe and secure in her house. She had slept with the windows open, and the sliding glass door in the living room was never closed in the summer. She involuntarily shivered as she thought of how stupid she had been. It was one thing for her to admit that she had been careless. It was another thing to listen to George Gibson lecture her about it.

To her surprise, he didn't comment on her silence but stood. She held her breath and waited for him to leave. She didn't want him to leave—maybe she had been knocked in the head too hard, but she couldn't stand the thought of being alone in the silence again, with only her thoughts and fears as companions. But he didn't leave. He picked up his plate again, then settled on a stool at the island.

"Heather mentioned something about a casserole," he said. "What does a brother have to do to get some food around here?"

She laughed to cover her nervousness at the fact that he had stayed. "Normally, I would throw the casserole dish at your head, but I'm weak right now, so I'll humor you and just say that the refrigerator is over there and the microwave is right there."

"Your hospitality skills need some work. What would Heather say?"

"Heather is very motherly. She would probably be horrified," Amelia confirmed. "Eileen and Vicki, on the other hand, would probably pat me on the back and pressure me to take it one step further by kicking you out of the house."

"Good thing Heather is the only one who makes sense," he told her with a wink.

He walked to the refrigerator and took out a casserole dish. She leaned against the counter and watched him move. She realized that she could become addicted to the sight of George moving around her kitchen.

His quiet voice broke the comfortable silence in the kitchen as he said, "Are you all right?"

"You said that I was two minutes ago," she reminded him.

He grimaced and muttered, "Just answer the question, Farrow."

"I'm fine." It was a lie, but she had a strange feeling that George needed to hear it. With her answer, the tension that she hadn't noticed became apparent as it seeped out of his expression. She wondered if he had been worried about her. She couldn't picture George worried about her. Maybe he felt guilty. From under her eyelids she examined his expression. He did feel guilt. She tried to think of a way to make him believe that it wasn't his fault, but she had never been good at comforting anyone. Just like her mother and father.

He said hesitantly, "Amelia, I feel . . . if I had been . . ." His voice trailed off and he stared at the floor.

She had the strange impression that he was attempting

to apologize. She smiled for the first time since she had stumbled into her attacker last night.

When he saw her smile, he cleared his throat and snapped, "You know what I mean."

She nodded. "I do, George."

He appeared relieved to get that "big talk" out of the way; then he said quietly, "Your attack could be related to what we heard in the stairwell yesterday."

She froze for a moment, then she said softly, "I've thought of that possibility."

"And?"

"And I don't think it's a realistic explanation for what happened," she said, attempting to sound like the matter was settled, that her father was right, even as every fiber in her body screamed that she was attacked because she had overheard a murder on the stairwell. But her father had been right about one thing. She was a Farrow. Farrows solved problems; they didn't create them. "In the last four months alone, I've sent four defendants to jail for murder, two of whom were gang members who would have the connections to . . . to . . ." Her voice trailed off because she couldn't force herself to say that someone had tried to kill her.

George placed the casserole dish in the oven, and turned it on. He turned to her and said, "I don't think this attack was the result of a grudge from an old case. It has to be related to your reporting what you heard on the stairwell, especially when you consider the subject— corrupt cops and judges. It's too much of a coincidence."

"Sometimes the simplest explanation is the right one. It makes more sense that one of the defendants I sent to jail wants revenge than some unbelievable conspiracy theory."

"Why is it unbelievable?"

"Why are you suddenly the big believer?" she demanded, ignoring his question. "You wanted to wait until Monday morning to report anything because you were so convinced that we heard nothing. Now you're trying to convert me?"

"I wasn't convinced that we heard anything dangerous on Friday, but seeing you with all of these bruises has convinced me. You and I heard something, maybe a murder, maybe not. You told courthouse security that you wanted a videotape of the courthouse entrances and you had the cops traipsing around doing all kinds of tests. If the men on the stairs can bribe cops, then courthouse security guards can't be any different. The wrong—or right—person heard about your inquiries. Maybe they thought you saw more than you were telling them and they sent someone to take care of you."

"This sounds like an episode of *The A-Team*."

"This has . . . Wait. I can't allow that one to pass. Did you just seriously cite *The A-Team* in our conversation?"

"Maybe," she said, then raised her chin one notch. She had a weakness for *The A-Team*. Maybe *obsession* was more the right word. Just because a woman who had more pearls than a senior citizens' center raced home on Saturday nights to catch the cable television reruns of the 1980s television series about a band of AWOL Vietnam vets running from the army and helping people . . . who did that hurt?

He stared at her for a full moment before he apparently decided to ignore it and said, "We heard the same thing, Amelia. You told, and I didn't. You were attacked the same night, and I wasn't. I'm convinced."

She forced a laugh as she shook her head in amazement and said in disbelief, "We don't even know if anyone was killed. The lab tests will confirm it, but the preliminary results show there was no one killed on that stairwell. You were right. I wasn't. You should be happy."

He stared at her. She had never seen him look so serious, even when they had run in the courthouse. "This isn't a game, Amelia. I'm not Mr. T and you're not that old guy who spent the whole show smoking a cigar while everyone else did all the work."

"They called him Hannibal. He was their lieutenant," she helpfully supplied.

He rolled his eyes, then continued. "Whatever we stumbled into is real, it's dangerous, and it could have cost your life."

"I just can't believe that . . ." Her voice trailed off and she concentrated on the remains of the cake on her plate.

"You were willing to believe it before you were attacked. And, now that it's real, you don't want to believe it? What changed?"

She didn't want to tell him about her conversation with her father and, instead, abruptly smiled and said, "Are you actually admitting that I was right to tell security about the conversation? That it was our duty to tell?"

He held up his hands in self-defense and said, laughing, "I must have left the kitchen for a little while, because I don't remember saying anything like that."

"But you believe me now? You believe that someone was murdered?"

"I always believed that we heard something that we

definitely shouldn't have heard. I also believed that we should have kept our mouths closed, gone home, and enjoyed our weekends and dealt with it on Monday. Crooked judges and cops don't bother me since I operate on the basic assumption that all judges and cops are crooked."

"My father is a judge," she told him through clenched teeth.

"So I've been told," he said with an uncaring shrug.

There was silence in the kitchen once more as the two stared at everything but each other. She should have made him leave, but then who would she eat the casserole with? Besides, if anyone could help her, would believe her, it was George. And she needed someone to believe her.

She hesitated, then confessed, "Before my friends came over, I did a little research. I wanted to find confirmation that what we heard on the stairwell was real."

She didn't miss his knowing smirk as he asked, "If you don't believe your attack is related to the stairwell incident, why are you doing research?"

"Whether someone attacked me or not because of what I heard, there still may be corrupt judges and jurors."

He sighed in obvious frustration, then leaned on the counter across from her and asked, "Did you find out anything?"

"I didn't find anything. There are a number of cases with questionable rulings, but most of those judges have been giving questionable rulings for the last fifteen years. Trying to find a case that looks like bribery in a system that is overworked and understaffed is like trying to find a needle in a haystack. Every case looks like bribery."

"We need the surveillance tapes."

"We?" she repeated, feeling a strange urge to smile at him.

"Maybe I want to clean the courts, too."

She snorted in disbelief. "Or more likely you're thinking about the fees you can charge clients for their appeals."

She flinched at her harsh tone. There was something about George Gibson that turned her into a shrew. Then she noticed a brief flash of something unrecognizable that crossed his face, almost as if he had been hurt by her comment. She quickly dismissed the thought when he sent her one of his smug grins.

"I did some research, too," he said with an uncaring shrug. "Some of my clients could have been sentenced by corrupt judges or convicted by bribed jurors. I could have their convictions overturned on appeal and, best of all, the state will pay my legal fees. Guaranteed money in the bank. It's a win-win situation. You didn't think I'd do this for free, did you?"

She suddenly felt cold. Alone. She had actually believed that George had come to her house concerned for her safety. She wanted to believe that George was someone she could trust, because she was attracted to him. She was old enough to know that lust had nothing to do with trust or comfort. She couldn't even blame George for her expectations and hopes. He never represented himself as anything other than what he was.

He continued, oblivious to her internal war. "Security told you that the backup tapes are kept in the basement of the courthouse. We have to assume that we can't trust any of the security or police at the courthouse. If we want those tapes, we have to find a way to get them ourselves."

"I know what that defense attorney mind of yours is thinking," she snapped, then emphatically stated, "We're not breaking into the courthouse and we're not stealing anything."

"How else do you propose we see the surveillance tapes to find out who did this to you?"

"I would never be able to identify my attacker from the tapes. He wore a mask. Besides, the person who attacked me may not be the same man from the stairwell."

She wrapped her arms around herself and leaned against the counter. She was tired. She wanted to sleep and forget that the past forty-eight hours had happened, especially the part where she actually thought George Gibson had come to inquire about her health, that he was actually human and not just a defense attorney. That he viewed her as more than just another annoying prosecutor. She shouldn't have thought that he would care. He didn't care that she was a Farrow, and in her experience the only men who ever paid attention to her were interested in her name and money.

She straightened her back once more, then said, "I'm not breaking into the courthouse, Gibson, not for any reason, especially not for videotapes that are considered property of the sheriff's department."

They engaged in a staring contest for a long moment and she actually felt her heart dip into the pit of her stomach from nerves. It was a strange moment for her to acknowledge how strongly attracted she was to this man. On a purely physical level, of course, but she was attracted to him and she couldn't deny it as she had been doing for the last year. And as he had made abundantly clear, he only cared about getting paid. She only entered situations that she could win, and she knew that when it came to her attraction to him, she could not win.

He abruptly grinned and said, "You're scared to break into the courthouse."

"I am not," she hotly protested.

"The thought of actually doing something fun has you scared out of your mind."

She vigorously shook her head and said, "What do you consider fun about breaking the law? I am an assistant district attorney; I can't just break into a courthouse—"

He began to move around the kitchen while making chicken noises. She didn't know if he wanted to make her angry or to make her laugh, but she found herself laughing at the sight of a grown man acting like such a child. He grinned at her, then leaned against the counter, too close to her again.

His gaze dropped to her mouth and the smile slowly faded from his face. She imagined him crossing the remaining distance and taking her into his arms. She imagined feeling his lips on hers and his hands roaming across her body. Her breathing suddenly became ragged. She should hate him. It was a natural response. When a beautiful man used her—usually for her connections but, in this case, because he wanted to free his probably guilty clients—it was appropriate for her to hate him. But she didn't.

She also shouldn't trust him, and she didn't. She raked a hand through her hair, then turned from his intense gaze to peer into the stove at the casserole.

"Another twenty minutes," she announced for no particular reason. "Heather made it. She's an excellent cook. She's opening a restaurant in Beverly Hills next week. We're all so excited for her. She's been dreaming about this for a long time."

"Heather can cook?"

She hid her smile at the surprise on his face before she said, "How else am I supposed to eat?"

"No, I just . . . She's so . . . She drives a convertible Lexus SC 430," he proclaimed.

"Of course," Amelia said, nodding as if she understood his strange explanation.

He broke into a small smile before he asked, "Does she need to work?"

"Of course not. She could live on the interest from her bank accounts alone."

"Then why does she want to open a restaurant? That sounds like a lot of work."

"Because she loves to cook," Amelia said simply.

"Some people throw dinner parties for friends and some people open restaurants," he muttered while shaking his head. Then he abruptly looked at her and murmured, "And some people become assistant district attorneys."

She didn't have a response and she didn't like the way he looked at her, as if staring at her long enough would answer all of his questions. She worked because she loved the law; she loved helping people. If she told George that, he would laugh in disbelief.

She told him, "I need to freshen up—"

"You have to use the bathroom?" he asked pointedly, obviously taking exception to her civil way of excusing herself for the bathroom.

She rolled her eyes at his pointed lack of manners. "Yes, George, I have to take a piss. Satisfied?"

"No problem. Just point me in the direction of your computer—"

"My computer? Why?"

"Because you were attacked and we're going to find who did it."

"So you can get paid," she added through clenched teeth, once more having to remind herself why he was at her house. Not to talk about Heather or Amelia's manners or even her aches and pains.

He sent her an unreadable look before he confirmed, "So I can get paid."

"Of course. I wouldn't want to stand between a defense attorney and his legal fees. I pride myself on knowing when to step aside before being trampled. The computer is upstairs in the study, second door on the right."

She had never seen George speechless before, but he was. He stared at her, and she could almost imagine that she saw hurt on his face. She reminded herself that he would need a heart to feel pain.

Once more, she told herself to throw him out of the house. To leave before she did something stupid—like forget his true colors. Instead, she turned and walked out of the kitchen. Whatever his reasons for being there, he was the only person she wanted there. He was the only person who would treat her normally.

George shouldn't have been surprised to realize that he and Amelia worked well together. He should have known that they would. She could predict his moves in court before he knew that he would make them. She matched his motions and arguments word for word. And after three hours spent in her study, which was almost as big as his entire apartment, the two had devised a system to search the most cases as efficiently as possible.

The little snatches of conversation they shared—all related to their research—were short and easy. For once, George didn't consider silence his enemy. He liked the silence with Amelia. As insane an idea as it was, he was beginning to think that he actually liked her. On the other hand, she appeared to vacillate between wanting to toss him out of her house and wanting to confide in him. It was strange to see the visible conflict play across her face. He had a feeling that, for now, she had decided that he was a necessary evil.

"Judge Banner has to be involved," Amelia said suddenly, turning from the computer to face him.

He smiled when he saw the wire-rimmed reading glasses perched on her nose. For some reason, the glasses made her seem more . . . human. They showed that the perfect Amelia Farrow had flaws like everyone else, even if it was something as out of her control as eyesight. That and the *Hunter* calendar taped to the wall next to the computer, with the stars of the 1980s cop drama standing back-to-back. He wondered if there was an eighties show she didn't watch.

"What?" she snapped, noticing his smile.

"You with eyeglasses . . . it's a different look."

"I wear contacts in court," she explained; then she frowned and abruptly said, "Do you have a problem with my glasses?"

He smiled. "No."

"Then why are you laughing?"

"I'm not laughing at you. . . . I am laughing at the *Hunter* calendar on the wall, though." He leaned back in the chair and studied her for a moment before he said, "I've never had the misfortune of arguing a case in front of your father in federal court, but I heard that compared to him, you're a walk in the park."

"My father has a . . . strict reputation," she acknowledged.

"Next you're going to say that it's all for show and that at home he's really a teddy bear."

A strange expression crossed her features before she murmured, "I wouldn't say that."

He wanted to ask her what made her frown, but he hesitated. It was none of his business what went on between Amelia and her father. And he doubted that she would tell him even if he asked.

Unfortunately, he had no control over his mouth and he pressed. "There has to be something to the man. He married Alice Lyle. At one of the foster homes I passed through when I was a kid, one of the older guys had a calendar of your mom on the wall. It was the only poster that Mr. Laurence allowed any kid to tape to the walls. I think that's only because he wished Mrs. Laurence would let him tape the poster to the wall in their bedroom."

He laughed at the memory, then frowned when he noticed the strange expression on her face. He silently cursed when he realized his slip. He had mentioned his past. He was not ashamed of his state-sponsored upbringing, but he also wanted to avoid the looks he inevitably received when people found out that he had been a foster child. No one seemed to truly believe that there were kids like Annie in the real world.

"I didn't know that you grew up in foster care," Amelia said.

He tried to find any hint of pity or distaste in her voice, but he found none. He reminded himself that Amelia would never broadcast such an emotion. She would think that it was too rude or unladylike. He lifted his shoulders in response, then muttered, "My clothes hide the scarlet *F* that's branded into my chest."

Then the unthinkable happened. In front of his eyes, Amelia laughed. A wide-open laugh that made George smile. All of her defenses and suspicion of him disappeared and she laughed like she probably did with Eileen, Heather, and Vicki. Her dark brown eyes sparkled with amusement and that incredible mouth slashed into an equally incredible smile. And George realized that he was having another brief bout of insanity, because he suddenly thought about all the things he wanted her mouth to do to him, instead of how he wanted to shut her up.

"I didn't mean it that way, George," she said through her giggles. "The image of you, looking ashamed, walking around with a scarlet *F* on your clothes. It's too ridiculous."

"I can look ashamed."

She sent him a doubtful look as she said, "Defense attorneys lose the ability as soon as they take their first client."

He laughed, then said, "In some circles, being a defense attorney is considered a noble job."

"I'm sure in the Folsom State Prison, everyone loves their defense attorney. . . . On second thought, if they're sitting in prison they probably *don't* love their attorneys."

He watched her laugh for a moment, then he mused, "You're on a roll today, huh?"

Because sitting in her quiet, large house and hearing her laughter suddenly seemed too right and too comfortable, he cleared his throat and said, "Why do you think Judge Banner is involved? He's the one judge I wouldn't have picked. He's too nervous . . . about everything."

She shook her head, as if to shake the last two minutes off; then she answered, "Judge Banner has handled three criminal cases in the last three months, all involving employees of Heller Helium who would be in jail right now, if not for borderline and inconsistent rulings.

"Heller Helium . . . that doesn't sound like a cradle of illegal activity. What is that? A balloon company?"

"Heller Helium houses one of the biggest drug operations in Los Angeles County. It's headed by Maurice Donaldson. He keeps an office front in the Rinaldi Building on Wilshire, but everyone in law enforcement knows that it's how he launders his money. He has ties to local gangs, to the Mafia, and to drug suppliers in Colombia. If anyone could pull strings like this—to make a body completely disappear in the middle of a courthouse—then he could."

George groaned at the mention of Maurice Donaldson. He had heard the name before from his clients. They always whispered it in hushed tones and darted quick looks over their shoulders. George also knew that if his clients hinted they worked for Donaldson, they were a lot more eager to simply go to jail than to testify.

"This keeps getting better and better," he groaned, dragging a hand down his face.

She glanced at the screen once more and summarized the contents to him, "The first case that Banner presided over with Heller Helium was thrown out on a questionable technicality. In the second case . . . the evidence was supposedly lost at the police station, so there was nothing for the prosecutor to present at trial and the case was dismissed.

"And during the last trial, which took place one month ago, a juror was killed in a carjacking. The juror's name was Thomas Chin. He stopped at a streetlight and two men ran up, shot him in the head, dumped the body in the street, and took off in the five-year-old Saturn. All three cases were handled by Judge Banner. The dead juror could have been the out-of-control part that the victim on the stairwell mentioned happening last month."

"Did Chin have a family?"

She nodded as she continued to read. "A wife and two little girls."

"Maybe the wife knows something."

Amelia turned from the computer to glare at him. "We are not going to disturb this woman while she's mourning her husband, George. It's barely been four weeks since his death."

"The events will still be fresh in her head."

"Her husband was murdered. . . . This is ridiculous. I can't believe I'm even entertaining this train of thought. My father was right—"

"Your father? Is he responsible for your sudden change of heart?"

"No," she lied. At George's doubtful look, she repeated firmly, "No."

"If it's so ridiculous, why did you spend the majority of your Saturday morning sitting in front of a computer researching criminal cases?" he shot back. "You know it's more than a coincidence that you were attacked the same night that you overheard a conversation about judge and jury corruption. We may not know if there was a murder or even if someone was shot, but your attack means that something happened."

She avoided his gaze as she said calmly, "All we have is a series of questionable rulings by one judge. We can't accuse a judge of bribery based on that. If we're wrong, we'll not only be disbarred, but we'll be laughed out of LA County."

"Maybe it's worth it to make certain that our courts are clean."

She laughed in disbelief. "Suddenly you're worried about cleaning the courts? I thought your only concern was the potential attorney fees."

He wanted to scream at her that he cared about more than money. But if he started trying to convince her, it would mean too much. He once more reminded himself that he didn't care what she thought. He didn't care what anyone thought.

He still couldn't stop himself from saying, "I've always cared about the bribery, Amelia; you just don't want to believe me."

She was silent as she stared at him, the disbelief evident

on her face. He sighed in resignation. There was nothing he could say or do to change her mind about him. In the past, he had liked seeing the distaste on her face whenever she saw him. It made him feel even more vindicated in treating her like a spoiled princess, but now . . . He shook his head because nothing had changed.

He told her what she wanted to hear. "Cleaning our courts means I get paid. There are at least five clients that I can think of right now who had Judge Banner presiding over their cases."

A flicker of distaste moved across her face. "I should have known."

"We both want to get rid of the corruption—"

"For different reasons," she stated firmly.

"Does it matter? Our different reasons for wanting to find out the truth don't change the fact that we have the same goal—to root out the corruption. We can try it alone, but we'll get a lot more done by working together."

She crossed her arms over her chest and narrowed her eyes in suspicion. He met her glare with an unconcerned shrug. He knew what she thought. She thought that he didn't care. She thought that he was in it for himself, just like everyone else did when they found out about his childhood and about his past. Half of the time, George wondered if he was in it for the money. Except a small part of him wondered: if he was in it for the money, why did he never have any?

The doorbell suddenly chimed, causing Amelia to visibly flinch. She stared toward the hallway with wide eyes, as if expecting a monster to suddenly walk into the room.

"Are you expecting anyone?" George asked, drawing her gaze back to him, wanting to reassure her.

"My parents and my friends have keys. They wouldn't ring the doorbell."

"I'll get rid of whoever it is," he said with a reassuring nod.

She stared at him for a long minute; then she reluctantly nodded and turned back to the computer. He noticed that her hands trembled when she stacked the papers on the desk into a neat pile. An anger, unlike any he had known, coursed through his body and he half-hoped that her attacker would return so that he could beat him with his bare hands. He hated seeing Amelia afraid. He hated how uncertain she was. He would rather have the sharp-tongued, politely insulting Amelia back than see her look frightened and alone.

He walked down the stairs to the front door. Through the pane of glass next to the door he saw a tall man with butterscotch brown skin, hazel eyes, and a tailored suit that cost more than George's car. The gleaming black BMW in the driveway obviously belonged to the man, who impatiently tapped his foot on the ground as he stared at the door.

George opened the door. The man glanced over George's shoulder toward the interior of the house before he demanded, "Where's Amelia?"

"Who are you?"

The man's eyes narrowed at George's tone. "My name is Brian Austell. I'm a friend of Amelia's. Now, where is she?"

George kept the pleasant smile on his face and slammed the door closed. He ignored the man's stunned expression, then took his time climbing the stairs before he ambled down the hall, where for a few seconds he examined the numerous framed paintings on the walls; then he finally arrived in the doorway of the study.

"Who was at the door?" Amelia asked.

"The door . . ." George pretended to mull over the question; then he said, "Some guy . . . Brian Austell."

Amelia appeared momentarily stunned; then she slowly took off her glasses and stood. "Brian is here?"

George nodded, surprised by the uncertainty that flashed across her face. He knew from that one look that whoever Brian Austell was, he wasn't just a family friend. There was a history between him and Amelia, and George's dislike for the man increased by another degree. Then he remembered her mentioning Brian before. The flowers. Brian was responsible for the nursery sprouting off the dining room table.

George quickly said, "If you want me to get rid of him—"

"No. I'm just surprised. I haven't seen him in over a year, not since the wedding party," she said, then began to brush stray strands of hair from her eyes and straighten her clothes. She turned to George and nervously asked, "How do I look?"

George mumbled a noncommittal response that Amelia obviously didn't care about, since she brushed past him and practically ran out of the room. He told himself to remain at the desk, to read through the stack of newspaper articles and cases that Amelia had assigned to him. But she had mentioned a wedding. He hoped that she was talking about someone else's wedding.

• • •

Amelia tried not to cringe when Brian wrapped his arms around her. She refused to return his embrace, but she couldn't help enjoying the familiar feel of him for at least a few seconds. Of course, she had to break the embrace first. She took several steps across the foyer to place as much distance between them as was respectable. Things with Brian always had to be respectable, which was why her father had always loved Brian more than she did.

He looked concerned as his gaze dropped to the bruises on her neck, then to her bandaged hand. He immediately closed whatever distance she had placed between them and placed one smooth, warm hand on her neck. He was beautiful. Another beautiful man who didn't want her. At least, George had been honest about it. She had to find out on her own, and after spending thousands of dollars on a wedding, the same thing about Brian.

"When I heard what happened . . . Are you all right?" His voice was soft and seductive, but she had long ago learned that he could turn on the charm when he wanted. Mostly when Kenneth Farrow was nearby to witness what a perfect man, friend, future son-in-law, and general all-around wonderful human being Brian could be. Otherwise, Brian was dedicated to pretending to work hard at making partner at his father's prestigious firm and to pursuing and catching as many women as possible—not necessarily in that order.

"I'm fine," she answered, once more moving from his hold.

Brian's smile and gentleness faded. "It's that job, Amelia," he said, grimly. "How many times have I told you? That damn job is going to kill you."

"Being an ADA is not the problem," came George's voice from behind Amelia on the stairs. Both she and Brian turned to stare at George, who should have been ashamed of his eavesdropping, but he continued unfazed. "The problem is all of the idiots out there who have no respect for the law or the people who enforce it."

She coughed over her laughter. George Gibson was defending police officers and attorneys from the DA's office? She quickly glanced out the window to see if pigs flew.

"Who are you again?" Brian demanded.

"George Gibson."

Amelia noticed that neither man offered a hand to the other, but instead the two simply glared at each other. When Brian shifted a speculative gaze from her to George, she couldn't withhold her laugh at his obvious thoughts.

She quickly explained, "George is an attorney that I occasionally argue cases against."

"What is an attorney, who you occasionally argue cases against, doing in your home the afternoon you're released from the hospital? You should be resting, recuperating. You should be at your parents' house, not here alone in this house," Brian said, sounding suspiciously like her father.

George snorted loudly in disgust. Amelia glared at him even though she secretly wanted to smile, to rejoice. Everyone loved Brian, her parents, her friends, her co-workers; even her gardener had asked about the "man with the BMW." George was the only person Amelia knew who had instantly disliked Brian, and no matter his other faults, Amelia suddenly liked George Gibson. A lot.

Brian ignored George and said to her, "Pack whatever you need for the next week. I'm going to take you to your parents' house."

"I already told my father—as I'm sure he told you, which is why you're here—that I'm not going anywhere."

Brian rolled his eyes and sighed impatiently. "You've proven that you can make it on your own. You've proven that you're a better and more socially conscious attorney than your father and me. Now it's time to stop these games and come to your senses. Until this maniac is caught, you should stay with your parents."

She hadn't seen him in over a year, since she had canceled the wedding, and it felt as if nothing had changed. He still ignored her. Brian wasn't a bad person. In fact, she liked him. He was one of her closest friends, or he had been. Sometimes she wondered if that was one of the reasons he had cheated on her. They had more fun laughing and talking outside the bedroom than they'd ever had inside the bedroom. She hated to admit it, even to herself, but she missed Brian. Not his kisses or his touch, but she missed his friendship.

"Brian, I'm not going anywhere," she said. "So drop the subject. Now."

"Yeah, drop the subject," George chimed in.

Brian glared at George, then turned to Amelia and demanded, "Who the hell is this man?"

"Asked and answered," George said, mimicking a courtroom objection.

Amelia interrupted Brian's response as she stepped

around him to open the door. "I'll tell my father that you stopped by and gave it a good try."

Brian did a good job of looking insulted as he angrily retorted, "I didn't come here for your father, Amelia."

"Of course not," she replied in a neutral tone.

"Amelia . . ." Brian's voice trailed off as he pinned George with a hard gaze that Amelia had seen make grown men sweat. She should have known that George would have no idea that Brian was an Austell of the Los Angeles Austells. Brian's politeness sounded forced as he muttered, "Can you give us some privacy, man?"

George looked at her for confirmation. She shrugged in response and he nodded, then walked back up the stairs.

She turned from George's retreating back to Brian, who looked angry enough to spit fire. The two had been thrown together numerous times as children when their parents left the two with the same nanny during their trips around the world. All through high school, college, and then law school, Brian had been a constant presence in her life. He was closer to her parents than his own, who had moved to Washington, D.C., when Mr. Austell became a congressman ten years ago.

Two years ago, she and Brian had become more than friends. It had been strange how natural the progression was from close friends to a couple. Too normal. There was no new-couple awkwardness or nervousness over family dinners. Besides the sex part, which Amelia figured would get better with time, things had been perfect between them. Too perfect.

They liked the same things—watching the Lakers and playing tennis. They knew all the same people. Her father loved Brian. Her mother thought he was too ordinary, but Alice dated foreign princes and professional athletes; anybody was ordinary to her, so her opinion did not count. Amelia's friends all loved him. And, most important for Amelia, she and Brian had never argued.

During their romantic relationship, she had never seen him look annoyed or angry with her. For that matter, she had never been annoyed or angry with Brian. Even when she opened the door to her bedroom in her parents' home the night of the wedding party and found Brian and Stella Brooks in bed together, she had been more irritated about the hassle of calling off the wedding—returning her bridal shower gifts, hoping the seamstress would take back the dress—than angry. Calm resolutions and nonconfrontations were very important to Amelia. She felt anger never solved anything, except with George. He only listened when she became angry.

"Who the hell is that?" Brian demanded in a harsh whisper while darting a glance toward the stairs where George had disappeared.

"He's a colleague."

Brian looked more confused by her answer. "What is he doing here?"

"Who I spend time with stopped being your business a long time ago."

He sighed in exasperation. "Are you going to hate me for the rest of our lives?"

"I don't hate you, but if I did, I think that I have the right."

"We've known each other for too long for us to have this weirdness between us. We go to too many of the same parties."

"I apologize for causing you such discomfort in your social life."

He took a deep breath and said quietly, "I didn't come over here to argue with you. I know that we haven't seen each other since . . . since the last time, but, whether you believe it or not, I still care about you. We've known each other since we were children, Amie; I can't just turn off my feelings for you. Maybe one day we can talk about what happened . . . that night . . . and then we can move past it."

"There's nothing to talk about. I appreciate your concern, but I'm fine. George and I are working on a project. It's taking my mind off the attack."

"You're working?" he asked in disbelief. "Someone tried to kill you last night and you're working?"

"What do you want me to do? Should I crawl under my covers until the police catch him? Should I quit my job, move back in with my father, and never leave the house? You know me better than that, Brian."

She had considered all of those possibilities and it felt good to hear herself sound so confident at their dismissal. She crossed her arms over her chest, then stared at Brian. He never had been able to win a staring contest with her. That hadn't changed, as he quickly averted his eyes.

"I just want you to be careful," he finally said. She nodded, then opened the door wider. He smiled at some unknown joke, then shook his head and muttered, "You never need anyone, do you, Amie?"

"Yes, I do," she said simply. "I just don't need anyone to mess up my life. I can do that on my own."

"You do fine on your own; that's probably why we . . ."

He took a deep breath, then sighed. "I should go."

She stared out the door as a hint for him to leave. She refused to talk about their past relationship or her needs, which she saw as weakness. She realized about a week after the almost-wedding that if she had been as needy and dependent as Stella Brooks, she and Brian would be happily married.

He visibly hesitated, then asked, "Can I call you again?"

She wanted to say no. She wanted to be as hard and unemotional as Eileen and Vicki told her that she needed to be, but instead she wrapped her arms around his neck and hugged him. Hard. Even if he only was her friend because they had been forced together as children, she had missed his conceited and sunny outlook on life, which only money and good looks could provide.

He smiled, a real smile; then he walked out of the house. She closed the door behind him and leaned against it for a moment to compose her feelings. She didn't notice that George stood on the bottom step until he cleared his throat.

"That's the guy who sent the small nursery in the dining room?" George asked in a strange voice that held none of his usual teasing but almost sounded strained. "Who is he?"

"My ex-fiancé."

She stared at George, expecting a sarcastic response. But he said nothing as his jaw clenched. For a moment, she almost imagined that he was jealous. She didn't know why he would be jealous. She characterized his tight expression as annoyance. She was keeping him from his quest for money. They had researched for hours and still had found nothing concrete. She had asked George to stay because she wanted his strength and his calm. Seeing Brian reminded her that she didn't need that. She didn't need to rely on that; she didn't want to rely on that.

"You look tired."

"I am," she said, avoiding his eyes. "I should probably rest for a while."

He appeared on the verge of speaking, but then he shrugged and walked toward the living room. He grabbed his keys from the coffee table, then walked toward the door. His face was pinched into a tight grimace as he said, "I'll see you Monday."

She nodded, then watched him walk out the door. His leaving hurt more than that of any other person who had left that day.

Chapter 6

"I've waited as long as courtesy dictates, but you're obviously going to make me beg. So start talking," Heather demanded as she and Amelia lounged on the chaises near Amelia's swimming pool behind her house the next afternoon.

Although Amelia counted a number of women—all from proper families—as her close friends, Heather was the one she had cried to when it finally hit her that she would soon be thirty years old with no children and one almost-marriage behind her. She had cried to Heather when her mother disappeared for yet another monthlong leave of absence with her latest boy toy. As Amelia's first nanny—who had remained with the family until Amelia turned 21 years old—would say, Heather knew "where all the bones were buried."

"I have no idea what you're talking about," Amelia said as she slipped on a pair of sunglasses.

It was almost a perfect day. The sun shone, she was lying in shorts and a tank top near her pool with her best friend, and she was alive. The remaining slight pain in her neck and at her right cheekbone flashed to remind her that things were not perfect. Someone had tried to kill her. And he was still out there. That put a damper on her mood.

"I thought we decided to stop being coy when we turned twenty-two," Heather reminded her. Amelia continued to ignore her, so Heather said clearly, "I'm talking about that gorgeous man who stood on your doorstep yesterday, looking like he was about to barrel through us all if we didn't move and let him reach you."

"You mean George?"

She laughed, then said, "Nice performance—a little too much surprise to be real, but nice try."

Amelia laughed, then shrugged. "Like I told you on the phone last night, he's just a colleague."

"So you claim," Heather said with a smirk.

"He was visiting an injured colleague. There's nothing out of the ordinary about that."

"Your other colleagues called, but only one stopped by," Heather pointed out.

Amelia shook her head. "You're completely wrong about this one, Heather."

"There were some definite sparks yesterday when you two saw each other. No one spoke for, at least, thirty seconds. I thought that only happened in the movies."

"What about you and Nicolas?"

As far as Amelia was concerned, Heather and her husband of three years had the perfect marriage, nothing like her parents' train wreck of a marriage. Heather and Nicolas were the one married couple Amelia looked to as having love, compatibility, and all other traits that were basically impossible to find now. Even though they, as a couple, were a fluke and Amelia knew she would never find that type of love, a small part of Amelia liked knowing that type of relationship could exist.

Heather's normally automatic smile at the mention of her husband was not present as she busied herself by pouring fresh-squeezed lemonade from the crystal pitcher into two glasses.

"Heather, are you feeling well?" Amelia asked, concerned.

Heather turned to her with a false smile and said, "Of course I'm feeling well. My restaurant is on track to open in a few days. I already have my menu planned and my orders in. What more could I want?"

Amelia recognized the sadness flirting around Heather's eyes. "If you want to talk—"

"I should be asking if you're all right," Heather interrupted, then rubbed Amelia's arm. "How are you, sweetie?"

"I'm good," Amelia lied through her smile. When she heard the loud silence, she whipped off her sunglasses and glared at Heather. "I am fine. Honest."

Heather inhaled deeply, then blurted out, "Amie, I've been thinking. Nicolas and I have so much room at our house . . . until this monster is found . . . maybe you should stay with us or your parents. I was worried sick last night thinking about you here all alone."

"Would you leave your house?" Amelia asked doubtfully.

"We're not talking about me," Heather immediately responded. "We're talking about you and this maniac still on the loose. What if he comes back to finish the job? I don't want you here if he does."

"I'm not changing my life because of this, and I'm not allowing you and Nicolas to, either. I've been taking care of myself for a long time."

"But—"

"Did my father talk to you like he talked to Brian?" Amelia demanded. "Next he's going to be calling my third-grade teacher to have her convince me to stay at his house."

"Yoo-hoo! Yoo-hoo!"

Amelia groaned when she heard the familiar greeting of her mother from the kitchen. She smoothed a hand over her hair and adjusted her headband. She would have spared herself the visit from her mother if she had known Alice was coming. It wasn't something she could prevent. Alice had a key and used it whenever she wanted.

"We're out here, Mom!" Amelia called into the kitchen, then glared at Heather, who only shrugged in response.

Alice walked onto the backyard wood deck wearing an outfit worthy of one of Magnum, PI's damsels in distress. Soft, flowing material that displayed the exact amount of breast that she wanted to show and probably more than she should have.

"Hello, ladies. It's a beautiful day to be in the sun, but you two should be at the beach picking up men, not hanging around here," Alice greeted them, then sat on the edge of Amelia's chair to reach over and place a kiss on her forehead. Alice pulled a slim black folder from her large designer handbag at Amelia's feet. "Guess what I finally received today?"

She didn't wait for Amelia to answer before she opened the folder and shoved it into Amelia's hand. Amelia and

Heather stared at the eight-by-ten glossy pictures of Alice. Amelia had to admit that the camera loved her mother. Alice was a gorgeous and striking woman, but there was something special between her and the camera in every shot taken of her that had made her the first black woman on the cover of several major fashion magazines. Amelia didn't begrudge her mother's success; she just wished she didn't have to hear about it so much.

"These are beautiful, Alice," Heather chimed in as Alice closely watched the two look at each picture.

"My agent told me *Sports Illustrated* will have a section devoted to older models in their swimsuit issue this year. Guess who is trying for one of the four spots?" Alice announced, then struck a pose that on any other woman would have made her look like a broken-limbed ostrich but made her look sultry and seductive.

Amelia and Heather exchanged glances. Amelia forced a smile, then glanced at her mother. "I thought you were retired."

"This is *Sports Illustrated*, Amie," Alice gushed, gracefully perching on the edge of Amelia's lounge chair. "The exposure would be terrific, and to be honest, I miss seeing my face in magazines."

"There's no doubt they will pick you," Heather said as she returned the folder to Alice.

Alice hugged the folder to her chest and flashed that 1,000-watt smile. "They would be fools not to. I'm flying to New York this evening to personally drop off my pictures, and Bev is in New York. I haven't seen her in ages."

"You're leaving?" Amelia asked, attempting to keep the panic and hurt out of her voice. She had told her parents she was a grown woman. She didn't need her mother to stay in town just because she had almost been killed, but as her stomach tied into knots Amelia realized that she was not as grown as she thought. Just once, she wanted her mother to be . . . a mother. Amelia didn't want oatmeal cookies and a bedtime story, but an, "Are you all right?" would have gone a long way.

"Just for a few days," Alice said, waving a hand dismissively. Her smile disappeared for a moment as she studied Amelia.

Then Alice's smile returned full force as if a brilliant idea had just popped into her head. She abruptly clapped her hands together with such excitement that Heather gasped in surprise.

Alice grinned and placed a hand on Amelia's leg. "Come with me to New York. We can go shopping and eat ourselves sick! My personal rule is that I can eat whatever I want when I'm in that town, because for so many years while I was modeling, I didn't eat anything. Besides, Bev hasn't seen you in years. What do you say, honey?"

Amelia felt herself smiling because her mother was so enthusiastic about the idea. It also provided some confirmation that Alice did remember that her daughter had almost been killed. Alice never invited Amelia on her jaunts, not that she would have gone.

"It sounds fun, Mom, but I can't," Amelia finally said, shaking her head. "I have a job—"

"Your job can wait," Alice dismissed with another wave of her manicured hand. "The one thing that Kenneth and I can agree on is that your job leaves much to be desired."

"My job had nothing to do with the attack," Amelia said firmly.

"Do you know who did this to you?" Heather asked.

"No," Amelia admitted.

"Then how do you know it's not related to your job?" Heather pressed. "Maybe going to New York with your mother is the answer. You can be far away until the police catch this idiot."

Amelia noticed her mother suddenly reach into her bag and begin to root around the contents, completely tuned out of the conversation.

Amelia turned to Heather and said, "I wish I could go, but I can't."

"Are the police, at least, doing something to catch this man?" Heather demanded.

"It's been two days, Heather," Amelia said, laughing.

"Aha!" Alice exclaimed as she pulled a lipstick tube from her purse. "Heather, how are the plans coming for your restaurant opening?"

Heather glanced at Amelia and Amelia instantly averted her gaze. She knew that she was a low priority to her mother, but she didn't need it to be proven to her friends. Her thoughts drifted to George, because his biggest complaint about her was her "perfection." She wished he would share her apparently irritating perfection with her parents.

George cursed, then turned off his computer. He couldn't concentrate. He usually spent Sundays at his office, catching up on work and preparing for the week ahead. Then in the afternoon he would go to the beach and hang out with Wayne or sit in a bookstore and read books that he never planned to buy. No commitments, no entanglements. That had seemed like the perfect leisurely Sunday until now. Now he felt restless. Like energy was bottled in his body with nowhere to go.

He glanced around his office. It wasn't really an office. It was more like one room with a desk, four chairs, a refrigerator in one corner, and a plant that he had carried with him from his college dorm to law school and finally to this office. He figured as long as the plant survived, then so would he. There was a wall of windows that showcased the courthouse only two blocks away and the other buildings buried under the Los Angeles shroud of smog. It wasn't much, but it was home, since he spent more time at work than in his apartment.

He turned from the window and began to rifle through the stack of mail that the floor secretary delivered for all of the various one-man and one-woman operations in the depressed building. When he realized that he had read the same bill twice, he tossed the bills onto the desk and buried his face in his hands.

He finally admitted it. He couldn't concentrate because he was thinking about Amelia. He hadn't wanted to leave her, but he had the feeling that she needed him to leave. Wanted him to leave. There had been a vulnerability on her face that made him want to hold her. The only reason he didn't was because he knew if he tried to touch her, she would have bodily thrown him out of the house. That and the fact that he was certain Brian Austell would fill the comfort void. A small, angry part of George wondered if Amelia had been in such a hurry to get rid of him because Brian would return.

George cursed once more at his thoughts. He was acting like a lovesick high school adolescent. She obviously thought that he was the scum of the earth. He wanted to be paid, he wanted to live comfortably, and for those reasons she thought that he was akin to an ambulance-chasing attorney whom other lawyers laughed at. Maybe George had followed an ambulance once or twice, but he hadn't done that in, at least, two or three years, since his criminal defense practice had taken off.

The telephone rang, intruding upon his self-loathing. He picked up the telephone, expecting to hear Wayne's voice. Only Wayne would know that he was in the office on a Sunday morning.

"Meet any women in church this morning?" George asked.

Wayne called to report every Sunday afternoon about the number of beautiful women in church in an attempt to entice George into accompanying him. George hadn't set foot in a church since he was ten years old, when he saw his married foster mother and the married choir director in the backseat of the car.

"No, I didn't go. . . . George, it's Amelia."

George almost fell from his tilted chair at the sound of Amelia's voice. He quickly righted himself, but not without knocking a few papers to the floor as he flailed for the desk.

"Hi," he said, attempting to cover his surprise at the sound of her voice. "How are you feeling?"

"I'm good, I'm fine. . . . I'm great."

"That's good to hear." There was a long pause and George wracked his brain for a reason that she would call. Maybe she wanted to discuss the O'Connor case or ask him to give her the ride of her life. . . . He frowned, because that thought had taken him by surprise. He finally asked, "What can I do for you, Amelia?"

"I've been thinking about what you said," she hesitantly told him.

When she didn't continue, he prodded, "I say a lot of things. You're going to have to give me a little more help than that."

"I've been thinking about talking to Thomas Chin's wife. Until I receive the lab results tomorrow, it wouldn't hurt to ask Mrs. Chin a few questions. She could know something that could help us interpret the results."

"Are you certain? You were against the idea yesterday."

"Stop it," she abruptly ordered.

"Stop what?" he asked with what he hoped was an air of innocence.

"Why are you treating me like this?"

"Like what?"

"Like . . . like we're friends, like you care."

"You called me, Amelia," he reminded her. The irritation was familiar, not the soft, squishy feelings. He clung to the emotion and used it to become angrier. "You were almost killed. I don't know how you expect me to treat you—"

"I want you to treat me normally, George."

He heard the pleading tone in her voice and he sighed in resignation. If she wanted to pretend everything was normal, then he found himself powerless to resist. If Amelia discovered that he couldn't resist her tear-roughened voice, then his clients would be in big trouble.

"I'll pick you up on the way to the Chins'," he told her. "The family lives near downtown."

"How do you know that?" she asked, sounding surprised.

"What can I say? I have friends in low places. I'll be there in thirty minutes."

Chapter 7

"So what happened with you and Austell?" George asked casually as he lounged in the passenger seat of her car.

He would never admit it, but her sleek luxury car rode as if they floated on a cloud and was worth every penny she must have spent for it. And he knew that it must have been a lot of pennies. After he arrived at her house, she had insisted on driving. At first he was insulted because he thought she didn't want to be seen in his car. Hell, *he* didn't want to be seen in his car, but it was the principle that bothered him.

Then he had realized about five minutes after she pulled her car into traffic that Amelia needed to drive, just like she needed to work. She needed to return to her normal routine. The tension seeped from her face and she actually looked happy as she navigated the car through Los Angeles Sunday street traffic, which in some parts was as bad as weekday traffic.

"What do you mean?" she asked.

"I mean, he was a fiancé and now he's an ex-fiancé;

usually something happens to make that title change."

"I don't want to talk about it."

"He cheated on you," George guessed.

For one second she took her eyes off the road to stare at him with an astonished expression. George actually laughed at her obvious surprise. A car horn blared behind them and she turned to the road again and drove through the intersection.

"How did you know that?" she finally asked.

"I eavesdropped on your conversation," he responded simply. She sent him a quick glare, which he returned with a grin. "You guys danced around the topic, neither of you came right out and said that he had an affair, but they pay me to put two and two together. Did you know her?"

"She was supposed to be a bridesmaid in my wedding party."

"Ouch."

"'Ouch' is one way to describe it. Brian said, 'Who needs a bachelor party? I have you.' We decided to just invite all of our friends over to my parents' house and have a combined bachelor and bachelorette party with food and games. I found the two of them. In my bed."

"That's very *Lifetime* movie of the week."

She actually smiled as she shot him a quick glance. "All of my friends thought so."

"But you didn't?" he asked, intrigued by her bemused expression. As if she didn't care. She had found the man she loved enough to marry in bed with another woman, and she didn't seem angry or bitter. Only amused.

"I could see the drama and the humor in the situation. Of course, the humor part came a little later."

He stared at her for a few moments, then murmured, "I can't believe you almost married Austell."

"Why not? He and I are perfect for each other."

George thought about Brian's neatly pressed slacks and meticulously arranged tie, then took in Amelia's sleeveless blue tank dress, matching cardigan, and headband. She had a point.

"Our problem was, Brian didn't want perfection. He wanted excitement and Stella Brooks, obviously. It's best that I found out about Brian when I did. Besides, I don't plan to marry for passion or love. I plan to marry for companionship."

"Companionship?" George asked, his expression blank.

"My parents were madly in love in the beginning. . . . It lasted long enough for my mother to get pregnant, and now they can't be in the same room with each other for more than five minutes without arguing. I loved Brian, but apparently that wasn't enough for him. So, I decided to stop looking for love and start looking for someone . . . compatible. Someone perfectly compatible with me." It sounded as if she had rehearsed her little speech a long time ago.

"Compatible?"

"O'Connor will accept attempted manslaughter." He stared at her, confused, and she smiled, then said, "Since you were repeating everything I say, I thought I'd give it a try."

He wasn't laughing. "I'm just trying to make certain that I'm not hearing things. You don't want to be in love with your husband?"

"If our interests are compatible, I believe that love will

follow. Eventually. But I'm not interested in love. I want respect and kindness. I want us to have mutual goals and an understanding that those goals can't be met without each other's support. Love is a . . . a nice emotion, but it confuses things and causes too many problems. Exhibit A: the O'Connor case. Your client claims he drove his truck into that house because of love for his wife."

"You're talking about a business deal, not a marriage."

"That's what marriage is—a business deal."

"What about sex?"

"Don't be crass," she said with a lift of her debutante chin that made George grin. Sometimes he purposely irritated her just to make certain that a touch of debutante still remained hidden beneath her public servant exterior.

"For the business deal, or marriage, to be ultimately successful, you have to have sex with your husband . . . if for no other reason than to carry on the family name or so your money won't fall into the hands of strangers," he said. "To have children, a couple must have sex at some point."

"If we truly respect each other and admire each other's intellect, I'm certain that the sex will be satisfactory."

He snorted in disbelief and leaned into the seat. "I don't know about you, Farrow, but I don't want my sex to be just 'satisfactory.' I like it sweaty and hard and loud. So good it makes your eyes roll to the back of your head. You can't have all that with satisfactory sex."

He stared at her and smiled when he noticed her flushed cheeks. Underneath the open sweater she wore he saw the suddenly rapid rise and fall of her breasts. He noticed that the golden-brown skin above her neckline looked soft and inviting. He tried not to dwell on the fact that his palms had begun to sweat. He couldn't prevent his voice from lowering to a husky whisper as he asked, "Have you ever had that kind of sex, Amelia?"

Her voice sounded an octave higher as she retorted, "I hope you don't expect an answer to that insulting question."

"I doubt it," he answered for her. "If you had, you would never accept satisfactory sex again."

Her mouth dropped open in protest, but before she could respond, George said, "Turn left here. This is the Chins' street."

A few minutes later, she parked the car in front of a single-level home in a tree-lined neighborhood. George got out of the car and put on his sunglasses to look less conspicuous as he surveyed the small house. He heard children laughing in the distance, and he turned to see a group of three boys ride by on their bicycles. His heart tumbled at the carefree expressions on their faces. He had grown up in this type of neighborhood, hardworking families mixed with gang members and drug addicts. The majority of people worked hard and were honest, but they were constantly terrorized by those who were not. His stomach clenched for a moment and he took several deep breaths. He had to force himself not to turn back to the car, and only because Amelia stood next to him.

He darted a glance at Amelia to make certain that she hadn't noticed his nostalgic expression. She looked pre-occupied as she stared at the house.

He turned back to the house and noticed the drawn curtains and dark windows. "It doesn't look like any-one's home," he said to her.

"I will have you know that I have had wonderful sex,"

she told him through clenched teeth. He hid his surprise as she walked around the car to stand in front of him. Her jaw was clenched and her arms were crossed over her chest. Typical courtroom Amelia battle pose, when she forgot she was supposed to be all sugar and sunshine.

"Yeah, right," he dryly responded.

"I have," she insisted.

"Cool, Farrow. I believe you. Do you think the Chins moved—"

"Blake Houston, my first year in law school."

"You expect me to believe that you had great sex with a guy named Blake? Did he have an ex-wife named Alexis?" George laughed at her obsession with eighties television.

"It was a very passionate affair. He was a tax attorney who spoke at my law school and—"

"A tax attorney?" George laughed in disbelief, then shook his head and said, "Now I can't even pretend that I believe you."

"All we did was have sex. We took turns. Some nights I did anything and everything he wanted. Some nights he did anything and everything I wanted. It didn't matter where we were or what time it was; we couldn't keep our hands off each other."

Maybe it was the way her mouth curled around the words *anything and everything,* but George found that he no longer had the air in his lungs to laugh. She was telling the truth. The black Mary Poppins of Los Angeles had done anything and everything some guy wanted.

"We would make love for hours. Days. He almost lost his job because of me. I almost flunked out of my first year of law school because of him. I finally broke things off because no matter how good the sex was, we had nothing else in common, and even if it kills me, I'm not settling. I'm going to have the whole package. And I will be happy."

She appeared on the verge of saying more, but she huffed in indignation, then brushed past him toward the house. He stared after her for a few moments, trying to envision Amelia wild and loose in bed, allowing a man to actually order her to do anything and everything. Except there wasn't some Brian look-alike with her. It was him. He cursed, then ran after her.

She climbed the porch steps and knocked on the door. He stopped beside her and snuck a peek at her from behind his sunglasses. His breathing still hadn't returned to normal since her admission. It was humiliating to think that Amelia Farrow had a more exciting sex life than he did. Since he worked fifty-hour weeks, he would bet that Bob Dole had a more exciting sex life than he did.

"Are you looking for the Chins?"

George spun around surprised that someone stood behind them and he hadn't heard the person approach. But, then again, since he could only think about Amelia promising to do "anything" he wanted, he shouldn't have been that surprised.

A woman with black hair that stood at attention in hundreds of solid curls stood on the bottom porch step. She wore a matching purple outfit that was a little too tight and showed a little too much chocolate skin, but George had a feeling that was the precise reason the woman had chosen the outfit. He couldn't place her age, but he would guess she was in her late forties and probably on the lookout for a new boyfriend, since she studied

George with barely concealed interest. She looked from Amelia to George, then back to Amelia again before she shifted the newspaper in her hands, as though it would defend her from them.

"My name is Amelia Farrow, and I'm with the district attorney's office," Amelia said smoothly as she flashed her identification. She motioned to George and said with a frown, "This is George Gibson."

"I'm Maddie. Now that we've introduced ourselves and exchanged blood types, what the hell do you people want now?" the woman asked, annoyed. "I'm sick of you all coming around here. You're making me nervous. If I get nervous, my boys get nervous, and you don't want that."

"Someone else has been here?" Amelia asked, surprised.

"I don't know," the woman said with a crafty smile as recognition sank in. She glanced from Amelia's gleaming luxury car to her Rolex watch and the obviously expensive clothes and shoes. "I may have seen someone and I may not have. In my old age, the vision gets clouded."

Amelia stared, confused, at the woman while George had to smile. This was a woman after his own heart. He pulled a ten-dollar bill from his wallet and handed it to her.

"Does that clear the fog a little?" he asked with a grin.

"I liked Anna and Tommy, so I promised myself that I'd keep an eye on the place. Anna didn't ask me to, but after Tommy's death she didn't really talk to anyone in the neighborhood. Two days after the boy died, she took the girls and left. She only took the clothes on her back.

No furniture, no dishes, not even the pictures still hanging on the wall," the woman said as she leaned against the porch railing as if prepared to talk for a while. "About a day later, this man came. Big, scary man. Deep voice. He looked through the windows and walked around the house. He came and banged on my door and asked me if I knew anything. I said that I didn't know the Chins. When I saw you, I thought maybe you were with him, but I should have known better." She paused to look George up and down and she added with a wink, "He wasn't half as cute as you, handsome."

George grinned at her in return while Amelia didn't bother to hide her look of annoyance. She asked, "Did you notice anything strange in the Chin household in the days immediately before Mr. Chin's death?"

Maddie snorted and said, "I was their neighbor, not their guidance counselor." She looked at George and said, "Where did you come up with this one?"

Amelia didn't give him time to answer: "Do you have any idea where Mrs. Chin went?"

Maddie belligerently shook her head, then once more glanced at George. He took off his sunglasses, then placed his arm around the woman's shoulders, turning her so that her back was to Amelia.

"We think that Mrs. Chin is in danger. We don't think that her husband was killed during a robbery."

"Of course he wasn't," Maddie said, causing George to look at her surprised. "The man drove a 1997 Saturn. Who would kill anyone for that? Anna hadn't even buried her husband and she took off to San Francisco, where her sister lives. Something or someone scared the poor woman to death."

"San Francisco," George said, then teased her with a squeeze to her shoulder. "You've been holding out on me, Maddie."

"I don't know where in San Francisco, but she told me that's where she was headed."

"Do you think that you could identify the man who came looking for her after Mr. Chin's death?" Amelia asked, stepping around George to once more insert herself into the conversation.

"Hell, no," Maddie said, vigorously shaking her head, sending ringlets of curls into her eyes.

George tried to send Amelia a silent warning to cease her prosecutorial bullying tactics, but Amelia ignored him as usual. "You may not have a choice in the matter. I can subpoena you—"

"Subpoena, my ass," Maddie exploded. "I'd be gone so fast your pretty little head would spin."

George cut off Amelia's response by grabbing her arm. She glared at him, but he ignored her and pasted a smile on his face for Maddie. "Are you holding out on me again, Maddie?" he cooed. "Did that man say something to you? Did he scare you, too?"

Maddie's face softened and she shook her head. "I told you the truth, I never spoke to him, but as he was driving away in a nice-looking burgundy Rolls-Royce— last three letters in the license plate JL5—my youngest came out and asked what did he want. I haven't seen my youngest scared of anything since he became too big for me to put over my knee, but he was scared when he saw that car. He told me to stay away from that man."

"Did he tell you why?" George prodded.

"He said the man worked for Donaldson. Maurice

Donaldson. I don't know anything about Donaldson, except that him and his kind come into our neighborhoods, flashing their money, driving their big cars, and trying to tempt my sons. It makes me sick to my stomach. They think they can do anything and everything and no one will stop them. They aren't scared of the cops, of death, of anything."

George glanced at Amelia, who met his gaze. He saw the same thoughts that he was thinking swirling behind her eyes. Donaldson's name was popping up too often for it to be a coincidence.

"Thank you, Maddie. And your boy is right. If you see that man or anyone else like that around here, just close the blinds and call the police. Understand?" George said. He pulled another ten-dollar bill out of his wallet. "Buy your kids a pizza."

"Kids, my ass. I'm getting my nails done." She waved to George, pointedly glared at Amelia, then sauntered across the yard.

George smiled to himself, then turned to Amelia, surprised to find her glaring at him. He suddenly felt nervous for no reason, which made him even more nervous. He forced a laugh and said, "Maddie's quite a character, huh?"

Amelia shook her head, then walked off the porch toward her car. He grinned, then followed her. He sat in the car and barely had time to close the door before she pulled away from the curb. He decided not to comment when he saw the warning look in her eyes.

"That was a dead end," he said to break the icy silence in the car, then quickly added, "No pun intended."

"It wasn't a wasted trip. You had the opportunity to shamelessly flirt with a potential witness."

He wasn't fooled by the sugar dripping from her voice. He decided to quickly change the subject. It didn't matter why she was angry, just that she was and he didn't want to deal with it.

"Since the Chins were no help, we have to get the videotapes. Maybe we'll get lucky and spot that burgundy Rolls-Royce that could be connection enough for the police to investigate or even for a grand jury."

"We can't just take the tapes. That's against the law."

He smiled at her serious expression, then said, "It's good to know that you ADAs are so quick on your feet, but as a defense attorney I have to correct you. We have no intention of permanently depriving the courthouse of those tapes, we're only borrowing them, so there are no grounds for a larceny conviction. We aren't planning to commit a felony, so there are no grounds for a breaking and entering conviction. Therefore, the most we could be convicted of is trespassing."

She shook her head. "Convincing me that we could only go to prison for trespassing is not enough of an incentive."

"There's no other choice, Farrow. If we want to know who was on the stairwell, we have to find the tapes. Whoever this person is probably killed Thomas Chin and tried to kill you. And if he didn't do it, then he probably knows who did."

"Maybe we should wait for the lab results from the stairwell before we do anything else, especially if it involves breaking the law. The police—"

"The police won't help because as far as they're concerned there's been no crime," he interrupted impatiently.

"I would think that you, of all people, would want to see this through."

She was silent for a moment as he hoped his words registered, then she reluctantly said, "I don't know about all of this, George. Breaking and entering, committing felonies . . . it's wrong—"

"What's wrong is that two little girls don't have a father because Donaldson decided that he needed to be killed. That's wrong. It's also wrong that my clients and other defendants got the short end of the stick while the truly guilty walk free because their boss has enough money to bribe enough judges and enough cops. That's wrong. You and me trying to figure out a way to put him behind bars is not wrong, Amelia."

He was surprised by his own ardent defense of his course of action. He cared. He cared more than he wanted to admit or wanted anyone to know.

"I'm going to do it with or without you. Are you in or out?"

"All right, George. I'm in."

He silently nodded, then stared out the car window. He thought of the numerous courtroom entrances and exits, he thought of what would happen if they were caught, but mostly he thought of the small spike of thrill he felt when he realized that it would require a return to his old way of life. It was a dangerous feeling.

Chapter 8

As his watch registered midnight, George tried hard not to laugh as Amelia slid into the passenger seat of his car. He could barely admit it to himself, but he had missed her. He had spent the rest of the evening after their visit to the Chins at his house finding the right tools for the job, contacting trusted associates who knew the layout of the courthouse, and worrying about Amelia. It was a strange feeling—the worry.

He worried about Wayne sometimes, worried that some idiot would kill him on the job. But George had never worried about anyone else, especially about a woman. And then along came Amelia. Sitting alone in the house where someone had tried to kill her only two nights before. Where was her family? Her friends? Her man? George couldn't see why people who supposedly loved her would allow her to be alone, no matter how much she insisted. Seeing her now in her cat burglar outfit, worthy of any Hollywood movie, made him realize that all the worry was worth it. Every minute was worth it to be around her again.

"What is so funny?" Amelia asked, shooting him a hard glare.

"What are you wearing?" he asked through his laughter as he eyed her all-black outfit—boots, pants, turtleneck, insulated vest, and ski mask rolled on top of her head. At least she wore pants. He had half-expected her to walk out of the house in a black sweater set and black skirt with a headband. He definitely liked her choice of pants. The tight fit emphasized more than a skirt ever could. He decided that he liked her pants a lot.

"What?" she asked blankly.

"You look like a cat burglar from every bad movie I've ever seen. We're borrowing a tape from the court's video collection, not stealing the crown jewels."

"Excuse me for not having the appropriate outfit to break and enter a courthouse," she snapped.

"As soon as the guards see you dressed like a character from *The Thomas Crown Affair*, they'll know something's going on, and we'll be carted off to jail before I can even attempt to get to the basement."

"I thought the point was the guards aren't supposed to see us." He kept his mouth closed. "Have you given any thought to how we're going to get into the storage room where the tapes are kept?"

"I figured we'd be where the guards are not," he replied with a casual shrug. "And eventually we'd make it to the lower level. I'd pick the lock on the door and—"

"You know how to pick locks?"

"We'll get the tapes," he continued, unfazed, "and

faster than you can say 'Harry Houdini,' we'll be out of there."

"You're basically telling me that you don't have a plan," she said. She shook her head and groaned. "I'm going to jail tonight."

"Of course I have a plan," he muttered, then added in a halting voice, "I just haven't thought of it yet."

She moaned again. "I should call my attorney now so he'll be ready to bail me out."

"OK, OK. . . . A guard sits in the video room at night to log and record all the tapes from that day. My sources tell me that he usually takes a break around midnight to meet his wife at the rear exit for a quickie."

"How do you know that?"

He ignored her question. "We can enter through the employee courthouse entrance. We'll have to somehow avoid the second guard, but he'll probably be waiting at the front entrance. We'll take the stairs down and we're in." He smiled at his own ingenuity and waited for her compliments. Even in the darkness of the car, he could see that she was not pleased. He sighed. "Do you have a better plan?"

As if she had been waiting for exactly that question, she eagerly told him, "I found old architectural drawings of the courthouse—"

"What?"

"I found floor plans on the Internet. . . . There's an air duct that begins in the elevator shaft and passes the room where the security tapes are stored. We can access the air duct through a door on the south side of the courthouse that leads to the elevator shaft."

"Hold it right there, Farrow," George said while shaking

his head. "This is sounding a little too complicated for me. I'm not climbing up any elevator shaft. Large, bone-crushing elevators are in elevator shafts."

"But the elevator in this shaft is broken, remember? That's why I was taking the stairs Friday. You can pick the lock to the door; we'll enter the air duct, climb up one level using the repair ladder, and then enter the air duct which leads directly to the room where the tapes are stored."

George was silent for a moment as he tried not to admit that her plan was better than his.

"What if the door is linked to the security alarm? As soon as we open it, the whole courthouse could light up like a Christmas tree and you'll get a firsthand look at all of the women you sent to jail last week."

"It's not linked to the security alarm."

"How do you know?" he asked doubtfully.

"You have your secrets, and I have mine," she said with a smug smile.

He silently nodded in acceptance, then glanced at her again as he carefully said, "We wouldn't have to break into courthouses and pick locks if we had someone powerful behind us, someone who could order security to turn over the tapes, who could order someone to find a man who works for Donaldson and drives a burgundy car . . . someone like your father."

"My father is not a part of this," she said, looking straight ahead.

"Have you told him what happened?"

"Of course I told him. At the hospital."

George watched her grind her teeth and he guessed. "You told him and he didn't believe you."

"He believes me. He won't admit it, but I can tell that he believes me. He just doesn't want me to rock the boat. My father has told me since I was a little girl that Farrows don't cause problems; Farrows solve problems."

"Having a few million stored in the bank can solve a lot of problems," George muttered.

She didn't respond but continued to stare out the windshield. From the lights of oncoming traffic George saw her stony expression. He told himself that he didn't want to hear about her "poor little rich girl" story, especially when he had started working at ten years old, but he also couldn't stand the strange look in her eyes. He recognized that look. Absolute loneliness.

"We don't need your father. We can do this without him," George said. "If he doesn't want to ensure that the criminal system is free of corruption, then that's his problem."

"You don't understand," she said softly, shaking her head.

"I understand, Farrow. He likes his life, his status, his position in the community. He likes having a perfect daughter. If you run around talking about corrupt judges and cops, you're not so perfect anymore. It'll affect him, too—whether you're right or wrong."

She stared at him across the car, then murmured, "Something like that."

"I understand more than you think about rich people. I've spent my whole life trying to understand them, so that if I ever have my own money I'll be nothing like them."

"You spend a lot of time thinking about money, Gibson," she noted.

He glanced at her, expecting to see the teasing on her face, but she appeared engrossed in the scenery of twinkling night lights outside the car windows.

"People who have no money usually think about it a lot," he dryly muttered.

"People who have money usually think about it a lot, too, George," she said, directing her gaze at him. He found himself once more at a loss for words and decided to go with the flow and keep his mouth shut.

"This is what I don't understand about you, Gibson," she continued, obviously not needing him to talk. "You want everyone for some reason to believe that you don't care and that you only are interested in money, yet you take on clients who can't pay you and never pretend that they can pay you. I would never admit this in public, but you're a good attorney; you could work at any big firm in this city and have all the money you want. If money is all you want, if it's the only thing that motivates you, why do you find and represent the only clients who can't pay you? Why do you want everyone to believe that?"

He shrugged at her questioning smile and turned on the radio. She immediately turned it off. "You work in that one-room office on Wilshire taking on indigent clients. Judging from this car, you can't be doing that well. You could have everything you ever wanted if you worked at a firm. Either you're an idiot or you're the most idealistic person I've ever met. Even more idealistic, I daresay, than me."

He smiled to himself at her half-disgusted and half-annoyed tone before he said, "I think you just paid me a compliment, Farrow . . . somewhere in there."

"By calling you an idiot?" she asked blankly.

He laughed as he parked the car on the deserted street behind the courthouse. He stared at the dimly lit building and, against his will, thought of all the possibilities that could occur when a woman walked into a building where she wasn't supposed to be and the people who were supposed to be in the building carried weapons. He looked at Amelia, who was checking the items in the small duffel bag in her lap.

"Maybe you should wait in the car," he said suddenly.

She looked at him with wide eyes, then shook her head and said, "You've known me for a year, Gibson. Do I seem like the type who would wait in the car?"

He rolled his eyes in answer, then pulled down the ski mask to cover his face. She actually smiled at him before she pulled down her own mask. Their eyes met for a moment, and he felt a jolt of arousal. He cleared his throat at that ridiculous emotion, then said gruffly, "First sign of trouble, I want you to run. Don't look back."

"I may not have taken Breaking and Entering one-oh-one, but I know that I'm not supposed to leave my partner."

"In Breaking and Entering one-oh-one, the first thing you learn is to save your own ass and leave your partner at the first sign of trouble," he told her, then smiled behind his mask and felt compelled to point out, "Not only are you breaking the law, but you just called a defense attorney your partner."

He heard her frustrated groan; then she muttered, "Come on."

He was surprised by her smooth athleticism as she raced across the parking lot, her all-black clothes blending in with the night. George tried not to admire her behind in the tight pants, because this was a serious situation. They were breaking the law, breaking into a courthouse. He was becoming involved with an assistant district attorney, whose father would probably eat him for breakfast. Still, he stared at her swaying hips for another moment, then ran after her.

Amelia would never admit the truth to George, but hanging on a tiny wobbly ladder in a chamber so dark that she couldn't see her hand in front of her face scared the hell out of her. When the two had reached the small maintenance door to the courthouse that had been next to a set of manicured bushes, she had prayed that George wouldn't be able to open the door with the extensive set of picks he had pulled from a case in the small backpack he carried. When the door magically popped open, George had whistled in obvious awe at himself while Amelia silently cursed.

Then she had hoped that the door wouldn't lead to the elevator shaft, that the floor plans she had received were wrong. Of course, after another picked lock George had opened the door to the stuffy, smelly, and extremely dark elevator shaft. Without a word, Amelia had found the ladder and begun to climb. Now she clung to the ladder, praying that she could continue to force herself to place each hand on the next rung. She could not press herself against the wall and plead with George to carry her out, because if she did, not only would she never be able to forgive herself, but she knew that she would never be able to face George in a courtroom again. Besides, Amelia Farrow did not give up. Not even when she was breaking the law.

She shone the pen flashlight in her hand overhead and almost dropped it when she saw the hulking mass of the elevator several feet above her head. It filled the entire chamber. If the elevator moved for any reason . . . She shook her head to clear away the thought and then shone the flashlight on the wall.

"I see the entrance to the air duct," she whispered excitedly. Her voice echoed in the wide chamber and she cringed for a moment at the volume.

"Can you make it there?" George whispered in return.

"I hope so," she murmured to herself, but the doubt in his voice propelled her to move faster up the ladder. She pulled a screwdriver from the duffel bag that hung on her arm and, with the light fixed in between her teeth, unscrewed the four nails that held the cover in place. She gingerly lifted the cover and placed it inside the passageway before she pulled herself into the duct with a grunt.

She climbed into the metal duct, cringing at every loud groan of the metal and ignoring the narrow, cramped confines that barely fit the width of her shoulders. If she barely squeezed through, she knew that George would have problems. She directed the light down the dark duct and froze for a moment. It was too hot, too cramped, and much too dark. Sweat rolled down her back as she remained frozen for several seconds. She wanted to be in her king-size bed at home, watching *The A-Team*, not crawling through a dirty air-conditioning duct in the dark.

Then she felt George's hand on her ankle. He squeezed

in reassurance, and instead of telling him that she didn't need his comfort, she began to carefully squirm through the duct. When she rounded a corner, she saw light streaming through a grate on one side. Through the grate cover she saw the familiar dull industrial beige paint of the interior of the courthouse and a stack of videotapes on a shelf. She had never been so relieved to see a video-tape as she was at that moment. She wouldn't swear to it, but a few minutes ago she'd thought she had felt something small and furry skitter across her glove. She had barely been able to contain the scream.

She stopped at the grate, her hands already on the cover to pull it open, when she saw a man in a security guard's uniform and a woman in a waitress uniform rolling on the floor in an amorous mutual attack. She muttered a curse and briefly closed her eyes for strength to withstand the X-rated show in front of her. She was hot and tired, more tired than she thought she would be. Who knew that breaking the law could be so exhausting?

"Pull off the grate. The second I entered this duct I realized that I'm claustrophobic," George whispered impatiently from his position at her feet.

"Someone's in there."

"I am burning up in here. . . . What did you say? Someone's in the room? Who?"

"A man that should be fired."

"What are you talking about . . . ?" His voice trailed off as he quietly pulled himself up the passageway. Since there was not enough room for him to lie by her side, he lay on top of her, basically squashing her, as he pulled himself up the duct. She pounded her closed hands into his chest, unable to orally express her anger, but he continued unimpeded until he lay over her body. Hip to hip. Leg to leg. And chest to chest. She felt his hot breath through his mask and hers as his mouth hovered above hers. His arms were planted on either side of her body, which gave her the impression that he was everywhere, that he surrounded her. Then he shifted against her body and Amelia stopped being angry and outraged by his invasion of her personal space and she became very . . . very aroused.

"What the hell is he doing?" George muttered as he slid his mask off. She stared at his classic profile as he continued to stare at the writhing couple through the grate. She had stared at his profile many times when she shot him a vicious glare in court, but she had never realized how perfect it was. How perfect he was. Suddenly he looked down at her and she realized that they were much closer than she had initially realized. His lips brushed her mask as he said, "That's Fields. He's the guard who's supposed to be in his car in the parking lot right now with his wife . . . except that's not his wife."

Amelia wriggled one hand free from the confines of his body to pull off her mask. She breathed in a cotton-free breath of air until she realized that her nostrils were filled with George's distinctive scent. She resisted the almost uncontrollable urge to claim his mouth, to feel his lips on hers, his tongue stroking her mouth. She arched her back to combat the lava flowing through her body and pooling in her center.

She felt the need to stretch—one long, feline stretch—in order to feel George on every part of her body, not just through her clothes. She tugged at the turtleneck and her eyes once more were drawn to his mouth, then to his eyes, and back to his mouth again. She felt out of control, untamable. She wasn't supposed to feel this way.

George appeared oblivious to her charged mood as he whispered, "What do you think? Should we wait?"

Her hands itched to touch him. She blamed it on the close confines, the attack the other night, even the visit from Brian. Whatever it was, she wanted George Gibson. And she wanted him now.

Her voice sounded hoarse to her own ears as she whispered, "George?"

He looked down at her and seemed to notice her discomfort. He tried to shift in the duct to give her more room, but he only succeeded in bumping his head. They both froze at the loud sound and looked through the grate at the happy couple, but the two appeared oblivious to anything except each other. Amelia quickly shut her eyes when she saw the man begin to unbuckle his pants.

George lowered his head until his mouth touched her ear. She involuntarily shivered.

He whispered, "Maybe we should leave. I'd hate to have to tell my cellmate that I'm in prison for breaking and entering and for being a Peeping Tom."

"I may not have the nerve to do this again," she admitted while keeping her eyes closed. Maybe if she didn't see him, she could stop the thoughts racing through her head. Then he shifted again and another electric jolt raced through her body. It wasn't just seeing him. It was feeling him, too. She had to get out of the duct.

"I'm crushing you," he said, attempting to shift his weight again.

She placed her hands on his waist and squeezed to keep him in place. When he looked at her again, this time in the distorted light coming through the grate, she saw a strange look in his eyes that must have matched her own. Then she felt his hardness expand between her legs, directly at that one place that burned the hottest on her body. Several seconds of silence passed between them with the grunting security guard and his not-wife in the background. Amelia didn't think it would happen. She would never kiss George Gibson.

In the end she wasn't certain who made the first move. All she knew was that one second they were staring at each other with identical bewildered expressions and the next second his mouth was on hers, his tongue inside of her mouth, plunging and exploring. He accomplished something with his incredibly slick tongue and questing mouth that he could never do in court. He won.

Neither could move their arms and hands, because there wasn't enough space, so they just lay in one spot, his mouth attacking hers, giving her no choice but to dwell in his kisses. His hips began to slowly and torturously grind against hers. She tried to open her legs farther, to bring him closer, but the confines of the duct prevented her from moving. She still felt that important part of him—the hardness of him against her.

She didn't know how long they kissed. She lost track of time, of how uncomfortable the air duct was. All she could think about was George Gibson lying on top of her, his body touching every part of hers, his hot mouth on hers. She didn't even consider that he didn't like her, didn't find her attractive. All that mattered was she had been asleep for years and suddenly George Gibson was the one who woke her up, who made her feel alive.

Slowly, his mouth drew from hers and his eyes scanned

her face, as if not entirely certain who she was. One of his hands moved to caress her face and then trace her right eyebrow with such gentleness that she was embarrassed to realize tears clogged her throat. The two ended their kiss as it had begun, by staring at each other with a strange incomprehensible silence between them.

Then as if a switch had been turned on, George cleared his throat and stared out the grate. His voice sounded strained as he said, "They're gone."

She looked into the room and saw that it was empty. Her face flushed with embarrassment and she refused to look at him again. While they had been sucking each other's mouths, the security guard and his not-wife had left the room unguarded. Anyone could have heard them or found them, and Amelia became more embarrassed because she realized that nothing could have torn her from George's arms while he had been kissing her. She would have battled heaven and earth not to move from George Gibson's arms while he kissed her. George Gibson. She squirmed under his weight, attempting to move as far from him as possible. She froze when she realized kissing had only increased the size of the problem pressed against her thigh.

As if he couldn't get away from her fast enough, George quickly unscrewed the grate and hopped onto the floor of the room. He didn't bother to help her from the duct but immediately turned to the shelves of video and began searching the labels. Amelia grunted as she half-fell and half-slid from the duct and landed on the desk. She straightened her clothes and tried not to notice that her knees felt like liquid and that her heart still pounded against her chest. She couldn't fool herself into thinking that her body's reactions were to the danger. It was because of George Gibson.

George suddenly cursed and she forced herself to look at him. He didn't meet her gaze as he muttered, "The tape is missing."

"What?"

"There's no tape of the stairwell entrances on any floor for the time period around five o' clock."

"It has to be there," Amelia protested.

"The tapes are lined up in order according to camera position in the courthouse and the date. The tape we want should be right here. It's not," he said while pointing to an empty spot among the other tapes on the shelf.

"Someone stole the tape?"

He actually had the nerve to laugh at her before he said dryly, "Imagine that. Someone stealing security tapes from a courthouse." When she glared at him, he cleared his throat and said, "The police could have taken you seriously, and they may have it."

"What about the entrance to the garage?" she asked excitedly, walking across the room to stare at the shelves. "No matter how many cops were bribed, they couldn't look the other way if a man dragged a dead body into the courthouse lobby. They must have gone out through the parking garage."

"If there *was* a dead body," he pointed out, sounding entirely too logical for a man who had just kissed her senseless less than a minute ago. He quickly scanned the tape labels, then shook his head. "Great minds think alike. That tape is gone."

"The parking garage tapes are duplicated and mailed to a warehouse in San Pedro at the end of the week," she murmured as she walked across the room to the mail carton. Several large packages sat in the bin.

"How do you know that? How do you know any of this?"

She thought it would be too anticlimactic to tell him that she simply had read the courthouse security manual earlier that evening. Instead, she murmured, "What can I say? I have friends in low places, too."

"Yeah, right," he muttered dryly.

She ignored his sarcasm and rifled through the sealed packages until she found the one that she wanted. She unclasped the lid and poured the tapes into his satchel. Then she pulled a few empty videotapes from the satchel, placed them in the envelope, and carefully closed it. She replaced the package exactly where she found it, then smiled in satisfaction.

"You've done this before," George abruptly said, a suspicious expression on his face.

She grinned and said simply, "Some of us make plans and some of us watch others make plans."

"I'm guessing that I'm the non–plan maker."

She ignored his comment and said, "I have to return these tapes tomorrow before the mail goes out."

"Just make certain to wipe the tapes clean of fingerprints," he muttered.

"I've prosecuted and lost enough criminal cases to know how not to get caught."

She found it too difficult to meet his dark gaze and she climbed onto the desk again. She dragged herself into the duct, then looked back at him to find him watching her.

"What?" she snapped, praying that he wouldn't mention the kiss.

Instead he sent her one of his infuriating grins and said, "You're getting good at this, Farrow."

She rolled her eyes and began to crawl toward the elevator shaft.

Chapter 9

George stared at his reflection in the bathroom mirror in Amelia's house and asked, "What have you done, Gibson?"

He needed air. He needed to stop thinking about that kiss. He pulled off the black sweater he wore and pulled the hem of his white T-shirt from his pants. He had kissed Amelia and just the thought of her response made him groan again. There were a few moments during the kiss when he thought if she kept responding like she ached for him, needed him, then the two would make love in the air-conditioning duct. He cursed as the memory of the kiss scorched a path through his brain and landed directly in his groin.

He should have felt ashamed. She wasn't his type. He didn't even find her attractive, except during his brief bouts of insanity that were suddenly not so brief anymore. Staring at his reflection in the bathroom mirror, he realized that he didn't look ashamed. In fact, he looked like a man who wanted a woman. A woman who hadn't looked at him since they left the courthouse. George had never been in a serious relationship. He preferred to date and to have fun, and to leave as soon as there was talk of commitments and forever. It had always been that way and he never questioned it. Although maybe a small part of him wondered if it was hard for him to think of being a husband and a father when he had no idea what a husband or father was supposed to be.

Amelia, on the other hand, had Kenneth Farrow as a father, whom everyone hailed as the epitome of fatherhood. She had almost married that idiot Brian, who could have been the walking poster for everything a mother would want for her daughter to marry.

George knew that someone like him had no chance with Amelia. Not that he wanted a chance, he quickly reminded himself. But he had to admit that he didn't dislike her as much as he had when the weekend began. In fact, he liked her a lot. And just maybe he was ready to admit that she was beautiful—in a conservative, headband-wearing way. Whatever way it was, he couldn't remember the other women he had dated; he didn't notice other women in the courtroom or on the street when she was around. But that didn't mean he should have kissed her.

For whatever reason, they had kissed. There had been no promises and no vows of undying love; it had been a nonpremeditated act that he was probably spending more time thinking about than Amelia was. Still, he had to admit that no kiss had ever thrown him for a curve like that one had. He never would have guessed that someone like Amelia, who never had a hair out of place or a button out of its slot, could kiss like she had lightning packaged in her slim body.

He gave himself one last censuring look, then opened the door and walked into the living room. Amelia stood near the front window and turned when she heard him enter the room. He noticed that she didn't hold his gaze for long. She was nervous, and instead of enjoying her nerves, he only became more uncomfortable.

"I didn't want to start the tape without you," she said, then quickly moved across the room to pick up the television remote control.

"Here I am."

She visibly hesitated, then abruptly blurted out, "About what happened in the air duct . . ." Her voice trailed off and she averted her eyes to study the remote control in her hands.

"What about it?" he prodded, not certain if he wanted to hear the rest of her statement.

He could have put her out of her misery. He could have chalked it up to being in a confined space with nowhere to go. And then he could have added that they were probably curious about each other after arguing for over a year. But he couldn't bring himself to dismiss the kiss. He had spent his entire life dismissing his feelings because it was always easier, but he couldn't easily forget or ignore the ones that Amelia had aroused.

"Should we talk about it or . . . It was kind of strange,. being in that air duct and hearing the other people making noises, and they were . . ."

"They were having sex." He had never seen Amelia at a loss for words before. He allowed her to squirm for a few seconds; then he tried to sound nonchalant as he said, "It was a nice kiss. I won't tell if you don't. OK?"

Their eyes met at the word *nice* because they both

knew the kiss had been a lot of things that went past just nice, but Amelia didn't call him on the inaccuracy.

In a no-nonsense voice she said, "I just don't want you to think that I go around kissing men . . . in air ducts."

"I hope not. You would probably be the only one in that fetish chat room on the Internet." He laughed at his own joke while she just stared at him, half-repulsed and half-irritated.

She hesitated for a second, then cleared her throat. "Let's just watch the tape."

She pointed the remote at the television and clicked a button. The grainy black-and-white images from the courthouse flashed across the screen. She pressed the "fast forward" button and the screen ran through images of people walking back and forth through the dark parking garage.

"Do you recognize anyone?" Amelia asked while staring at the screen.

"No. . . . Wait. What about those two men?"

"That's Vance Harkin. I've argued several cases against him. I would have recognized his voice." She sped through the tape to another picture of two men walking out of the stairwell. "What about them?"

"Both of those men are LAPD detectives. My clients have been arrested by both; I would have recognized their voices. It wasn't either one of them."

There was a long silence as both concentrated on the television screen. George darted an occasional glance at Amelia, but her eyes remained glued to the screen. She finally sighed in defeat, then switched tapes in the recorder. The image showed an empty hallway in the courthouse. After a few minutes, the screen showed

George and Amelia racing through the hallway and tugging on locked doors. Eventually, they disappeared into a courtroom, the door closing behind them. He was surprised at the fear that he hadn't known was apparent on his face.

George heard Amelia's sharp intake of breath as a man walked into the hallway. He was a tall, heavy man whom George would not want to meet in a dark alley. The man wore a dark suit and long overcoat that may have added or hidden the majority of his muscle. He wore dark leather gloves over his hands as he calmly and coolly checked each locked door, hunting George and Amelia, stalking them. George didn't think he scared easily, but he briefly glanced at the dark shadows outside the windows to make certain no one watched.

"Turn around," George muttered to the man on the screen. As if in response, the man partially turned toward the camera, giving them a view of his profile. "I don't recognize him. Do you?"

When Amelia remained silent, George tore his gaze from the screen to look at her. He was surprised to see that her mouth hung open in a soundless gasp. He immediately knelt in front of her and placed his hands on her shoulders. She looked haunted. She looked frightened. And it made George angrier than he had been before. He reined in his anger and took her clammy hands in his.

"You don't have to deal with this right now—"

"That's the man," she whispered, her eyes still on the screen. "That's the man who attacked me."

George whipped around and stared at the screen. His eyes narrowed. "Are you certain?"

"I know it's him. From the way he moves, his weight,

his height. I bet he would even smell the same. . . ." She finally looked at George with tears glistening in her eyes. "I was right, George. . . . Even when I pushed and tried to convince you, the police, my father, a part of me always hoped that I was wrong because I just didn't want to believe it, but I was right. The attack was not about my job; it was about what we heard. This means that everything the men said on the stairs is true. There are dead jurors, including Thomas Chin, corrupt judges, and it all connects to Maurice Donaldson."

George couldn't resist fingering a few strands of her hair and smoothing them toward her ponytail. He didn't know if it soothed her, but it made him feel better to touch her. He withdrew his hand when he realized that he touched her as if he needed to. He didn't need anyone or anything.

"We can take this to the cops now. We have your ID, my testimony, and the videotapes that prove there was someone following us. The lab results from the stairs will add the extra evidence we need to push this over the edge for the cops to start investigating and find out who this mystery man is. They can probably stroll into Donaldson's office and find this idiot sitting at the front desk."

"How will we explain the tape being in our possession?" she asked.

He smiled because even in the midst of everything, she was still the prosecutor who drove him crazy in court. "I've explained away worse in court. Besides, no one will care how we got the tapes, once we explain what they mean."

Her eyes once more wandered toward the television screen and the large man. George took the remote from her hands and clicked off the television. He gently guided her chin toward him until she looked at him.

"We don't have to decide anything now," he said softly. "We're both tired. We need rest. We'll tackle this tomorrow."

"Are you leaving now?"

He hesitated when he saw her eyes widen in temporary fear before she managed to mask the feeling.

"I'm tired and I really don't feel like driving home," he lied. "I'll crash on the sofa, if that's all right with you?"

"You don't have to sleep on the sofa."

For one second, he couldn't draw air into his lungs. As he stared at her full lips and her dark eyes, he tried to remember every reason that he shouldn't become involved with a spoiled princess like Amelia. Instead he could only picture her long legs wrapped around him as they tangled with each other in the middle of her bed, sharing more explosive kisses that set his soul on fire.

"There are two guest bedrooms—one downstairs and one upstairs. You can have your pick," she continued, oblivious to the fact that she had just burst his bubble with the mention of guest bedrooms. He almost laughed, because he hadn't known what else he expected. She was his opposing counsel. His adversary. He shouldn't want to sleep with her. Or kiss her in air ducts.

"I'll stay down here," he finally said.

"The maid changes the sheets in the guest bedrooms every other week. I'll bring you a towel—"

"Don't worry about me, Amelia," he said, then couldn't resist caressing her skin one last time. He could become addicted to touching her skin, to touching her. It was a strange moment to realize as he stood in Amelia's dark living room that he had never touched a woman in his life just for the sake of touching her. He had never thought he had the right, but with Amelia he did. Or maybe he just wanted the right.

"I am tired," she admitted reluctantly, moving away from his touch. "I'll see you in the morning."

He watched her walk up the stairs, then he fell onto the sofa. There was no way he would be able to sleep. He didn't easily fall asleep on a normal night, not when he worried about bills and clients in jail and Wayne working as a police officer. Now there was another reason he would lose sleep tonight. And that reason was stripping naked in her bedroom right now.

George groaned as he squinted through sleep-clouded eyes at the early-morning light streaming through the open windows. He glanced at the expensive overstuffed chair in the corner of the room near the window, which was framed with sheer curtains, and wondered what five-star hotel he had been dumped in by aliens.

He suddenly remembered that he wasn't at his apartment, in his bedroom with his drawn curtains. He rubbed his face, then stretched his sore arms over his head. As his stiff neck testified, he had fallen asleep on Amelia's sofa. He suddenly registered the droning sound of morning talk radio drifting from the kitchen and the scent of coffee. He glanced at his watch, then groaned. It was eight o'clock. He had a court appointment at nine. A great start to a Monday morning . . . being yelled at by an irate judge.

He found a wide-awake, freshly showered, and bright-eyed Amelia standing in the kitchen, concentrating on a bowl of batter. She looked cute and cuddly in a gray sleeveless dress; then he wondered what could ever make him think of Amelia Farrow as the cute and cuddly type. But in her own kitchen she looked unguarded. Almost relaxed. Even the ole headband didn't bother him so much anymore.

He yawned and walked farther into the kitchen. She took one look at him, then pointed toward the coffeepot on the counter. He found a mug and poured the steaming hot liquid into it, then took a long gulp. He sighed in satisfaction and reveled in the feel of the warm sun rays dancing around the kitchen. He would probably be half an hour late to court, and it didn't bother him one bit.

"I'm not human until, at least, my second cup of coffee," he grumbled when he realized that Amelia stared at him.

"I know," she murmured as she bent over a bowl of pancake batter. He noticed her careful movements with her bandaged hand as she stirred the contents of the bowl.

He eyed her for a moment, then poured another cup as he asked, "How do you know that? Been doing research on me?"

"Don't flatter yourself. I've stood across from you during morning arguments and, let's just say, you actually look human during your afternoon appointments, while in the morning you look . . . you look how you look right now."

He fought his smile but failed before he sobered, then asked, "Did you sleep well last night?"

"Yes, thank you. If you hadn't been here . . ." Her voice trailed off and she whipped the batter with more energy than he thought necessary, probably irritating the cut on her hand. "Thank you for staying, George."

"You did me a favor. That sofa sleeps better than my bed," he said truthfully, deflecting her solicitousness because he had never been able to accept anyone's gratitude. "How's your hand? Last night in the elevator shaft . . ."

"It's fine," she said, too brightly. "I'm making waffles with fresh blueberries."

"Homemade?" She gave him an insulted look and he laughed and said, "Give me a good place to sleep, a nice homemade meal, and you'll never get rid of me, counselor."

He saw the flash of uncertainty cross her face and he instantly cursed himself for opening his big mouth. He would have thought he'd be used to it by now. Since his mother left him, he hadn't allowed himself to be hurt by something as simple as rejection. But thinking of Amelia rejecting him too surprisingly hurt. A lot.

He finished the coffee with a quick gulp and said, "Actually, I can't stay. I have a court appearance at nine o'clock, and even if I take the jet—which I'm sure you have parked in the back—to my apartment to change clothes and shower, I'll still be late."

"I was planning to explain the present situation, excluding the corruption parts, to Judge Stants's clerk and see if we can reschedule our trial dates until the end of the week. Would that work for you?"

"I can live with that." He stalled for a few moments by washing his coffee cup. Then there was nothing to make him stay. Amelia continued to whip the batter. He cleared his throat and she looked at him. His chest tightened. Not only did the sunlight make the kitchen look bright, but it made her look bright. "Call me as soon as you hear about the test results from the stairwell."

She sent him a small smile, which nearly broke his heart, and she pointed to the door. "Go, George. I'll be all right."

He walked toward the door, then turned and abruptly asked, "Do you have my cell phone number?"

She laughed as she rolled her eyes. "Yes, George, I have your cell phone number. Leave. Now."

There was a knock on the kitchen door and George whirled around, prepared to jump the newsboy, if he had to. When an attractive older woman opened the door and waved her key, it took him several seconds to control the tremors of anger and surprise that raced through his body. He had been on the verge of launching a war against a middle-aged woman who . . . who George realized when he stared at her looked exactly like Alice Lyle.

She was as beautiful as he remembered from the poster. He would always remember that poster. She had worn a tangerine bathing suit that had shown every curve and valley in close detail. Her long hair had been blowing in the balmy Caribbean wind and there had been a smile on her face that George had always found strange, more than sexy, but the other boys in the foster home had assured him it was sexy. Alice Lyle had been on the top of every adolescent boy's dream list in the early 1970s, and George thought even now she could give the present-day models a run for their money.

"Mother." Amelia sounded surprised. "I wasn't expecting you."

"How are you feeling, darling?" Alice asked, breezing across the kitchen to brush an air kiss on Amelia's cheeks.

"Fine. . . . What are you doing here? I thought you were leaving for New York last night."

"You know how I absolutely hate flying at night. I thought I'd come over here, eat breakfast with you, then catch the noon flight. I could even get in a little shopping before I drive to the airport."

An awkward silence hung in the kitchen, and the same confusion on Amelia's face crossed her mother's face. George smiled because he suddenly saw the clear resemblance between the mother and daughter. The same high cheekbones and almost too-long nose. At the sound of his movement, Alice turned to him. She sent him a dazzling smile that actually made him blush.

"You must think I'm terribly rude," Alice said with a high-pitched laugh. "I didn't know that Amelia had company."

"George was just leaving," Amelia said with a pointed glance at George. "He's running late—"

He ignored her and said to Alice, "I'm George Gibson. Your daughter and I have argued numerous cases against each other over the last year."

"Alice Lyle Farrow." She gently squeezed his hand, which hardly compared to the powerful grip that Amelia used to crush her opponent's hand in court. Alice's sharp eyes examined George's rumpled clothing; then she said, "You're the young man that the girls and Brian met the other day . . . and you're still here."

"I bet I made a big impression with the girls and Brian," George dryly said.

"Did you and Daddy grill the pizza deliveryman who

was here last night, too?" Amelia coolly asked.

"No," Alice said with a dismissive wave of her hand.

When George saw Amelia's annoyed expression, he laughed, then regretfully said, "It was nice to meet you, Mrs. Farrow, but I have to leave if I want to make it to court on time."

"You sound like my husband. Which firm are you with?" Alice asked, apparently in no hurry to release George from the parental inquisition.

"Mother, please allow the man to leave," Amelia said impatiently.

"I don't work in a firm," George answered her mother's question. "I have my own practice."

"Really?" Alice asked, sounding amazed at the concept of an attorney not working in a large corporate firm. "How do you like that, Mr. Gibson?"

"I like the hours, and I can't beat the boss," he answered with a shrug.

Alice smiled again, then turned to Amelia and said, "He's delightful. Why have you been keeping him a secret?"

"There's nothing to keep secret." Amelia groaned. "We're colleagues."

"Brian warned me that you would attempt to sell us that line," Alice said. She winked at George and added, "She's a lot of work, but she's worth every minute. Just like her mother."

"Mother—"

George interrupted Amelia's protest at her mother's misinterpretation of the situation by placing a kiss on her forehead. She immediately stopped talking and stared at him with wide eyes that promised pain at a later date. He sent her a private smile, then turned to smile at Alice. "I hope that we can talk later, Mrs. Farrow—"

"Please call me Alice. We're practically family."

George grinned at her and ignored Amelia's narrowed eyes. "Practically," he managed to say without collapsing into laughter. The only way that he was "practically" family with Alice was if "practically" meant "no way in hell."

"It was lovely to meet you, George," Alice sang.

George winked at a smoldering Amelia, smiled again at Alice, then walked out of the kitchen feeling happier than he had minutes before.

Chapter 10

Amelia stared at the reports on her desk in disbelief. There were no traces of blood on the stairwell, no gunpowder residue, not even a single hair left on the stairs. There was something the report didn't state. The stairwell was too clean for a stairwell in a Los Angeles County courthouse. No fingerprints, no hair, nothing, not even a dust ball. A chill swept through her body as she closed the folders. She reassured herself that she was not in the Twilight Zone by glancing out the open door of her office cramped in the chaos of the Los Angeles County District Attorney's Office to see her colleagues walking past, the sounds of ringing telephones and clicking computers in the background.

She once more glanced out her door, this time to make certain that no one was paying attention to her; then she picked up the telephone. She dialed the number she had memorized.

"What?" came George's short greeting in the telephone.

She gripped the receiver, then said, "It's Amelia."

She heard his sigh of relief; then he asked, "Are you all right?"

"I'm fine, George. You can stop asking me that question every two hours."

"I'm trying to show concern for another human being," he muttered in response. "Sue me. . . . Wait. Forget I said that."

She rolled her eyes, then said, "I received the test results. All negative. No traces of blood or gunpowder or any sign of a struggle. In fact, there are no traces of anything on the stairwell. As if someone cleaned it right before the samples were taken."

"Or as if someone at the lab didn't do their job," George said.

Through her open door, Amelia saw Richard Grayson, the district attorney of Los Angeles County and her boss, walking across the office, through the cubicles, his eyes on her. She silently cursed, then said into the receiver, "I have to go."

"Dinner tonight?" At her obvious hesitation, George added, "I have a few photos for us to look through of Donaldson's known associates. Maybe one of them will match the man on the tape."

She almost told him to simply send her the information, but she wanted to see him again. Unfortunately. She raked a hand through her hair, then said, "Fine. I'll try to have some information, too."

"How about that Chinese restaurant near your house at the bottom of the hill?"

"Seven o'clock."

"I'll see you then."

The line went dead just as Richard walked into her

office. She forced a smile, then replaced the receiver. Richard had shocking white hair and a trimmed matching mustache. He stood as straight as a rod due to his previous military training, which translated into his barking orders at everyone from the mayor to the night custodian, and an almost comical need for neatness.

He barely stood eye level with Amelia, but when he walked into a room everyone noticed his presence. Amelia respected him because he was shrewd, intelligent, and he reported to her father only half of the things she did in the office even though he and her father were close friends. Her burning guilt from her illegal activities last night didn't bother her as much as the fact that she felt the need to confess to Richard that she had a date with George Gibson later that night.

"Are you all right, Amelia?" Richard asked as he settled into the chair across from her desk. "I had to find out from the receptionist that you had been attacked over the weekend. This is unacceptable. One of our own attacked . . . I want to assure you that we'll find out who did this and they'll pay."

She wanted to tell him about her suspicions, about George. She trusted Richard. He had taken her under his wing, and even though she was a Farrow, he had treated her like any other attorney in his office. She would always love him for that.

"I understand that you rescheduled some of your trial dates. Do you need help covering your cases? Anything you want, Amelia."

"I have everything under control," she told him. "I don't expect anything in my schedule to significantly change, I just needed some time—"

"Anything you want, Amelia," he repeated, more firmly.

"Time is all I want right now."

"Do you have any idea who did this to you? Can you think of anyone from your old cases who could do this to you?"

"I have no idea," she said.

"I heard about the incident on the stairwell."

She clenched her hands into fists underneath her desk. She wondered if there was anyone in Los Angeles County whom her father hadn't spoken to besides her.

"Richard—" He held up his hand and she immediately stopped talking.

"I believe that you heard something, Amelia, and I believe that we should investigate . . . when we have more proof, or any proof. I received a copy of the test results of the samples taken from the stairwell. I trust your instincts, but maybe this time . . . a cigar is just a cigar. We have a tough job, and we deal with tough people."

"Of course," she murmured.

"We have a psychiatrist—"

"Thanks, Richard. If I need someone to talk to, I'll remember that."

He smiled, then stood, suddenly uncomfortable. He hesitated, then abruptly turned and walked out of the room. She sighed, then focused on the mound of paperwork on her desk.

George snapped his briefcase closed and shook hands with his client as the two men stood in the courthouse hallway. George couldn't deny the triumphant feeling that coursed through his body when he kept an innocent man out of jail. An almost innocent man, at least.

"You're all right, Gibson," his client said with a relieved grin.

"Next time you start a fight with a man in a parking lot over a spot, make certain he's not the chief of police."

Harold Lowes grinned, then walked down the hallway to no doubt drink to his good fortune, become drunk, and pick a fight with someone else who would beat him senseless and then arrest him. George shook his head, then opened his appointment book as he walked toward the next courtroom for a preliminary hearing. He looked up just in time to barely avoid running into an Asian woman standing in his path. She wore large dark sunglasses and all-black clothes. Her shiny black hair was swept into a ponytail at the nape of her neck. She was petite and George had the feeling he could blow her away with one breath.

"Are you George Gibson?" she asked in a quiet voice.

He glanced at her hands to make certain she didn't hold any subpoenas. He sighed, then admitted, "Yes."

She took off her sunglasses and George noticed her bloodshot dark eyes. "I understand that you've been looking for me. I'm Anna Chin."

"Thomas Chin's wife," George guessed, then quickly glanced around the crowded hall to make certain that no one watched. He took her arm and led her toward a secluded corner of the hall that he and other lawyers often used for client conferences.

"I can't stay," she whispered, avoiding his gaze. "I shouldn't even be here, but Maddie said that you would find Tommy's killers."

"I'm trying."

"We were in debt. Serious debt. And to find a way out, Tommy took money from the wrong people, and when they wanted their money back, he took money from even worse people."

"Donaldson?" George asked.

She shook her head as she pulled a tissue from her pocket and dabbed at her tear-filled eyes. "I don't know who they were. I just know that he went to jury duty one day worried about paying back the loan, and when he came home that evening, he had enough money for the loan and to pay off the rest of our bills. I didn't ask him because I didn't want to know—" She suddenly gasped and began to weep silently into her hands.

George awkwardly rubbed her shoulders and stared at the ground until Anna composed herself. She sniffed loudly, then continued. "Tommy just told me that after he was picked for a jury, the clerk approached him in the parking lot and asked him if he wanted to make money. It was supposed to be simple. He was just supposed to vote 'not guilty,' convince the other jurors to, or hold up a unanimous verdict. No one was supposed to get hurt."

"The clerk was from the courtroom where your husband was hearing the trial?"

"That's what he told me."

"Mrs. Chin, I know this is hard for you, but I need you to come with me and tell this to the district attorney's office—"

She took several steps from him, the fear plainly visible on her face. "I only came to tell you this because Maddie said I could trust you. I'm the only one my children have left."

"We can protect you."

"Do you think I'm stupid?" she demanded, anger replacing the sadness. "I don't know who these men are, but I know they're dangerous and I know they killed my husband. The day he told the clerk that he wanted out, he was murdered."

The anger appeared to fade as quickly as it had started and her shoulders sagged as if all the air had deflated out of her. She once more dabbed at her tears, then said, "Tommy had a change of heart. He couldn't do it anymore. He told me that he was going to fix everything. That was the last time I saw him."

"You're the best chance we have to catch these men for your husband's murder, Mrs. Chin. You're the only one who can connect the murder of Mr. Chin to the trial in Judge Banner's courtroom," George pleaded.

She didn't immediately answer, but he saw the truth in her eyes. She was going back into hiding. She was going to protect her children. She didn't want to become involved, and George couldn't blame her. He could have had her detained as a material witness. He could have made certain she didn't go anywhere, but he didn't have the heart. She was a woman who had children and a dead husband. He and Amelia would have to find another way, and he had no doubt that Amelia would.

"I have to go," Anna said simply.

He pulled a card from his suit jacket pocket and forced it into her hand, even though she tried to walk away. "If you change your mind, please call me. You could help a lot of people."

"I can't help anyone. I can barely help myself, Mr. Gibson," she whispered, shaking her head. She sent him

one last mournful look, then walked out of the courthouse.

Later that evening, Amelia stood outside the Chinese
restaurant and stared at her reflection in the glass doors.
She groaned because she suddenly wished she could go
home, put on a real dress instead of a suit, comb her hair,
have her eyebrows . . . She settled for smoothing down
flyaway strands of hair with her hand and applying lipstick. Then she rolled her eyes at her reflection.

Having dinner with George was technically not a date,
but it was something. It may have even been a tacit
agreement to work with him. She hadn't told Richard her
suspicions that afternoon; she hadn't told him about the
videotape. She had kept secrets from her office and had
trusted George. And he was going to disappoint her. She
kept forgetting his main goal—to make money. He had
never hidden that from her, but she chose to forget it
when she was swayed by his beautiful eyes or smile.

She briefly closed her eyes and vowed not to be fooled
tonight. She would remember why George wanted to
help, why he even cared. Not because of her. With men
who looked like him, it was never just about her. She
entered the dimly lit restaurant and immediately spotted
George through the other diners at a table in a dark corner of the restaurant. Her stomach wavered from desire
and she placed a hand over it. If seeing him made her
body go into hyperdrive and replay images of their kiss,
she didn't know what would happen if he ever touched
her again. She would probably jump him.

He smiled when he saw her, and she barely resisted

the urge to throw herself at him. There was something about him that drove her insane, that took over her body's responses. She forced a return smile, then sat in the seat across from him.

"Long day?" he asked with an almost sympathetic expression on his face.

She thought it would be better to only talk business; then she could not pretend that their dinner was anything else. She handed him a manila folder. "The test results."

He ignored the folder and asked, "Are you hungry?"

"Starved," she admitted.

"Any particular dish that you want?"

"Whatever you're having is fine."

He smiled and she found herself smiling in return, not knowing why. "You have no opinion on what we should order? Don't tell me you're one of those women. You pretend that you're really easy, everything is fine, but then I'll order something and you'll spend the whole dinner talking about how nasty it is."

"Can you see me as that type of woman?" she asked, raising one eyebrow.

He grinned and said, "No. You say what you want. That's what I like about you. It's frustrating but very attractive."

She stared at her chopsticks and tried to stop the flush of heat to her face. He didn't mean anything, she told herself. He didn't mean to flirt with her or to stare at her as if she were more than a means to a paycheck. Still, she snuck a glance across the table at him and she wished that he had meant it. The waiter saved Amelia by choosing that opportunity to set down their glasses of water and a bottle of beer for George. By the time George gave the waiter their order, Amelia had controlled her racing heart enough to actually look at him.

He took a long gulp from his bottle, then reached into the briefcase next to his feet on the floor. He pulled out an envelope and set it on the table in front of her.

"Those are the pictures of Donaldson's associates that I told you about. Maybe we can match one of the men in the pictures to the man from the videotape. Once we find out who he is, we'll find out the connection to Donaldson."

She stared at the sealed envelope, unable to force herself to open it. She had dreamed about the man's face last night. She looked up from the envelope to find George watching her. Because he looked too sympathetic, too human, she opened the flap and pulled out the grainy black-and-white pictures of several men in various states—getting in cars, talking to other men, all unaware of the camera.

"These look like police surveillance pictures. How did you get these?" she asked, mostly to hear her voice and ignore her trembling hands.

He avoided her eyes and said, "It's better you don't know."

"Possession of confidential police property. . . . We're definitely going to be disbarred."

He snorted in disbelief. "If we were going to be disbarred, it would be for breaking and entering the courthouse last night and not because we're looking at a few police surveillance photos from a closed investigation that no one will miss."

"If you're trying to scare me, George, it's working—"

She barely hid her sigh of relief when she reached the end of the stack of photos and had seen no sign of the man who'd attacked her. She shook her head and stuck the photos into the envelope. "He's not any of those men."

"I didn't see him, either, but I have more important news. I had a surprise visitor in the courthouse this afternoon."

"Who?"

"Anna Chin, the dead juror's wife."

Amelia almost choked on the water that she had just taken. "What?"

"Maddie proved to be helpful after all. She told Mrs. Chin to talk to me."

"What did she say?"

"That we're on the right track," he said simply. "Thomas Chin accepted a bribe from the clerk in the courtroom where he was placed on a jury. Judge Banner's court. The same day that Chin told his wife he was going to pull out of the deal, he was murdered."

"This is the trial involving one of Donaldson's men, presided over by Judge Banner?"

"The one and the same," George confirmed. "I checked the dates."

"Who is Banner's clerk?"

"It will take me five minutes to find out," he said with a wink, then pulled out his cell phone.

She smiled in gratitude as the waiter placed bowls of soup in front of them. She silently sipped her soup as George leaned back in his chair and began to talk into his cell phone. He laughed into the phone and, for a brief moment, she was jealous. Longer than a brief moment until she heard him say, "Thanks, Bill," and she relaxed. There couldn't be many women named Bill.

When George finally met her gaze, she didn't turn away

or make a sarcastic remark. Her breath caught in her chest as his eyes dropped to her mouth. She told herself that she didn't want him to kiss her again or to want her, but it would have been a lie. She licked her lips and his gaze instantly dropped to the soup on the table. She quickly snapped herself from whatever lunacy had taken over, and straightened in her chair.

This incredible overpowering heat had been the ignition with Blake all of those years ago. She hadn't been able to control herself around Blake. The heat had taken over, and she would temporarily lose control of her body. But things seemed different with George. Instead of draining all common sense and dignity from her body, as being in the relationship with Blake had done to her, George made her feel sexier and smarter. Being around Blake, Amelia had felt like she lost a chunk of herself, mostly because he wanted to control her. Brian hadn't cared what she did, which she initially took as trust but later saw it for what it was—disinterest.

George was different. Beside the fact that neither Blake nor Brian would be caught dead in rubber-soled shoes, George listened to her. Really listened. She could have given him the weather report and he would give her that look that indicated she actually had said something important. Even his kisses were different. She only had two other men to compare him to, but George kissed her like she was the powerful one and he had to hang on to her. And he never treated her as less than an equal in the courtroom even when other male attorneys and judges would attempt to insult her because she was a woman. If she didn't know better, she would think that she was falling in love with him.

A heavy silence lay between them until he cleared his throat and said, "Nathan Finnegan. He never retrieved his car from the courthouse parking garage Friday night. It was towed. And he didn't report to work this morning. I already tried his home number. There was no answer. No one has seen him since Friday evening."

"He's our victim." She watched George shovel food into his mouth, apparently unaffected by the fact that a man could be dead. She cleared her throat, then hesitantly asked, "Do you think that Nathan Finnegan is dead, George?"

"I don't know, but I have his address."

She shook her head and said, "No, Gibson, one felony a year is enough for me."

"There could be hard evidence in Finnegan's apartment—"

"Or he could call the police on us when he hears you picking the lock."

"We'll knock first or, at the very least, peek through his windows."

"We're not going to do any of that. We're going to call Finnegan's supervisors tomorrow and ask them to contact him, if he's not at work. If they can't, then we'll ask them to call the police to go to Finnegan's apartment. If anyone should break and enter, it's the police."

"You're right," he said with a loud, dramatic sigh. "We should leave the investigating to the police and hope that they care, hope that they don't show the same apathy that they show for every other victim on the street. But you're an ADA; maybe they'll treat this case differently. Maybe they'll care, that is, if the cops on the force who aren't working for Donaldson are assigned to your case."

She drained the glass of water, then slammed it on the table, with more force than necessary. He didn't flinch but watched her, almost as if he knew what she would say. She loved practicing the law, but she admitted she had felt a small thrill crawling through the air duct—when she hadn't been half scared out of her mind or kissing George.

"This is the last crime we commit, Gibson," she said firmly.

He held up his hand in a version of a pledge and said solemnly, "Scout's honor."

She narrowed her eyes and suspiciously asked, "Were you ever a Boy Scout?"

"For about two days, until I saw the uniform. I still think it would have been cool to learn how to make a microwave if I was lost in the forest."

She laughed at the image of George Gibson in a Boy Scout's uniform. "Do you ever go to the forest?"

"Once I went camping."

"Judging from your expression, I have a feeling that you're not going again."

"If I can sleep indoors in a nice, warm bed with my own shower and access to coffee and meals that don't require creating fire while doing it, then sign me up."

"I like camping." She laughed when she saw the surprise on his face. "I was a Girl Scout."

His deep laughter joined hers and for a moment she thought she heard music in their combined laughter. She became self-conscious when she realized that he had long since stopped laughing and he just sat and openly studied her.

"What?" she demanded. "You're staring."

"Nothing," he muttered, then returned to his food, avoiding her eyes, his smile abruptly gone.

"What?" she pressed curiously.

He sighed in resignation, then said, "I was just wondering if you wear a headband when you're camping."

Both hands flew to her head. When she assured herself that it was still in place, she said, "I hate having hair in my eyes." At his silence, she said, "You don't like it."

He looked confused as he said, "Actually, I do."

She decided not to ask what he meant, since he looked like he wouldn't answer, and she said, "I did some snooping of my own. I found out who owns a burgundy Rolls-Royce with the last three license plate letters JL5."

"Who?" he asked, surprised.

"Kevin Parker."

"That name sounds familiar."

"He was one of the Heller Helium defendants that Judge Banner set free. I also looked at the videotapes from the courthouse parking garage. There was a burgundy Rolls-Royce in one of the stalls caught on tape. That means Parker was there at the same time as the murder."

"Parker could be the man who Maddie saw outside the Chins' house. The one who attacked you. . . . We should find him—"

"No," she firmly stated.

"Why?"

"We stay away from big, mean-looking men."

"You don't think that I can handle him?" George asked with a wounded look.

"You can play heavyweight champion on your time. We're only trying to gather enough evidence to take to the police, not get ourselves killed. The last link we need is proof that Banner knew Finnegan was helping one of Donaldson's men walk free. That's it. OK?"

"OK, but I have seen *Matrix* five times. I can handle Parker."

She tried hard not to laugh but failed miserably.

Chapter 11

"I cannot believe that I allowed you to talk me into this," Amelia hissed twenty minutes later, then elbowed George in the side and ordered, "Hurry up!"

He knelt at her side picking the lock to Nathan Finnegan's apartment while Amelia partially shielded him and served as lookout in the hallway the apartment door faced. She was a "lookout"—the idea alone would have given her father a heart attack. A few days ago, it would have given her a heart attack. She silently cursed at the thankfully empty, quiet hallway; then she glanced over her shoulder at George. Another undesirable trait. Cursing.

George's face was scrunched in concentration as he continued to fiddle with the door lock. She berated herself for it, but she took a moment to enjoy the slope of his forehead and the long eyelashes that batted against his cheeks. She barely prevented a sigh from escaping. She straightened her shoulders and glanced down the hallway again.

"Hurry up!" she prodded again as she heard the elevator doors around the corner of the hallway slide open.

She noticed that Finnegan's apartment door was in the middle of the hallway, with nowhere to hide in case someone did suddenly leave their apartment or round the corner from the elevator. She figured that she and George would have to either run like hell or . . . She hadn't gotten to a second option.

"This isn't as easy as it looks," he snapped in return.

She heard footsteps on the hall's hardwood floor and she tugged on his sleeve. "I think someone's coming."

"Go stall them."

"What?"

"Hurry, Amelia. I'm almost done."

She stumbled from the door, then quickly rounded the corner. She collided with a man who held a stack of papers in his hands. The papers flew in every direction and Amelia immediately knelt and spread the papers with the pretense of helping in their retrieval. The harried-looking man didn't appear to notice as he tried to gather as much of the paperwork as he could.

"I am so sorry," she sighed, hoping that she sounded like her mother when she was anything but sorry. "I didn't see you."

Amelia stared at the man with her attempt at an innocent expression. It must have worked, because the man's brown face broke into a large smile behind his black wire-rimmed eyeglasses. With wide brown eyes, closely shaven hair, and a neatly trimmed mustache, the man was cute in a way that reminded her of the slightly homely forensic scientists who testified in trials about gun residue and other subjects that put jurors to sleep.

"It was my fault," he said shyly. "I should have watched where I was going."

She instantly felt guilty, because he seemed like a nice man and it had been her fault. She glanced over her shoulder, but unfortunately, she couldn't see around the corner. She couldn't tell if George was inside the apartment or not. She turned around to find the man staring at her. He bashfully hung his head when he realized that she had caught him. She almost laughed. The first man to find her attractive in almost a year had to be the one person who could send her to jail.

"You live here, right? I've seen you," she said. Before he could respond, she offered her hand and said, "I'm Dana. I live down the hall."

"In Four-oh-two? Mr. Carson's old place?"

"That's me," she lied, while trying to hide her cringe of horror at her behavior. Lying was officially added to her list of distasteful traits. "Four-oh-two."

"My name is Sam." He gathered the last of his papers and helped her to stand as he himself rose. He was obviously a nice guy. She could have made herself like him, if her lips didn't tingle every time she thought of George. He told her with a shy smile, "I've been meaning to come introduce myself. Just because we live in LA doesn't mean we can't be neighborly."

"That's what I always say." She forced herself to laugh, one of those high-pitched laughs that men responded to like Pavlov's dogs when her mother did it. Instead, Sam looked at her as if she had suddenly sprouted a new head. She placed a hand on her throat and quickly explained, "I have a sinus thing."

"That's too bad." Sam shuffled the papers in his hand

and Amelia had the sinking feeling that he was trying to find the nerve to ask her on a date. "Listen, Dana, since you're new to the building—"

"Hey, sweetheart. Sorry it took me so long." Amelia grinned in relief at the sound of George's voice. He stood at her side and snaked an arm around her waist as he planted a loud kiss on her mouth that involved just enough tongue to be inappropriate and make her chest heave with desire. Even as her lips tingled from the contact, she sent him a hard glare before she turned to smile at Sam.

"Sam, this is—"

"I'm her brother," George said, even as he squeezed her closer to him. She looked at him horrified as Sam's eyes grew wide behind his glasses. "Were you about to ask my sister out, Sam?"

Sam quickly shook his head and mumbled, "No, no—"

"Of course you were, buddy. I say go for it. Ever since her boyfriend dumped her, she's been a shell of her old, vivacious self," George said with a sad smile. "I've been trying to get her out there to meet people, but you're the first man I've seen her pay attention to in months."

"Really?" Sam asked, not looking very eager at the prospect of asking out a woman who tongued her brother.

Amelia tugged hard on George's hand as she told Sam, "It was nice to meet you, but we have to go."

Sam shot them one last look, then practically ran toward his apartment as she half-dragged and half-led George down the hallway.

She pushed him onto the waiting elevator and the doors slid closed before George could embarrass her further.

She waited until they sat in his car before she glared at

him across the seat. He laughed. Hard. Tears formed in his eyes.

"Did you see his face when I said you were my sister?" he asked as his body shook with laughter.

"That wasn't funny," Amelia snapped.

"Yes, it was. You didn't see his expression when I kissed you."

"You're impossible."

"I'm also good. Very good." George pulled several envelopes from inside his coat pocket. Amelia gasped in shock when she read the address labels.

"This is Nathan Finnegan's mail," she told him. "We can't take Finnegan's mail. . . . That's a federal offense."

"Since we can assume that Finnegan is dead, he's not going to tell. Maybe we should worry about this letter to his neighbor Maris Johnson, though. Finnegan must have taken her mail by accident and never returned it."

"I'm serious, George."

"He has about three ads for a dating service. Have you ever thought about one of those?" he abruptly asked.

"One of what?"

"A dating service. It could do wonders for your social life."

"My social life is just fine, thank you," she stiffly replied.

"Are you sure?" he asked doubtfully. "I remember that guy you brought to the Christmas party at Sharon Walter's house last year."

"He was an adult. . . . Of course you'd have a problem with him."

Surprise, then confusion crossed his face before he asked, "What's that supposed to mean?"

"Just that I'm surprised your date's parents allowed her to stay out that late past curfew on a school night and everything."

"She was twenty-two years old. Legal in all fifty states," he protested.

"I'm sure that she'll wait for you while we're in jail for tampering with someone's mail," Amelia said pointedly. "By the time we serve our sentence, she may even be old enough to drive to the jail to pick you up."

"Forget the mail," he said, tucking the envelopes back inside his coat pockets.

"I can't forget the mail."

"The apartment had been completely trashed."

"By the police?" she asked hopefully.

"No one's filed a missing person's report on Finnegan. Why would the police come to his apartment and trash it? Whoever was there before us was looking for something."

"Like what?"

"I don't know." George pulled a tape cassette out of his jacket pocket and ignored Amelia's groans of protest. He popped the tape into his cassette player. "I found this tape underneath the sofa." He pressed the "play" button.

She sighed heavily but leaned against the seat to listen, resigned. A curt voice that sounded eerily similar to the nervous voice on the stairs came from the machine: "You know what to do at the beep."

"Finn, this is Harry. The basketball game has been moved to Tuesday so Lincoln can make it home to clean the gutters before his wife returns from her parents'. Love and marriage, huh? I'll take single. See ya Tuesday," came the cheerful voice of someone who obviously had no idea that Nathan Finnegan was missing.

There was another beep and then a familiar male voice said, "Finnegan, we need to talk. Meet me at six on Friday."

Amelia stared at George with wide eyes and pointed toward the tape. "That's Judge Banner."

"Exactly."

"Six was the time we heard the men on the stairwell. Did Finnegan go to the stairwell expecting to meet Judge Banner?"

"Which could mean that Judge Banner sent Finnegan to his death when he told Parker that Finnegan wanted out."

"We don't know that for certain," she said, shaking her head. "We can't even prove that Donaldson or Parker is involved."

"Donaldson has his tentacles in any and all criminal activity that takes place in Los Angeles. I read through some of my old case files today. Some of my less innocent clients at one time or another had some contact with Donaldson or his men."

She raked a hand through her hair, because she knew that he was right. Over the years, Donaldson had gone unchallenged by the police and the district attorney's office. If she found evidence to implicate him in a crime, she would have job security for the next decade.

"I think that's enough to take to Grayson for indictments, at least against Judge Banner and Kevin Parker," George said with a smug smile.

"No, it's not," she said while shaking her head.

"We have Judge Banner on tape scheduling the meeting where Finnegan was killed."

"The judge will argue that Finnegan never arrived, that he waited, but Finnegan was busy being killed, and that he knows nothing about the meeting on the stairs. Assuming Finnegan is dead. We have no body, no proof—except a towed car—that there's been foul play. What if he's simply out of town?"

George cursed, then said desperately, "The answering message gives us enough for a search warrant, right?"

"He's a judge, George. The normal rules don't apply."

He rolled his eyes in disbelief, then said, "I'm going to remember you said that the next time I try to have the evidence from an illegal search thrown out at trial for one of my nonjudge clients."

The ring of her cellular telephone from inside her handbag interrupted her retort. She pulled it out, grateful for the interruption.

"Good evening. This is Amelia Farrow."

"Ms. Farrow, this is Judge Roland Banner," came the bark from the opposite end of the receiver. At the sound of the man's familiar husky voice, she quickly turned to George, who sent her a questioning look.

"Judge Banner," she greeted him, pointedly looking at George. He frowned in return. "This is a pleasant surprise."

"I heard about what happened to you this past weekend in the courthouse," the judge said, never one for pleasantries. "It's horrible."

"It was awful."

"I've also heard that you've been asking questions. . . ." For the first time since Amelia had encountered him, Judge Banner sounded hesitant. "I heard that you believe you overheard a conversation in the courthouse on Friday which led to your attack."

"It's surprising how much you have heard, Judge Banner."

His laughter sounded forced over the telephone. "I wanted to make certain that you were recovering."

"I am." She waved at George to be quiet, since he kept mouthing questions for her to ask Banner.

"Maybe you should take some time off, Ms. Farrow. Leave Los Angeles for a while, just until the animal who attacked you is caught."

She gripped the telephone and said through clenched teeth, "Is that a threat or a piece of advice?"

His gasp of outrage did not impress her. "Would you mind telling me what you're talking about, Ms. Farrow?"

"Did you know that your clerk, Nathan Finnegan, is missing? No one has seen him since Friday." From the corner of her eyes she saw George throw up his hands in frustration and hit the steering wheel.

"I don't like what you're implying. I called as a professional courtesy to inquire about your safety."

"Is that really the only reason you called, Judge Banner?" Amelia pressed. "I think you called either to warn me that someone is trying to hurt me or to ask for my help because with Finnegan's disappearance you suddenly realize how deep you're in."

There was a long silence and Amelia glanced at George, who was shaking his head in disbelief. She frowned at him.

"Only because I respect your father will I hang up this telephone right now and pretend this conversation never happened. Good night, Ms. Farrow."

Amelia flinched at the loud click and then the humming dial tone. She closed the phone, then forced a smile at George, who looked satisfied that she had just been hung up on.

"That went well," she murmured, avoiding George's knowing gaze.

"Great job, Amelia," George said dryly. "Like every prosecutor, you attempt to bully your way into a confession."

"And you think that if he had called you, you would have gotten him to confess?"

He shrugged. "I am known for my powers of persuasion."

She shook her head in disbelief, then said abruptly, "Turn left here."

George obeyed, speeding across several lanes of angrily honking motorists to do it. "Where are we going?" he asked.

"Highland."

"The street?"

"Yes."

"Why?"

"Because we're going to confront Judge Banner." When he didn't immediately respond, she looked at him. In the rapidly fading sunlight she saw the disbelief and amazement in his expression. She actually smiled.

"What do you think that will accomplish, Amelia, except us spending the night in jail because he'll call the police on us? He's a judge. He's not going to admit to anything, whether he's guilty or not, and we don't know for certain that he is guilty."

"We need Banner to turn. We're after Donaldson, and Banner is the only one smart enough to recognize the deal we're going to offer to give him to us. Judge Banner

has never called me on my cell phone. He called me tonight because he's scared. Maybe he noticed Finnegan
wasn't at work this morning. Maybe he started wondering if he was next."

"The hanging up in your face was a cry for help?"
George asked doubtfully, the laughter playing on the corners of his mouth.

"Just watch the road," she ordered, ignoring his doubtful expression.

Judge Roland Banner lived in a bungalow-style spilt-
level house in the old-fashioned Hancock Park area of
Los Angeles. His lawn was neat and well maintained,
with tall bushes that shielded the yard from the neighbors. All of the windows in the house were dark and
the driveway was empty, which hinted that no one was
home. From all outward appearances, Judge Banner
didn't live above his means or give any other signs of
an unexplainable cash flow. She was slightly disappointed.

George got out of the car and motioned for her to follow. She crept behind him toward the back door where he
once more pulled out his lock-picking tools. She grabbed
his arm and pointed to her watch.

"He just called me. Do you think they're already
asleep? It's just ten o'clock," she whispered.

"Maybe he didn't call you from home. They may not
even be here," he said while shaking his head.

"Knock."

"Knock? Are you crazy—"

In the middle of his sentence, she knocked on the back
door. There was a moment of silence and she knocked
again, which made George cringe and scan the dark

backyard. When she still didn't hear an answer, she glanced at George, who stared at her.

"Are you happy?" he asked dryly. "Now we know that the Banners aren't home, but their neighbors know that we're here."

At that moment, they both heard a movie-quality horrified scream from inside the house. Amelia stared at the upstairs window where it sounded like the scream originated, just as George kicked open the door with a loud crash. The door flew open as wood pieces scattered in different directions.

"Stay here," he ordered, then ran into the house.

She stood unmoving for half a second before she realized what she'd done; then she ran after him.

The two skirted around pieces of furniture that were visible in the moonlight glow through the windows. Amelia heard the sound of struggling and more screaming from the second level. George found the stairs in the living room and bounded up them two at a time. She tried to keep up, but he rounded the corner a few paces ahead of her. By the time she ran into the hallway George had run through an open door. She followed him and collided into his back as he stood in the middle of the room.

She looked around his shoulders to see what had stopped him, and her mouth dropped open. Mrs. Banner, crying hysterically and clutching her frosted blond curls, crouched on the bed in the center of the room while a man dressed all in black, with a black ski mask covering his face, stood over a prone figure on the ground. Despite the blood and cuts on the man's wrinkled face Amelia recognized the balding white head of the man on the ground as that of Judge Banner. As if he suddenly realized the danger of the situation, George flew across the bedroom and knocked the man in the mask off the judge.

The two men tumbled to the ground and slammed into a table against the nearby wall. A lamp flew in one direction and shattered on the carpet while the other items on the table fell in various directions. Mrs. Banner screamed again while Judge Banner groaned from his position on the ground and tried to crawl toward his wife. Amelia shook herself out of her own fog and searched for the clasp to her purse. After several tries, she finally grabbed her cell phone, then tried to remember how to dial 911. She'd told herself that this wasn't her trapped in the nightmare when she had been attacked in her own house, but her pounding heart and throbbing head told her different. She couldn't make her fingers move to call the police.

The two men continued to struggle across the bedroom. Amelia finally forced her fingers to move, but it seemed like it took her forever to punch out the three numbers. The masked man gained the upper hand and delivered a fist to George's face. George flew onto the bed and became tangled in the sheets with Mrs. Banner, which made her scream again. Without a pause, the man ran across the room toward Amelia just as she heard an operator answer, "Nine-one-one, what's your emergency?"

Time froze as the man came closer and closer to Amelia, toward the door, to his escape. It probably only took a second, less than a second, but she could hear each of her breaths as if it lasted a lifetime. She stumbled back and almost fell into the hallway as he took a step toward her. But as if a light had been switched off, he suddenly dropped to the ground in an unconscious heap.

Amelia looked up, her breath coming in short gasps, waiting to thank her rescuer. She stared at Mrs. Banner, in all of her nude fifty-plus-year-old glory, the broken halves of a vase in her hands.

"Roland's mother gave us that vase," she told Amelia in a matter-of-fact voice. "I always hated it."

Then the older woman collapsed to the floor, only feet away from the masked man.

Chapter 12

Amelia groaned when she saw Richard Grayson enter the living room of Judge Banner's house an hour later. She searched for a hiding place and settled for a small corner behind a potted tree in one inconspicuous corner of the living room.

The Banner house was no longer dark and quiet. Now each room was filled with two or three police officers and other chattering men. The paramedics had pronounced that Judge Banner had a broken arm and enough bruises to start a collection, but the older man had refused to go to the hospital. He sat in a wide chair in the corner of his living room, occasionally sipping from a cup of brandy with a trembling hand. He had never been a handsome man, but now he looked grotesque. His face was swollen and multicolored. One eye was completely swollen shut, and she figured the other eye would have trouble seeing when that side of his face began to swell, too.

Mrs. Banner walked into the living room with a tray of full coffee cups. The older woman had changed into a pink jogging suit that made her look more vulnerable than being nude had. She nearly dropped the tray before she set it on the living room table. The judge sent her a small smile and she nodded in reassurance before she sat on the sofa and stared at the far wall. Amelia knew exactly how the woman felt. She wondered if the judge could make Mrs. Banner feel as safe as George made Amelia feel.

"Amelia, what the hell is going on here?" Grayson demanded, obviously spotting her in her hiding place. He stalked across the living room to stand in front of her.

"Someone attacked Judge Banner in his home."

"I know that," Grayson snapped. He had never been a patient man. It was no wonder that he and her father were such good friends. "I want to know what you're doing here."

Amelia glanced around the room for George, but he was nowhere to be found. After the fourth cop car had arrived, he had mumbled something about "too many cops give me the hives"; then he had walked out of the house. She had wanted to follow him, but she'd stayed behind precisely because she wanted to follow him.

"Judge Banner called me earlier this evening, and I wanted to stop by and continue our conversation."

"About what?"

She took a deep breath, then blurted out, "I believe that I know who the two men were on the stairwell. One was a man named Nathan Finnegan, who was a clerk for Judge Banner at the courthouse. The other man works for Maurice Donaldson. His name is Kevin Parker and he drives a burgundy Rolls-Royce. Parker may also be implicated in the death of a juror—Thomas Chin."

"Donaldson," Grayson repeated, confused. He slowly nodded as he said, "The man who attacked Banner is Milton Tucker. He's a known muscle man for Donaldson."

"He may know the man who attacked me, too," she said quietly.

"We'll find out," Grayson promised with a steel glint in his eyes that made her believe him. "How do you believe the judge plays into all of this? Why was he a target tonight?"

"His clerk, Nathan Finnegan, who hasn't been seen since Friday, worked for Donaldson. Banner has to be involved. I wasn't certain until tonight." She bit her lower lip when she glanced at Mrs. Banner, who sat on the sofa still staring at the wall. Amelia felt a flash of sympathy for the woman. It was a strange moment to realize that the defendants she stood across from in court sometimes made mistakes and deserved leniency. Mrs. Banner had saved Amelia's life and Amelia would repay her by sending her husband to jail.

"How is Banner involved?" Grayson prodded.

"I'm not sure," Amelia answered truthfully. "There was a message on Nathan Finnegan's answering machine from Judge Banner. They were supposed to meet the day that Finnegan went missing. I wanted to ask him about their meeting."

She purposely left out the time of the meeting. The police would eventually discover that, but she didn't want to be the one to tell Grayson. Maybe Mrs. Banner would get to spend one more night with her husband. Amelia felt that she owed her that much. And she hoped that after the beating Judge Banner had taken that night, he wouldn't be too ready to jump on the Donaldson money wagon any longer.

"I'll talk to him," Grayson said with a heavy sigh. There was a speculative gleam in his eyes as he focused on Amelia. "How did you find out about all of this? How do you know what's on Finnegan's answering machine? Or about Thomas Chin and Kevin Parker?"

She glanced at her watch and feigned amazement at the late hour. "It's been a long day—"

"The lead detective told me that you and George Gibson interrupted Judge Banner's attack. What were you doing with George Gibson?"

"He's a . . ." She couldn't bring herself to say the *f* word, so she simply said, "He's a colleague."

"Colleague or not . . . watch your back with him, Amelia. I know his type. They're all about money and the quickest way to make a buck. Like we said when I was about your age, being a defense attorney is not an occupation; it's a lifestyle."

She silently nodded, attempting to hide her confusion from Grayson. She could have given herself the same speech. She could have warned herself about George. There was always that small part of her that wanted to scream that George was different. But he wasn't. Even he had told her that he only cared about the money in this case.

"Do you want to sit in on Tucker's interrogation?" Grayson asked.

"I'm tired," she said truthfully. "Is Quintero going to observe for our office?"

"Yes."

"I'll call him tomorrow morning."

"Get some sleep, Amelia."

She forced a smile, then turned to leave. Her eyes rested on Mrs. Banner, who watched her. She wanted to sit next to the woman and reassure her that everything would be all right, but it wouldn't be all right, because her husband was a criminal and Amelia or someone else in her office would prove it. Instead, she nodded at the older woman, who sent her a weak smile in return; then Amelia walked out the door.

She immediately wrapped her arms around herself. Even though she wore her suit jacket, the brisk March air chilled her. She wondered if she would ever be warm again. Not since she had walked into her living room to find a lightbulb a few nights ago had she felt warm. She dug inside her purse for a cell phone to call a taxi—because despite most people's preconceptions, people in Los Angeles took taxis.

"I thought you were going to stay in there all night," George said, his voice surprisingly close to her ear.

She barely restrained her smile of relief when she whirled around to see him standing next to a uniformed police officer on the porch. She drank in the sight of George even though it had only been an hour since she last had seen him. A faint bruise was blossoming on his jaw where Milton Tucker had hit him. She wanted to do something ridiculous—like kiss his injured jaw.

"Were you waiting for me?" she asked, surprised.

"I brought you here. I'm supposed to take you home," he said with a shrug. At her bewildered silence, he motioned to the man standing next to him. "This is Wayne Phillips. We were friends before he became a cop. Wayne, you know Amelia."

She sent him a polite smile and shook the handsome man's hand while he rolled his eyes at George. For a brief moment she wondered if Wayne knew about their illegal activities. When she sent George a questioning look, he shook his head for her silence, then directed his attention to Wayne.

Wayne told her with a long-suffering grin, "He always introduces me that way. As if someone would hold it against him if he became friends with me *after* I became a police officer."

"With my clients, it's a possibility," George responded with a careless shrug that made Wayne shake his head.

Wayne was a handsome man. She had prosecuted a case once where he had been the arresting officer. She had noticed him then. He was tall, sexy, built like a tank, with dark brown skin, and he had the type of respectable job that matched hers. He caught the criminals and she put the criminals behind bars. Like Brian, Wayne would have been perfect for her. Except no matter how hard she stared at Wayne's even white teeth and perfect smile, he couldn't make her forget George's gaze on her.

Wayne looked concerned as he studied Amelia, making her slightly self-conscious. "Are you all right? I heard things got a little hairy up there."

"I'm fine," she answered, not meeting either man's gaze.

"You're a brave lady," Wayne continued, obviously responding to the not-fine look on her face. "I wish we had a few more ADAs like you. We could actually do some good in this city."

She was forced to respond to Wayne's warm smile with one of her own. She was surprised when George placed a hand on her arm. He had never voluntarily touched her except in the air duct, and that had been . . . That had been the Air Duct Incident.

"We've had a long night, Wayne," George said with a smile that looked forced. "I'm going to drop Amelia at home and then go to my place and sleep for about forty-eight hours."

"You two did a good job tonight . . . besides the few felonies along the way," Wayne said with a pointed look at George.

George waved a dismissive hand and said, "We have no idea what you're talking about, Officer Phillips."

"Yeah, right. You're as innocent as a newborn," Wayne dryly muttered; then he abruptly grinned and pointed at George. "Call me tomorrow morning."

George nodded in acknowledgment, then led Amelia down the sidewalk and toward his car. She hadn't realized how tired she was until she sat in the passenger seat of his car and George slammed the door for her. She closed her eyes and leaned her head on the rest. She briefly stirred when she heard George sit behind the steering wheel.

"You told Wayne that we broke into Finnegan's apartment?" she asked, trying to care about the answer even though sleep prevented her from opening her eyes to look at him.

"Are you kidding me? He's a cop."

"You don't trust him?"

"I trust Wayne with my life," he said immediately, aiming a brief glance in her direction. "But he's spent the majority of his life thinking that he needs to protect me. And he has, but I don't want to involve him in this, not if his friends and colleagues may be involved. I told him that we had Finnegan's answering machine tape and it led us to Judge Banner. He didn't ask how I got it, and I didn't tell him."

She tried to think of an admonishment, but all she could do was smile at the sound of his deep baritone voice.

"How do you know him?"

"We grew up together."

"Was he in foster care, too?"

"I met him in the first foster home I was placed in when I was six years old. He was six, too. We were the youngest in the house and, therefore, seen as the weakest. We had to fight to prove differently." He laughed at the memory and she focused on his laughter and not the pain she felt upon thinking of a six-year-old George Gibson only knowing how to respond to a new situation by fighting. "He protected me when I was too weak to protect myself and I protected him when he was too weak to protect himself."

She opened her eyes and stared at his profile for a moment before she asked, "What happened?"

"My dad was never in the picture," he said quietly. "My mother was young; she drank a lot. Social Services found out. The rest is history."

She didn't know why his flippant response made her ache more for him, but it did. She would have touched him if she thought he would allow it.

"You were so young," she whispered sadly. He shrugged in response and avoided her gaze. "Where is your mother now?"

"I haven't seen her since I was six years old. She came

for a visit. She brought me a Winnie the Pooh bear."

"She never came back?" Amelia asked, horrified that a mother could leave her child, could leave George.

"Maybe it was an even trade? I still have the bear," he said with a shrug.

"And Wayne."

He smiled, a genuine smile, as he said, "Wayne was always smarter than me. He realized soon enough that if we backed each other up, we had a better chance. He was right. We stayed in that orphanage for a few years; then we were separated into different homes, but we still attended the same elementary school. Through the years, we always stayed in touch. We even lived together during high school for almost two years at the Ednas'."

She closed her eyes at the smile in his voice at the mention of the Ednas. "You liked them? The Ednas?"

"They were a nice couple. Older. They had a small house. Wayne and I had to share a room, but it was . . . it was as perfect as things got for me for a little while."

"What happened?"

"Mr. Edna had a heart attack and died. Mrs. Edna was destroyed. Her son made her move in with him and his family in Riverside. She died six months later. That whole family was nice, and I always wished . . ."

"Wished what?" she prodded.

"Nothing. I don't waste time on wishes," he said quickly. "When you grow up the way I did, you realize it's not worth your time to wish for things that can never happen."

"And it's not worth your time to care, either?" she asked. She saw the discomfort cross his expression as he shifted in his seat.

He snorted in disbelief. "I care, Amelia."

"I know you do, but you don't like to admit it. You don't like for other people to know." She could feel his nerves more than see he was nervous. She filed it away for future reference, then asked, "Did you always want to be a lawyer?"

He was silent for a few moments as if lost in memories; then he said, "If it wasn't for Wayne, I never would have gone to college. He always thought there was more for us than working at some dead-end job in the neighborhood or not working and being dead in the neighborhood."

"I worked with him on a case before. He was well prepared during his testimony. The jury immediately trusted him. He's the type of officer who I like to have on the witness stand to make my cases."

"He's the closest thing I've ever had to a family."

With those softly spoken words she smiled in her semiasleep state. "It sounds like you have a nice family," she murmured.

"What about you? Daddy Warbucks and Mommy Moneybags? You must have had the type of childhood that most kids dream about. Any toy you want, anytime, right?"

Her smile disappeared, but her eyes remained closed as she whispered, "You'd be surprised."

"What do you mean?"

"I love my parents and I know they love me, but it's hard to talk to your father when he's one of the smartest judges sitting on the bench, and it's hard to talk to your mother when she's one of the most beautiful women in the world, as dubbed by *People* a few years ago."

She felt his hand gently remove her headband. He gently stroked back the hair that fell into her face without the barrier. She didn't want to open her eyes because she was afraid that he would stop. He did. His hand withdrew from her face and she felt cold again.

"And so you try to be perfect because you don't think you're as smart as your father or as beautiful as your mother," he said, surprisingly close enough to her true feelings that she flinched. "But you are smart, Amelia, and you are beautiful. They should have told you that."

She opened her eyes to find a strange expression on his face as he stroked her hair. Before she could speak, he whispered, "Go to sleep, Amelia. I'll wake you up when we reach your house." His soft voice drifted across the car and wrapped around her like a warm blanket.

She didn't think she would be able to sleep after receiving the most wonderful compliment in her life, but she did.

Amelia's eyes fluttered open and for one second she was confused until she felt George next to her. Her second thought was that she was lying on her bed in her own bedroom. The room was dark and she still wore her work clothes, except the suit jacket. She turned over and smiled when she saw George. He had pulled the easy chair that usually sat in the corner of the bedroom next to her bed. He lay stretched from the chair to the bed. One of her blankets covered him.

The moonlight that flooded the room softened his masculine features and mouth. In his sleep, the usual smirk he wore to show the world he didn't care was gone. In fact, he looked almost vulnerable. As if he were still a little boy with a Winnie the Pooh bear. Her parents had never needed her. No one had ever needed her. She suddenly wondered if maybe George Gibson needed her.

She gasped softly in surprise when George's eyes suddenly opened. Her heart thumped against her chest and she froze in her position on the bed. He had caught her staring at him. For some reason, he didn't move, either. He just held her gaze in the moonlight. She slowly dragged her tongue across her bottom lip as silence hovered in the bedroom.

He abruptly tossed the blanket aside and rose to his feet. His laughter sounded nervous and forced as he dragged a hand over his face.

"I should get home," he said, his voice sounding strained. "I just didn't want you to wake up and be alone . . . not after everything."

She slowly sat up in the bed, being careful not to move too much for fear that she would break the mood in the room. She felt that if she breathed too hard she would upset the delicate balance. Whether that would have been good or bad, she didn't know.

"Thank you," she finally whispered.

"Your father called while you were asleep."

"You answered the phone?" she asked while trying not to be horrified at the thought of her father's reaction when he heard a strange man answer her telephone. "What did he say?"

"He said that your bodyguards will be here at eight o'clock tomorrow morning to drive you to work."

She groaned and buried her face in her hands. She

glared at him when she heard the suspicious sound of laughter coming from him.

"He sounded proud of himself," George offered helpfully.

"Tell me that you're lying."

"I think it's a good idea."

"Are you serious?" she asked in disbelief. "It's over. Donaldson has no reason to want me dead anymore. We have Milton Tucker, Judge Banner is probably confessing as we speak, and Finnegan's whereabouts—dead or alive—will be solved."

He visibly hesitated, then said, "You're right. It is over. We caught the bad guys. Grayson knows that you're responsible, and I'm sure you'll receive a promotion or a raise. And I'll have every one of my cases with Judge Banner, and whoever else gets caught in the dragnet, reversed, with the state of California footing the bill. And Anna Chin may be able to sleep at night."

Amelia forced a smile, then stood, to draw his attention and hers from the bed. She cleared her throat, then said, "So I guess I'll see you in court."

"Right." He stuffed his hands into his pants pockets and another awkward silence hung over the room.

Amelia had the strange feeling that they were a boy and girl standing on the front porch of her parents' house, each trying to find a way to kiss the other without appearing to make the first move. Or, at least, how Amelia had imagined the scene when she was a child. Her parents had never been the type to wait for her to return from a date in the living room with the lights burning. Her mother had never wanted to hear the details or giggle over girl talk.

Her father had never attempted to intimidate a date. Although, Amelia reminded herself, she hadn't been asked on many dates in high school, so maybe her parents never had the chance.

George laughed again, then walked out the bedroom door. She silently followed him down the stairs toward the front door. He walked outside the door and she thought that he would simply leave without saying another word, but at the last minute he turned to face her.

"Make sure you put on the alarm," he said. "Even though there's no—"

"I will."

"If you have one of those things, you should use it."

She nodded and he nodded.

He turned to leave, then abruptly turned around and asked, "What ever happened to that guy? The guy you brought to the Christmas party last year?"

She was surprised by the question, but she haltingly answered, "We dated for a few weeks and . . . we had nothing in common besides two stressful jobs. He was a heart surgeon. Why?"

"I just wondered if someone else should be here with you. . . . That woman, the twenty-two-year-old . . . it was nothing. We met on the beach one day, dated a few times, and then I took her to the banquet."

She didn't know why he told her or why the news made her so relieved and depressed at once. Instead, she silently nodded and leaned against the door. He searched her face for something; then he stuffed his hands in his pants pockets.

"Do you have a lot of one-night stands?" she asked, obviously surprising him, as well as herself, with the question. Normally, she would have withdrawn it as none of her business, but not this night.

"More than some, a lot less than others."

"And you find them . . . fulfilling?"

He sent her a sexy grin that was hot enough to burn off her eyebrows before he said, "Depends on what you're looking for."

"You know what I mean," she muttered, then abruptly confessed, "I've only been with two men in my life."

"What a waste," he murmured.

She couldn't decide if that was a compliment or an insult, so she repeated, "Do you find them fulfilling?"

He studied her for a few moments, which made her squirm, before he murmured, "Why the cross-examination, Farrow?"

"Just answer the question please."

"I don't know," he finally said with a shrug. "I guess I must enjoy it or I wouldn't do it, right? One night is about as long as I can stand without feeling claustrophobic, probably something to do with my abandonment and trust issues. A psychiatrist would probably have a field day in this head."

When she didn't respond, he glanced toward his car, then murmured, "I should leave."

"Good-bye, George." She flinched at the note of finality in her voice, but it was the end. Whatever aspects of friendship that had blossomed between them over the weekend had ended. They weren't friends. They weren't enemies. They were just attorneys on opposite sides of the law who sometimes argued cases against each other.

He nodded, then turned and walked toward his car. He opened the car door, and before he could sit in the car she found herself walking down the entry walk toward him. She didn't know what propelled her to move, especially when she should have allowed him to leave, should have wanted him to leave. She stopped next to him as he turned to sit in the car. He looked at her.

"Is everything all right?" he asked, concerned, staring back at the house as if expecting a monster to be standing in the door.

"I wish you hadn't been so nice to me," she blurted out.

He looked slightly confused; then he smiled and said, "Believe it or not, Amelia, I'm a nice guy. Maybe being in court brings out the worst—"

She didn't give him time to finish but clutched his shirtfront and dragged him down to her lips. His mouth met hers and it was another powerful explosion that raced through her body at the touch of his soft, moist lips. His mouth opened above hers and she plunged her tongue into the warmth. His tongue bathed hers, battled with hers, and then eventually made love to hers.

Her hands no longer had the power to hold anything and flattened against his chest. She could feel the pounding of his heart, the heat from under his clothes, as their kiss deepened and he wrapped his arms around her, pulling her closer. The first kiss in the air duct had taken her by surprise, but this kiss . . . She had expected the fireworks, the out-of-control passion, and the dizziness that circled behind her closed eyes.

Then she felt his hands travel from her waist to underneath her shirt. She gasped into his mouth as his callused hands began to massage the delicate skin on her stomach and waist. Each contact with his rough hands caused little sparks to travel down her spine.

She should have pushed him away in shock—he was feeling her up in public—but she didn't. She couldn't move from his mouth. George made love to her with one kiss and she was about to lose all control. Then one of his hands moved the lace of her bra to one side and she felt his hand on her nipple, on her breast. Her nipple felt like a hard, nerve-filled pebble against his large and gentle palm. He continued to move his other hand in circles on her still-covered breasts as if he wanted to memorize each one in a different state of undress.

Amelia gasped again into his mouth, then moved her hands along his broad shoulders to wrap around his neck, moving him closer. She felt the hardness of him against her. He began to move against her, and her body of its own will responded. Like an erotic dance, or like most rap videos, the two moved against each other, first slowly, and then George began to make certain he touched her most intimate place.

Amelia's mouth fell open in amazement at the feelings, and his hungry, questing tongue took full advantage. She didn't know if she could handle the emotions any longer. She tried to respond to his kiss, but she couldn't do anything but hold on for the ride. The ache with which she needed to feel him in the one place he didn't touch was almost unbearable. She wanted him inside of her. And she almost told him, except it suddenly became too much of him. In and around too many places. The dam she had been holding back burst and she screamed out his name as the explosion of emotion burst from the protected shell of her body.

His kisses became softer and softer as he coaxed her back to earth. His touch became less and less; his hands moved from under her clothes until he gently held her shoulders. Her heart pounded against her chest and her ears felt like they were permanently clogged from the release of emotions. She buried her head against his chest as she tried to comprehend what the hell had just happened. She'd had an orgasm in the middle of the street with an avowed enemy, with all of her clothes on. She couldn't bear to think what George thought of her, what she thought of herself. No matter how she tried to tell herself it was the twenty-first century and she was liberated to do whatever she wanted, she still felt guilty.

His gentleness, his soft nuzzling of her hair, was too much. She looked away and refused to meet his eyes.

Instead, she reached to adjust her headband, but it still sat in his car, so her hands uselessly dropped to her sides. She said in a hoarse voice, "Drive safely."

Since she was too embarrassed to meet his gaze, she turned and half-sprinted toward her front door. She entered the house, then slammed the door behind her and barred it with her body. She didn't release her breath until she heard his car engine start, then eventually fade away into the distance. She sighed in relief, then turned on the house alarm before she ran to her bathroom for a nice long, cold shower.

Chapter 13

Amelia ignored the stares directed at her as she walked through the lobby of the downtown building that housed the district attorney's office and other municipal services. She wasn't certain if the stares were because everyone in the building somehow knew that she had attacked George in front of her house last night or because of the two large men trailing behind her who had set off the security metal detectors.

Her father's bodyguards had promptly rung the doorbell at eight o'clock. She had attempted to explain to the two men that she didn't need their services, but after talking to their blank faces for fifteen minutes she had given up and allowed them to drive her to work. Her father had conveniently not answered his phone so that she could force him to call off the guard dogs.

She held up her chin and made her strides as long and powerful as the tight black skirt she wore would allow her to move. In the bright sun of the morning her behavior the night before seemed more wanton and shameful.

Granted, George hadn't exactly been a protesting partici-
pant, but he was a man. He wouldn't stop any woman
from throwing herself at him. He had touched her and
she had allowed him to touch . . . Her embarrassment
over the incident quickly turned to erotic memory as she
remembered the feel of his hands on her breasts. She had
spent all night remembering.

The elevator doors slid open and she instantly wiped
all thoughts of George from her mind. She wouldn't
allow anyone to interfere with her job, especially not
George Gibson, no matter if one of his kisses could make
her lose control. She stepped off the elevator and walked
into the doors marked for the district attorney's office.
The receptionist, who had sat at the large desk at the
entrance for more than ten years, openly gasped when
she saw Amelia and the two men behind her.

"Good morning, Dionne," Amelia said in her normal
businesslike, somber greeting. "Do I have any messages?"

"Messages?" Dionne blankly repeated, her attention
focused on the bodyguards and not Amelia. She sent the
man who had introduced himself as Jenkins a flirtatious
smile that Amelia wouldn't have thought the grand-
mother of four capable of.

Amelia loudly cleared her throat and Dionne begrudg-
ingly tore her gaze from the men to Amelia.

"Do I have any messages this morning, Dionne?"
Amelia repeated in a loud voice.

Dionne shook her head as if to pull herself out of a
trance; then she said to Amelia, "Mr. Grayson is waiting
for you in his office."

"Thank you."

Amelia walked past the attorney and legal secretary cubicles, ignoring their curious glances in her direction. She reached the double doors of the district attorney's office and motioned for her bodyguards to wait outside the door.

She said, "There are some seats over there—"

"I'm sorry, Ms. Farrow, but if you're going inside that room, then we're going inside that room," Jenkins told her in the same monotone he had used all morning.

"This is going to be a repeat of this morning if I attempt to argue, isn't it?" she asked coolly.

She thought that he almost smiled before he nodded. The other one, who had been introduced only as Morse, simply stood in one place and stared around the office as if an assassin would jump out at any second. She sighed in frustration, then walked into the office. It was the most spacious office in the building, but since it was still a government building, it wasn't that large. Grayson had made the most of it with the dark, masculine colors and enough mahogany to make her practically see the testosterone in the air.

Grayson sat behind the large oak desk wearing the same three-piece dark gray suit that he had worn the day Amelia interviewed for her job five years ago. He didn't look happy. In fact, he looked upset. She immediately sat in one of the leather chairs across the desk from him.

"What happened?" she instantly asked.

He heavily sighed, then paused when he saw the men towering behind her. He shook his head and murmured, "Your father?"

"You told him about the attack on Banner," she accused.

He shrugged with a small guilty smile, then became sober as he said, "There's no case, Amelia."

"What do you mean?"

"There's no case."

"But when I left the house last night—"

"Banner refused to cooperate. He claimed not to know who Milton Tucker was or why he attacked him."

"He's lying. Milton Tucker didn't wake up last night and decide to attack a judge in his home for the hell of it! There was a reason."

"Maybe he didn't like one of Banner's rulings for one of his friends. Who knows how these maniacs think? It's getting harder and harder to predict," Grayson said with a helpless shrug. "But that doesn't change the fact that we have nothing."

"If Banner wants to hang himself by not cooperating, then we'll let him. Tucker is our ticket. What did he say?" Amelia asked desperately. "Offer him a plea and he'll rat out his mother. I've seen people like Tucker—"

"Tucker escaped," Grayson softly responded. "On the drive to the county jail. He knocked out his driver and somehow got out of the car. The last anyone saw him, he was headed down Western."

"How could he escape?" she gasped in confusion.

"We think some of Donaldson's contacts in the police force helped," Grayson answered.

She was horrified that tears filled her eyes, not because she was sad but because she was so angry.

"What about Finnegan?" she pressed. "He's missing—"

"Exactly, Amelia, he's missing. No body. No crime. The lab results taken from the stairwell came back clean. Of course, Donaldson could have gotten to the lab, but at some point we can't blame everything on him. Maybe there was no crime."

She rolled her eyes and got to her feet. She began to stalk the room, unbuttoning her suit jacket in the process. It was the only way she could think. She had to pace. She had to unbutton her jacket.

"There has to be another way. . . . Bring in Kevin Parker and I'll ID his voice and match it to the voice on the stairwell."

Grayson straightened in his chair and said hesitantly, "We have no cause to bring him in. The last thing this office needs is another black man claiming police harassment—"

"That's exactly why they want to kill me, Richard, because they know that I can match Parker's voice to the murder."

"We still haven't conclusively proven that Parker or Tucker was the one who attacked you, or that there has been a murder, or that any of this relates to Donaldson."

"There was a murder and it relates to Donaldson," she said with a confirming nod. "Finnegan has been missing for almost five days. I heard his voice on the stairwell that night. Parker was on the stairwell with him. And if I could hear his voice, I could identify him—"

"How do you know that? How do you know any of it?" Grayson asked, his voice deadly and quiet.

"Because I saw his profile on the court videotapes—" Amelia didn't realize what she had done until it was too late.

Grayson's expression hardened and he said through clenched teeth, "What are you talking about, Farrow? The police are questioning courthouse employees about missing tapes that were mysteriously returned yesterday. Don't tell me that you know where they were. Please don't tell me that. I do not want to hear that my star ADA is stealing sheriff's property."

"I have a lot of work to finish before my morning arguments," she said, grabbing her briefcase and purse.

"Stay away from George Gibson, Amelia," Grayson ordered in a flat voice. "I know that you wouldn't have done any of this without his . . . guidance. You have a good career here. In fact, I think that you could be the first female that this county would vote into this office. Don't ruin it."

She nodded stiffly, then turned and walked out of the room. She made certain to hold the door open for her two shadows.

George searched the courthouse cafeteria for Amelia. He found himself looking for her throughout the day whenever he left a courtroom or walked the halls. He also was surprised to realize that he had done it before. And often. He always paused, just a step, to look for Amelia when he entered the courthouse.

The woman had gotten into his blood last night. He had barely been able to sit behind the steering wheel after he left her house the night before. He had spent most of the night dreaming about the look on her face that night. He had never seen a woman with such pure abandon and delight on her face. She had enjoyed every second and it had made him enjoy every second. He hadn't even "sealed the deal," and for the first time since he had ever been with a woman, he hadn't wanted to.

Kissing her and being able to touch her had been enough. Of course, his body had cursed him, but there had been something to just holding her in his arms, having the right to kiss her, and seeing that he gave her enjoyment. He had made her smile like that.

Then he saw her. Across the cafeteria. She sent the cashier a brief smile as she paid for her food, not the full smile to which George had become accustomed but one of her stingy smiles that she reserved for strangers. In the span of one night, he had missed her. She had seen to that when she stopped him from leaving and gave him the best fifteen minutes of mouth-to-mouth he could remember since Latasha Jenkins in the eleventh grade.

"What happened to your face, Gibson?" one of the attorneys, who openly examined the bruise courtesy of Milton Tucker, asked at the table where George sat.

"Jealous husband came home and found you with his wife?" another man asked with a nudge in George's side.

"Just because that happened last night with your wife, Hamilton, don't take your anger out on me," George retorted, causing the table to collapse in laughter.

His attention was diverted when he noticed Amelia heading toward the exit. He realized that he might not see her until tomorrow at lunch and suddenly that seemed too long. He finished his sandwich in one bite, gulped down the soda fast enough to give himself a severe case of heartburn, then stood and grabbed his briefcase.

"You just sat down," Hamilton said, surprised.

"I forgot that I have a . . . a thing," he mumbled in response, then hurried across the cafeteria.

He felt like he was back in high school as he maneuvered his way through the cafeteria crowd and tried to find a way to "accidentally" bump into Amelia. He was only a few steps from her side and she still hadn't noticed him when he felt a hand on his shoulder. A very heavy hand that belonged to a very large man. George turned to look at him.

"May I help you?" the older man asked in a baritone voice that told George that the man would help him lose a tooth or two.

"It's all right, Jenkins," Amelia said from behind George.

He winced when he realized that she had turned around. He faced her, and whatever mindless greeting he had planned drifted out of his mind. He wondered why he had ever thought she was not beautiful, that she couldn't compete with the women he had dated. She left every one of them in the dust. It wasn't just the fact that she could kiss like nobody's business, which was not apparent from her prissy suits and headbands, but she could make him laugh. He hadn't mentioned his mother in almost twenty years, but he had told Amelia. Not even Wayne knew about Winnie the Pooh.

George glanced at Jenkins and the older man reluctantly removed his hand, but George felt the remnants of the pressure in his sore shoulder. For the first time, he noticed the other large man standing on the other side of him. Both men continued to watch him as if waiting for him to breathe wrong just so they could break his neck.

"These must be the bodyguards," George said, finding the strength to face Amelia again.

"Jenkins and Morse," she introduced the two men. "Is there something that you wanted, Mr. Gibson?"

He noticed that she avoided his eyes and George

wondered what he had done wrong, besides exist. Apparently, she regretted last night. Of course she regretted allowing him to touch her. She was Amelia Farrow. No man could touch her without completing a ten-page application and having a charge account at Brooks Brothers.

"I wanted to see if there's been any news about Tucker or Banner."

"There's no case against Judge Banner since he won't cooperate. There's not enough evidence of a crime to even force Donaldson to come to the station for questioning. And Milton Tucker escaped on the way to jail last night."

George felt his mouth drop open in shock and he quickly closed it. He quickly glanced around the crowded hall and decided there were too many people nearby for comfort. He grabbed her arm and led her to the men's restroom down the hall. He left her outside while he searched the wooden stalls to find them empty. He motioned for her to come inside. She hesitated for only a second before she stalked into the bathroom. He watched her bodyguards take guard posts at the entrance as the door swung closed.

She glanced around the bathroom and he saw the flash of discomfort cross her face. He wanted to tell her that for a public men's restroom in a Los Angeles courthouse, this one was relatively clean and relatively smell-free, but instead he cracked open one of the two windows. She crossed her arms over her chest and faced him head-on.

"Tucker escaped?" he asked in disbelief. His voice echoed in the large, empty bathroom and he flinched, then repeated in a whisper, "Tucker escaped?"

Her expression remained frozen as she added, "And no

one can find the still-missing Nathan Finnegan. To summarize, we have no case. You should have forced Anna Chin to give a statement while you had the chance."

He ran a hand over his hair as he tried to collect his thoughts. He finally asked, "What are we going to do?"

"We aren't going to do anything."

"You're going to give up that easily?" he asked, surprised.

"It's not our job anymore. The police are conducting an investigation—"

"The police are the exact people who need to be investigated," he said.

George said in a rushed whisper, "I've never known you to give up on anything."

"I'm a prosecutor, George, not a police officer. I don't investigate crimes and I don't break into buildings. That's not in my job description," she hissed in return. He was, at least, glad that some of the old fire he had seen that weekend had returned and she no longer treated him like a servant at a debutante ball.

"They tried to kill you, Amelia, and you're going to let them get away with that?"

"They're not going to get away with anything. The police will gather evidence in the proper way, and when they do, my office will prosecute the offenders."

"This is bullshit and you know it," he said angrily. "Banner isn't playing ball because your people aren't making him. He's a judge, right? He probably wasn't even brought to the station for questioning. It's real easy for him to refuse to tell the truth when he's sitting in the comfort of his own home."

"Are you accusing my office of some sort of wrongdoing?" she asked, indignation flashing across her face.

"Everyone else is on the take; why not the DA's office?"

"As if you can talk," she said through clenched teeth while poking one finger into his chest. "The only reason you care about any of this is because you won't be able to put your guilty clients back onto the streets and you won't be able to sue the state for more money."

His anger subsided when he saw the accusation in her eyes. He stuffed his hands in his pants pockets and took a step away from her. He asked quietly, "After the last few days, you still think that's all I care about?"

He saw her sharp intake of breath and it gave him a small glimmer of satisfaction that she wasn't as unaffected by what had happened between them as she pretended. It shouldn't have, but it pleased him because he had been affected. Very affected.

"What other reason could there be?" she finally retorted, her face a blank mask. "You've made it clear from the start what you cared about. And it wasn't justice or the integrity of the system. It was always about money."

"Don't talk to me about money. It's real easy for a rich person to feel sanctimonious about their money."

"It always goes back to that with you, doesn't it?" she asked coolly while crossing her arms over her chest. "All of this time, I thought you hated me because we're on opposite sides. But the truth comes out. You hate me because I have money and you don't."

"I don't hate you. I never hated you," he said fiercely.

She turned to leave, but he grabbed her arm once more and forced her to look at him. He said in a softer voice,

"Amelia, I don't hate you. Sometimes you can irritate the hell out of me and you make me want to hit my head against a brick wall, but I don't hate you. No one could hate you. It's like hating Santa Claus. There's no point."

"Never mind," she said, shaking her head. Her expression was unreadable, her jaw clenched tight. He had never seen her so angry, except he didn't know if she was angry with him or herself. "Don't worry, George. The cops will catch the bad guys and you'll get paid. And you'll even get a good story out of this."

He knew she meant what had happened between them, and the fact that she thought he would use it as fodder for jokes infuriated him.

"Be careful, Amelia," he warned, narrowing his eyes at her. "I wasn't the only one almost naked against that car last night."

Her eyes widened and her breath quickened. Then she brushed past him and walked out of the bathroom. He began to go after her, but instead he stuffed his hands into his pants pockets. She was right about him. She could save the world on her own.

George stared at his blank computer screen and resisted the urge to turn off the computer. After a full day of court appointments and counseling clients, he had returned to his office. He had three motions to write and file by the next morning, but he had been sitting in his office for an hour and the only slightly constructive thing he had done was water his faithful plant. He blamed Amelia. She had no right to make him like her, to make him even admit that he was attracted to her, and then snatch her friendship—her smile and laughter—from him. It wasn't fair.

The door to his office suddenly flew open. He didn't have any scheduled appointments, so he got to his feet to direct the person to the bathroom, since, for better or worse, his office was next door to the one bathroom in the hallway. But the three men who filled the doorway obviously weren't looking for the bathroom. He also could tell that they didn't need his services, since their dark, expensive suits suggested that they could afford better.

Two of the men were only slightly smaller versions of the Incredible Hulk. Their muscles barely fit inside their dark, tailored suits, and George's practiced eye caught the distinct outlines of guns underneath their jackets. The man who stood in the middle of the other two was the one George knew he should worry about. His fudge-colored brown skin and bright amber-colored eyes hinted at an innocence that George would bet the man had never known. His dark suit was the most expensive-looking of those worn by the three men, but the clothes couldn't hide the truth. These men came from the streets and, despite their fancy clothes, belonged on the streets.

No one spoke as the man settled in the one chair facing George's desk. The two hulks remained posted on either side of the door. Their eyes never remained in one place for long but constantly scanned the room, the hallways, and even outside the sixth-floor window.

"My name is Maurice Donaldson," the man finally said.

George stared at the man for a second longer, then slowly sat in his chair. He had faced men like Maurice his entire life. He had grown up with men like him. They didn't normally pay visits to lawyers like George. Their lawyers practiced in the downtown high-rises and billed hundreds of dollars an hour, which men like Maurice could pay without batting an eyelash.

"You've heard of me," Maurice said with a knowing smile as he met George's eyes.

"I've recently had a lot of contact with your employees."

"That's right. . . . Your choice of acquaintances has gotten you into some trouble."

George's jaw clenched, but he kept his expression impassive. The most important lesson he had learned on the streets and in court was to never show a weakness, and he was quickly realizing that Amelia Farrow was his weakness.

"What can I do for you, Mr. Donaldson?"

"From what I've heard, you're a good lawyer. I can only imagine that you work in this hellhole because you don't collect fees from your clients, who probably all have a sob story every time it comes around to payday."

"I like my office."

Maurice laughed, a smile that never quite reached his eyes, but they both knew that neither of them believed George's lame protests. The smile disappeared as quickly as it had formed, and Maurice seriously regarded George for a moment before he said, "I have a proposition for you, Mr. Gibson."

"I don't think—"

"Everything I've heard about you tells me that you're a man of intelligence. You don't let the rules get in the way of serving your clients."

"I don't know what you've heard, but I've never broken any law while representing a client."

Maurice held up his hands in defense and said, "I'm not the state bar looking to revoke your license. The point

I'm trying to make is that you take care of your clients. You care for them and they care for you. I think you deserve more than a one-room office, cheap suits, and a run-down apartment. I can put you where you belong."

"Are you in legal trouble?"

Maurice laughed again and shook his head. "I'm a legitimate businessman, Mr. Gibson. What legal trouble would I have?"

"Then how can you help me?"

"As you indicated, my employees have a habit of encountering the law. I have ten employees at Heller Helium and almost one hundred other employees across Los Angeles County. Most of them have misunderstandings with the law on a regular basis. You can help us with that, Mr. Gibson. You can be the sole representative for all of my employees."

For a moment, George was stunned into silence. He had been expecting to hear many things from Maurice Donaldson, but a job offer was not one of them.

"You want me to be your general counsel?" George clarified, just in case his fantasies had intruded upon reality.

"I thought that was what I said," Donaldson said with a smile.

"Why?" George asked blankly. "You have enough money to hire whoever you want. Why me?"

"I've done some research on you. You remind me of myself. No family. No one to look out for you. You had to fight and scrap for everything in this world, just like I did. We have to stick together. When one of us makes it, he has to hold his hand out for the next brother."

George didn't bother to hide his snort of disbelief. The

goons flexed their muscles at him while Maurice once more pasted that fake smile on his face.

"You don't believe me," Maurice said.

"I'm not saying that I'm not good, but you need someone more established and experienced. I don't have the staff—I don't have any staff—to come close to handling your volume of business."

"We'll hire the staff."

George couldn't shake the feeling that he should run out of his office as fast as he could. He knew Donaldson's type. They were all smiles and attempts at civility when the deal was going their way, but the second it didn't, their real personalities appeared.

"I appreciate the . . . the offer, but I like my practice the way it is—"

"I would give you one million dollars—cash—today as a retainer."

All attempts at nonchalance flew out the window as George quickly unscrewed the bottle of water on his desk and took a quick swallow to wet his suddenly dry throat. He set down the bottle and studied Maurice's face for any sign of a joke.

George's voice cracked as he repeated, "One million dollars?"

"Just to make yourself available if we should need you."

"One million dollars." Suddenly George was wondering, praying that he and Amelia had made a mistake. Maybe Maurice Donaldson wasn't involved. Maybe another criminal mastermind was responsible for Chin's death and Finnegan's disappearance.

"That's just the beginning. Vacations, cars, women . . .

it's all a part of the fringe benefits package when you work for me. Like I said, you're a bright guy, Mr. Gibson, and a bright guy wouldn't pass up this opportunity. You've spent your whole life scrimping and saving. If you come to work for me, you don't have to think about money another day in your life," Maurice said with his toothpaste-commercial–bright smile.

"And in return, what do you want?" George asked, hoping that Maurice didn't notice the sweat on his forehead. One million dollars was a lot of money.

"Besides your legal services? Nothing at all."

George laughed in disbelief, which made Maurice smile. George abruptly stopped laughing and said simply, "You claim that we come from the same place; then you know that where we come from, nothing is that simple; there's always something more involved."

Maurice's pleasant expression didn't change. "If our positions were reversed, Mr. Gibson—if I were the attorney and you were me—what would you think that I'd want?"

"You want me to stop searching for Nathan Finnegan."

It was imperceptible, but George saw Maurice flinch before he said, "I have no idea what you're talking about."

"Of course not," George said with a smile. He stood and stared at his Timex watch. He would have loved to have bought himself a Rolex. "I have an appointment in five minutes. It was nice of you to stop by."

Maurice remained seated and his goons remained at their positions at the door. "What's your price, Mr. Gibson?"

"I do have one, but I'm not the kind of attorney you're

looking for. Every person deserves a fair trial, and I've defended some people who didn't even deserve that, but I don't protect men who leave little girls fatherless and who intimidate and bully their way through the court system."

There was a moment of silence as George steadied himself for an onslaught from the twin goons. He figured he would go down in about four shots, but he would take one of them with him. He had been in worse situations before. He even felt some of the old adrenaline racing through his veins.

Then Maurice smiled and said, "Because only attorneys can intimidate and bully their way through the court system?"

George didn't smile as he responded, "We pay a lot of money and go to school for a long time to do that."

Donaldson laughed, then slowly stood. He took a moment to brush imaginary lint off his jacket. Maurice finally looked at George and sighed. "I thought you and I could come to an understanding. We come from the same place. We know that inside the courtroom nothing ensures a fair trial except money."

With a smile and shrug that conveyed he wasn't offended, he walked out of the office followed by the two giants. George sat at his desk and suddenly realized that the back of his shirt was wet with sweat. And his hands were trembling. So much for his macho act. He had been as scared as hell. The prospect of being beaten to a bloody pulp did that to him.

He glanced around his office, almost expecting Donaldson to jump out from under the sofa. It was so quiet that George could have pretended that he'd never had the visit, but he had. He tried not to think about the money. He tried not to think about Amelia. She would hate him forever if he worked for Donaldson, but he was tempted. Tempted enough to shift through his bills to determine how much of the million dollars he would have left over once he paid them.

Chapter 14

"I'm so nervous," Heather whispered as she clutched Amelia's hand with a grip worthy of a professional wrestler.

The two stood in the middle of Earthly Delights, the newest restaurant to open in the competitive world of Beverly Hills dining. Even though Amelia had no financial stake in the success of the small bistro, she was as nervous as Heather. The sound of clinking silverware as people stood in the crowded restaurant for the opening and the soft sounds of the string quartet served to ease Amelia's nerves.

"Everyone is having a wonderful time," Amelia assured Heather and herself, but it was the truth. She heard the laughter and saw the smiling faces as proof. Besides, the small appetizers that Heather had chosen to serve and the circulating champagne would make anyone have a good time. Even if no one had fun, they would go away with their stomachs satisfied.

"Is the food really good?" Heather asked, turning to Amelia with an anxious expression on her beautiful features.

Amelia smiled and squeezed her hand. "For the tenth time, the food is excellent, Heather. This is going to be a good thing for you."

"I hope so." Heather sighed as her eyes scanned the room. "After everything I went through with Nicolas . . ."

"What do you mean?" Amelia asked, noticing that her friend's voice trailed off.

"Forget I said anything. Let's just enjoy tonight."

"Where is Nicolas, Heather?" Amelia asked suddenly, looking around the room at the majority of familiar faces.

"He's not here. He had to work."

"Work? This is your opening—"

"Let it go, Amelia," Heather said firmly, squarely meeting Amelia's gaze. "I want to enjoy tonight, and I want to enjoy it with my best friend, who . . . who was almost taken from me. Let's not ruin it, not right now, OK?"

Amelia debated questioning Heather further, but if she and Nicolas had marital problems, Amelia did not want to grill Heather in front of all of their friends and acquaintances. But Amelia didn't need to ask. She could see from Heather's drawn expression that there was a problem. And it broke Amelia's heart. Partially because she felt for her best friend, but Amelia had spent the last three years viewing Heather and Nicolas as an example of a perfect couple. They knew all the right people, came from the right families, and looked good enough standing next to each other to be constantly photographed for the society pages. If Heather and Nicolas had problems, then Amelia didn't know how she could ever find someone. No one was as predictably perfect as Heather and Nicolas.

"I don't believe it," Heather said suddenly, a wide smile on her face.

Amelia followed her gaze and her mouth dropped open when she saw George walk into the restaurant. He paused at the entrance to turn and smile down at . . . Amelia crossed her arms over her chest when she saw who stood next to him, a gushing Constance Dailey. Amelia had never had a problem with Constance. Most days the criminal defense attorney wore her skirts too short and her suits too tight, but through various legally related social events, Amelia had come to know the woman and liked her. But when Constance briefly touched George's arm, Amelia decided that she despised the woman.

As if sensing Amelia's gaze on them, George glanced across the room until his gaze met hers. The heat flushed her face and other parts of her body when she remembered her behavior the previous night. She wondered if she would ever be able to look at him again without feeling such mortification. Without acknowledging her presence, George turned to Constance again.

"Is he dating Constance?" Heather asked, surprised.

"I have to find Eileen," Amelia muttered, and had turned to slink into the crowd just as she heard a woman call her name.

"Amelia! Amelia Farrow!"

Amelia cringed and turned in time to see Constance push her way through the crowd, tugging on George's hand as he trailed behind her.

Constance threw her arms around Amelia in a bear

hug and rocked her back and forth several times. Amelia gasped at the strength of the hug and her gaze naturally sought out George. His expression was impassive as he flickered a glance at her; then he smiled in greeting at Heather.

"I just heard about what happened over the weekend," Constance said as she finally released Amelia. Constance was a beautiful woman with cinnamon brown skin, long hair that was always messy in that just-had-a-man-mess-it-up look, and chocolate brown eyes. She was one of those delicate, petite women who always made Amelia feel like a large, lumbering elephant because she towered over them by several inches. "How horrible! Are you doing OK? Do you need anything?"

"I'm fine. Thanks," Amelia said, forcing a smile even as she noticed how Constance immediately moved back to George's side. Amelia once more glanced at him and was surprised to find him staring at her. He immediately averted his gaze and stuffed his hands in his pants pockets.

"Are you sure that you're OK?" Constance pressed. "I would be a total mess right now if I had been attacked, almost strangled to death, possibly raped in my own home."

Amelia flinched at the words. Any of the situations could have happened, but hearing the blunt words spoken made it seem too real.

"Heather, nice to see you again," George said before Constance could make Amelia feel "better" enough to cry. He smiled as he glanced at the high ceilings and large windows of the restaurant. "Congratulations on your opening. It appears as if you already have a success on your hands."

"I hope so," Heather said, smiling, then looped her arm through Constance's arm. "Constance, last month you asked me about that thing."

"What thing?" Constance asked, confused.

Heather laughed—her high-pitched, fake laugh that instantly aroused Amelia's suspicions. She knew that Heather wasn't above matchmaking, even if it meant forcibly removing obstacles—which in this case was Constance.

"The thing, you know," Heather said. "You asked me about it. . . . Well, it's over there."

"The thing is?" Constance asked uncertainly.

"Right." Heather winked at Amelia, then dragged a confused Constance to the other side of the room.

Amelia shook her head and tried not to laugh at Heather's blatant ploy to get her and George alone. When she once more forced herself to look at George, she realized that Heather's work had been for nothing. George looked everywhere but at her, and when he did glance at her, he looked pained.

"I should grab more napkins," she murmured, then abruptly turned and walked toward the kitchen. She veered toward Heather's small office in the back of the restaurant to hide out for the rest of the night. When she tried to close the door, a brown-skinned hand caught it. George walked into the office and closed the door behind him, locking it.

She sharply inhaled as the once-quite-comfortable room suddenly shrank and his presence occupied every inch. There was barely any furniture in the room, but it suddenly felt too crowded.

He leaned against the door, as if to tell her that the only way she was getting out of the room was through him. She drank in the sight of him. From his finger-calling hair, to his mouth that she could still remember on hers, to his lean hips and long legs.

"You shouldn't be in here, George," she said, attempting to sound calm. "This is Heather's private office."

"You're trying to avoid me," he said simply.

She forced an ungraceful snort of disbelief before she demanded, "Why would I avoid you?"

"Because you must realize how angry I am."

"Excuse me?"

He moved from the door to walk across the room and tower over her. She didn't budge from her spot, even though she wanted to. Not because she was scared, but because he was too gorgeous this close. *He* was too much for her this close.

"You pissed me off this afternoon," he said, enunciating each word as if she were a small child. "How dare you act like I'm using you? Maybe I'm interested in Donaldson and Finnegan for the money, but I've always been honest about that. I don't need to seduce you to get my fees. Believe it or not, but I kissed you—and you kissed me back, I might add—because I wanted to."

She rolled her eyes in disbelief, then said simply, "You should get back to Constance. I'm sure she's looking all over the restaurant for you."

"Constance is not my date," he quickly informed her. Amelia actually paused at the news, even though she told herself not to care. "We're friends. She told me she wanted someone to go with her to a restaurant opening; I didn't know it was for Heather's restaurant."

"So you're saying if you had known that I would be here, you wouldn't have come?"

He groaned, then ran a hand down his face. "Why do you make things so difficult, Amelia? Do you want me or not? One second, you're spouting nonsense in the middle of the courthouse that I kissed you as an excuse to learn what you know in the Donaldson investigation. The next second, you're acting hurt because I don't flirt with you."

"I never asked you to flirt with me," she said, horrified at the image of attempting to flirt with George. She would be too tongue-tied, too wrapped up in remembering how his tongue felt, to be able to respond.

"Every time you look at me, your eyes are begging for me to flirt. . . . Actually, you want a lot more than flirting."

"Not only are you arrogant, but you're delusional," she retorted.

He stepped closer to her and this time she did move, her thighs bumping into the edge of the desk. She caught the edge of the desk to steady herself, but unless she bent over backward, she had no way to escape George. He appeared to take pleasure in this fact as he moved even closer, until the edges of her breasts touched his hard chest. Her nipples instantly hardened beneath the silk of her dress.

"I like you, Farrow," he said in a deep voice that made her skin burn. "After last night, I would think you could tell that."

"About last night . . . that was a momentary bout of insanity that we should both forget—"

"I can't forget it. I've tried. If you tell me that you can forget what it felt like touching each other like that, then you're a liar." He appeared to wait for her to contradict him, and when she didn't, he grinned. One of his smirky grins that she pretended to find irritating but secretly turned her into a boneless mass of flesh. His hand gently rested on the back of her neck and softly began to massage the area near the faint bruises still left from her attacker's hands. "The two of us . . . Let's just accept that whatever is going on between us is too good and too strong for us to deny right now."

"I will not allow myself to be controlled by lust," she told him, then shuddered in delight at the feel of his hand massaging her neck.

He sent her that grin again as his mouth moved to within inches of hers, close enough for her to accidentally kiss him if she breathed too hard.

"That's the problem with lust. You never have much choice in the matter when it wants something."

"Maybe not for someone like you," she told him haughtily. "But I am an adult. I can control my actions—"

"Control this," he said, then used the hand at her neck to push her toward his mouth. She didn't resist.

The two clung to each other as their mouths battled in a duel of wills. As his tongue swept through her mouth with a voracious conveyed desperation, she admitted that she couldn't control her reaction to him. Her body moved against his with a welcoming that she never would have given of her own free will. She wanted him. She wanted this man, and as his hands began to roam against his body, she couldn't find one reason that she shouldn't have him.

She dragged her mouth from his and brushed aside his suit jacket, then fumbled with his belt buckle. She licked her lips dry from his mouth as she saw his erection push out the dark pants.

"Did you lock the door?" she groaned, the desire making her voice rough and hoarse.

"What are you doing?" She never thought she would hear him sound anything but arrogant and cocky, but he suddenly sounded confused and slightly out of control.

She met his eyes and smiled. "If you don't know, then it's been longer than I thought since you've done this," she said softly.

"We can't do this here. . . . There are people outside the door," he said, glancing around the room.

Amelia agreed with him. It was wrong. It was something practically perfect Amelia Farrow would not do, but when she finally released his buckle, her hand reached into his pants and she felt him. His hardness. His eyes fluttered closed and he deeply exhaled. His hands came to rest on her shoulders and he squeezed. Hard.

She drank from his lips again before she whispered, "Don't tell me you're afraid to get caught, George?"

He stared at her and when she saw the somber look in his eyes, for a brief moment, the smile faded from her face. She didn't want him to think so hard. She didn't want him to question her. For once, she didn't want to think. She didn't want to be the responsible, perfect Amelia.

As if he read her mind, his hands suddenly gripped her bottom and pulled her against his body. She gasped at the strength in his grasp and his hardness in the one place she needed to feel him. He sent her one of his patented grins before he forcibly moved her onto the edge of the desk. He pushed her legs apart and moved into the open V space.

She smiled, then grabbed the back of his neck and pulled him to her. Their kiss this time was hard. Almost carnal. Without the questions, the unspoken truce between them released any reservations. Amelia had been kissed before, she had been touched before, but never like this.

Never with the certainty that this was right where she should be, even if that location was in Heather's office with almost 100 people outside the room.

He slid the spaghetti straps of her dress down her arms, then pulled down the bodice of the dress. She gasped when he almost ripped off the strapless bra; then his too-hot mouth clamped on one nipple and she barely kept herself from screaming. He sucked; then his tongue drifted across the nipple before he moved to the other breast. She wrapped her arms around his head and willed him to never release her, even as she whispered pleas of mercy.

She didn't know when he had removed her underpants, but she felt him push the hem of her silk dress to her waist. The cool air in the office swirled around her thighs but was instantly heated when his hands played on the soft skin. She watched as he impatiently pulled a condom from his wallet. She didn't know when his own pants were pulled down or when she opened his shirt, but when her hands branded his chest, he entered her in one long smooth stroke.

She gasped into his mouth at the sheer possession and rightness in his movements. Her position on the desk pushed her hips into the almost sinfully perfect position to accept him. She placed one hand behind her to hold the majority of her weight and wrapped the other hand around his neck as she matched his movements. Their rhythm was natural, fast, too good. Sweat beaded on her forehead as she looked down to watch their thrusting hips. Then she closed her eyes to enjoy the feelings that having him inside of her aroused, better than her dreams and fantasies.

She felt his mouth against her neck as he laid his head

against hers. She wrapped her legs around his waist to take his penetration even deeper into her body. He grunted as his mouth opened and planted itself on her neck. She grinned and wrapped her arm tighter around his neck. She wanted to tell him that she would have a hickey, but she liked the feel of his tongue and his lips on her neck. One hickey was worth it.

Then it happened. The feelings emanating from their union began to spark throughout her body, began to focus in a pinpoint of ecstasy that was so close to pain that she cried out his name. His mouth curled into a smile against her neck before he placed his mouth over hers, half to kiss her and half to silence her.

His smile did it. Just knowing that he smiled made her scream his name in completion. After a few more smooth thrusts, she heard him gasp her name as his hands clenched her waist.

George was too stunned, too relaxed, to move for a few moments even when he finally remembered where on earth he was. He was standing in the middle of some- body's office, still inside of Amelia Farrow. Just what the hell had he done? He abruptly moved from between her legs. He grabbed tissue from the box on the desk and turned from Amelia to handle the condom. He zipped up his pants and stared at the ground as she gingerly moved off the desk and straightened her own clothes.

He discreetly watched her as she smoothed down her hair with jerky movements. He blamed this whole inci- dent on the lack of a headband. When he had walked into the restaurant and spotted her across the room, he had been shocked into disbelief. She didn't have on the ridiculous headband, and her hair fell in what had been smooth waves before his hands had completely destroyed whatever hairstyle she had worn. She wore a short, black dress that should have been simple, but it plunged to depths and rose to heights that George didn't particularly like when he had noticed the other men in the restaurant watching her from the corners of their eyes. George had wondered when he ever thought that she was plain and ordinary.

She took a compact from her purse and gasped at the image. He wanted to tell her that she had never looked more beautiful. Her skin shone with sensual exertion, her hair was mussed, and her mouth was swollen with his kisses. Just staring at that mouth made him want to kiss her again. Staring at her breasts once more encased in the black material made him want to grab her. He wanted to do everything again, but instead he walked into the private bathroom attached to the office.

When he walked out, she snapped the compact closed before she zipped her purse. He forced himself to turn and face her. He had spent half of his "romantic" life perfecting the speech that allowed him to ease out of the room with no promises of tomorrow or future entanglements. For the first time, that speech fled his mind. It sounded stupid and false. He didn't want to ease out of the room with Amelia. He wanted to grab her silky waist and plunge into honey again.

"I should return to the party," she said in that nervous debutante voice that she used whenever she felt that she had done something she shouldn't have with him.

He should have allowed her to leave, if only because

she looked so uncomfortable. Her hands kept smoothing her hair down as if she missed the headband.

"I should, too," he murmured.

She walked to the door with long strides that instantly made him harden again, just watching those legs in motion. He quickly crossed the room and grabbed her arm. She stared up at him and he almost ignored the silent plea he saw in her eyes. Almost. Except he couldn't ignore it. Being with her, the feelings she caused, he wanted to feel them again. Never in his life had he wanted anything else so much, except to feel how she made him feel. As if he were normal.

"We can't ignore this," he said simply.

She visibly swallowed and silently nodded before she opened the door and walked out of the room. He dragged a hand over his face, then leaned against the wall. Amelia had officially driven him crazy.

Chapter 15

"You disappeared in the middle of the party last night. Where did you go?" Heather asked as she sat at Amelia's kitchen counter and picked grapes off the vine in a bowl on the counter the next morning.

When Amelia had stepped out of the shower, her doorbell had rung. She should have known that Heather would come over before work to talk about the previous night. She would gossip and Amelia would think about George and what she had done. She never would have guessed that she'd lose all restraint at twenty-nine years old or that she would just now find the man she loved more than she thought possible.

Amelia flexed her hand, still sore from the stitches, as she chopped pineapple for a fruit salad.

"I needed fresh air," she lied. Badly. She instantly tried to change the subject. "It was a great party. We even got a small section in the society pages. That's great advertisement for your restaurant—"

"So, you went . . . where? Outside?"

"Yeah. Outside. I went outside for a while."

"That's funny, because your father told me that he saw you heading toward my office, with George close on your heels. Then I saw your two shadows standing guard at the office. And, forty-five minutes later, your mother told me that she saw you leave the office, looking . . . flustered and very, very relaxed. And then she saw George leave the office looking flustered and very, very relaxed. I just want to know one thing: do I need to buy a new desk?"

Amelia whirled around to face Heather, who laughed through a mouthful of grapes. She buried her face in her hands as her body shook with laughter and humiliation. She had forgotten about Jenkins and Morse during her . . . encounter with George. The two men had blended so well into the party that the thought never crossed her mind that they would follow her and George to the office, but she should have known. That was their job. Now she could never look at the two men again.

"My mother and father were there?" Amelia asked, surprised. "Mother is supposed to be in New York, and my dad hates crowds."

"She told me that she didn't want to miss my opening." Before she continued to chop the pineapple, Amelia shook her head at the strange idea of her mother thinking of someone else's feelings. "I don't remember the excuse your father gave. I thought it was kind of sweet. Neither wants you to know how worried they really are."

"I will never understand those two people," she said, shaking her head. "Why didn't they say anything to me?"

Heather grinned again as she said, "Maybe they didn't want to disturb you."

Amelia felt her face flush in embarrassment even as she said, "Whatever you're thinking happened between George and me didn't."

"You should step to the side, because the lightning is about to strike," Heather warned with another huge, smug grin. "You can't lie to anyone, Amie, but especially not me. I can tell. That tight, pained look that comes from your attempt to be absolutely perfect is gone. George worked it out of you?"

"Heather!" Amelia gasped in shock and half-laughter.

"I'm not judging. I think it should have happened a long time ago. He's gorgeous, Amie. Not bad, not bad at all."

"I don't want to talk about this."

"There hasn't been anyone since Brian, right?" Heather prodded.

Amelia glared at her best friend, but when Heather simply returned her glare, Amelia sighed, then shook her head.

"Why not, Amie?" Heather sighed in disappointment. "It's been over a year."

"I've been busy; I've been—"

"You've been punishing yourself because you think it was your fault that the marriage didn't happen. You and Brian never should have gotten that far anyway."

Amelia set down the knife and whirled around to face Heather, sagging against the counter. She searched Heather's face for any signs of joking.

"I didn't know you felt that way. I thought you liked Brian. Everyone likes Brian."

"Brian is a wonderful man, but he's not for you."

Amelia tried not to feel hurt or upset that Heather had

kept such a secret from her. While Amelia had been cheerfully planning her wedding, her best friend had been biting her tongue about the fate of the marriage. Regardless that Heather was right, Amelia felt betrayed.

Instead, she snapped, "You could have told me that before I invited half of Los Angeles to our wedding, Heather."

Heather didn't meet Amelia's gaze as she softly said, "It was never Brian that you wanted. You wanted the idea of Brian. He's from the right family, with the right credentials and even the right clothes. But love isn't about that, Amie. Love is not this neat little emotion that you can stick inside a Tiffany's box with a little white bow. It's about tears and pain. . . . It's sloppy and dirty. It's yelling at three o'clock in the morning; it's sex in offices and baby spit-up on your favorite Chanel suit. And if you're very lucky, it's the most not-perfect thing in your life, because that's when it's real."

Amelia's anger instantly disappeared when she saw the tears shining in Heather's eyes. She instantly crossed the kitchen and wrapped her arms around Heather. She didn't know why Heather cried, but her best friend hurt and it hurt Amelia.

"You're right," Amelia whispered, smoothing down Heather's hair. "I wanted the dream of Brian, what being with him meant."

Heather abruptly pulled from Amelia and crossed the room to grab a dish towel from the counter. She delicately dabbed the tears in the corners of her eyes as she laughed woodenly. "I think I got mascara all over your suit," Heather apologetically said.

"I'll change," Amelia said with a smile.

"I'm sorry. I know you have to leave for work and I have thousands of things to do before the restaurant opens for dinner tonight," she whispered, shaking her head. "This is not the time or the place, is it?"

"Tell me what's wrong, Heather."

"Nicolas and I are getting a divorce."

Amelia covered her suddenly open mouth with one hand.

"That's why he wasn't at the opening," Amelia finally whispered in shock.

"He loves someone else," Heather said with a laugh of disbelief. "Or, at least, he does now. He said she's . . . she's fun. He said that she doesn't always worry about what others think, and that he doesn't care anymore, either. She's a stockbroker. She works every day. He said that he doesn't feel like being with her is a chore like being with me is, keeping up the image of us. Her name is Mercedes. He's leaving me for a woman named after a car."

Amelia instantly crossed the kitchen and wrapped her arms around Heather once more. "He's a fool, Heather, and we'll make him pay. I know a great divorce attorney who salivates at the opportunity to destroy cheating husbands. We'll take the bastard for every penny."

Heather didn't answer but rested her head on Amelia's shoulder and cried. Not the perfect, quiet tears like in the movies, but real, hard tears that broke Amelia's heart.

With a tired sigh George locked his car in the parking garage underneath his apartment that evening and headed toward the stairs that led to the lobby of the building. His steps echoed across the deathly still garage. All day his thoughts had been preoccupied. He had just made love to Amelia Farrow. It hadn't been sex. It hadn't been the other impersonal terms people used to describe it. It was making love. Plain and simple. Nothing that felt like that could be anything but . . . He cringed at the word *love*.

For the first time in weeks, he had no reason to go to the courthouse. He had tried to fabricate a reason, just to try to run into Amelia, but then he wondered if it was best to keep his distance. For now. Knowing Amelia, he figured that she probably needed time to think about what had happened and all of the reasons that it shouldn't have.

George was snapped from his thoughts when he heard heavy breathing behind him. Someone was standing directly behind him, and with his luck, there was a gun pointed at his head. He tried to tell himself it was his fault. If he hadn't been behaving like a high school boy obsessed with his first girlfriend, he wouldn't have been taken by surprise. And instead of being scared, he was mad as hell. George abruptly spun around and saw a tall man in a hat. George didn't think; he grabbed the man's raised arm and then used his other hand to punch him in the face.

With a yelp of pain, the man fell to the ground. George straddled the man, prepared to hit him again, when the hat fell off to reveal the bruised face of Judge Roland Banner.

"I could hold you in contempt, Gibson," Banner snapped as he fingered the blood at the corner of his mouth.

George rolled his eyes, then stood, not bothering to help the judge to his feet.

"What the hell are you doing in my parking garage?" George demanded.

Banner struggled to his feet as he told him, "I've been following you all day. This is the first time that I've felt that it was safe enough to approach you. By the way, you drive too fast, Mr. Gibson. We hit sixty miles an hour on Third Street—"

"We both know that you're the last person I should receive a lecture from on obeying the law."

The judge's face flushed red with anger, but he took a deep breath and, instead, he said, "I wanted to thank you for what you and Ms. Farrow did for me and my wife. I'll always remember it, Mr. Gibson."

"You're welcome. Next time try to accept bribes from nicer people," George muttered, then started for his car.

Judge Banner grabbed George's arm and said with narrowed eyes, "I know what I did was wrong. I don't need to hear it from you, of all people."

"You're standing in my parking garage," George reminded him.

The anger drained from the older man's face and he released George's arm. He leaned against the wall and heavily sighed.

"That man was going to kill me, wasn't he?"

George's irritation with the judge disappeared when he saw the utter hopelessness in the man's eyes. He hesitated, then said, "This isn't my area, but if you help the police, they'll help you—"

"I can't, George. You know how men like Donaldson operate. I sent my wife to stay with her sister out of state, but I can't leave. I don't want to go to jail, and I need to fix some of the things . . ."

George actually felt sympathy for the older man. Maybe that was the reason he had decided to become a defense attorney, because he could understand desperation.

"Did you send Finnegan to his death?"

"No," the judge gasped, and if he feigned the grief that swam in his dark gaze, then George thought the man deserved an Academy Award. "I wanted to tell Nathan to keep his mouth shut and not cause trouble for himself. The day before Nathan disappeared, Maurice Donaldson called me and said that Nathan was causing problems, talking too loud, saying that he wanted out. Nathan had found out that not all of the employees from Heller Helium were as innocent as Maurice wanted us to believe. I wanted to tell Nathan to be quiet, for his own sake. I was beginning to suspect that Donaldson was not as genial as he pretended to be."

"You two thought that Maurice Donaldson's employees were innocent?" George asked in disbelief.

"I knew they weren't altar boys, but Donaldson insisted that his employees were being harassed by the police for crimes committed by Donaldson in his youth. He said that he wanted to go legit and the police wouldn't allow him to. The same thing happened to my father. He had been a gangster in his youth and the police never forgot. They harassed him until he was an old man. Looking back on it now, I realize how naive I was to believe Donaldson. He knew about my father and used that to make me feel sympathetic toward him."

"Then there was the money," George added, to keep Judge Banner and himself on track.

Judge Banner actually smiled and said, "As I'm sure

you can understand, the money was too good. Nathan and I decided to help Donaldson on a few cases. Turn a few verdicts that wouldn't hurt anyone."

"You never searched the records of these stellar individuals who you released on the streets. Armed robbery, assault . . . the whole gambit."

"Nathan tried to tell me, but I didn't want to know," Judge Banner admitted. "I was wrong, George. I have the painful reminders now every time I look in the mirror. Not to mention Nathan. . . . He was ambitious, but he was a good kid."

"What about Thomas Chin?"

"Who?"

"The juror from one of your cases who was killed midtrial."

"That was a robbery. It had nothing to do with our trial," he protested.

George sighed and said, "It had everything to do with your trial. I spoke to Chin's wife. Chin was a bribed juror. The day he planned to refuse to cooperate with Donaldson anymore, he was murdered. Maurice Donaldson is a dangerous man, and he'll kill anyone who gets in his way, including you and Nathan."

"I didn't know. You have to believe me. I would never be a part of murder."

George didn't know if his senses were dull or if the judge was a convincing liar, but he did believe him. "You should go to the police and tell them everything that you just told me."

"I can't cooperate with the police, not now when I'm in too deep, but I owe you. You saved my life and my wife's life. I want to give you this."

George stared at the car key that the judge had handed him. "A car key? Who does it belong to?"

"I've told you all that I can, Mr. Gibson." The judge turned to walk out of the garage; then he hesitated and said, "Donaldson wants Amelia. He feels like she's a loose end, and he hates loose ends. Without Milton, Finnegan's body, or any other evidence, her testimony is the only thing the DA's got."

George felt his heart drop to his stomach at the mention of Amelia's name. He ran his hands over his face. "I was on the stairwell, too. I heard everything."

Banner stared at George with wide, surprised eyes. "But all this time I thought that she was the only witness. Or, at least, that's what Donaldson thinks."

"How can I make him stop thinking that? How can I make him concentrate on me—"

"Are you crazy?" Judge Banner said, perplexed. "Ms. Farrow is only alive because of luck and because her father has been able to protect her. You . . . you're nobody. You won't last five minutes if word gets around that you're a witness."

"Thanks for the vote of confidence, but I need your advice, not your doubts. I have enough of those on my own," he said.

Judge Banner was silent for a moment; then he actually smiled. "You're in love, aren't you?" he said. "You're in love with Amelia Farrow."

"I have no idea what you're talking about," George said flatly.

"You have to be. There's no reason George Gibson would put himself on the line unless it was because of the one emotion that makes us all human." The older man studied George for a moment, then said, "I've been wrong about you, haven't I?"

George glowered at the judge. He was *not* in love with Amelia. Judge Banner was a crook. He didn't know about love. Except George had seen the tortured look in the man's eyes after the attack, as he saw the fear on his wife's face.

"Take care of yourself," George said, ignoring the judge's questions.

"You take care of Amelia."

"She could give you a good deal if you give her something to work with."

The judge laughed in disbelief. "Amelia Farrow? She'll chew me up and spit me out. Unlike everyone else in this county, I've never been fooled by her supposedly sweet exterior. That woman has the heart of a lion."

"She can help you."

"I'm too old to go to jail."

"If we find evidence implicating you, then you'll go to jail anyway."

"George Gibson trying to strike a deal for the DA's office. I've seen it all," Judge Banner mused while shaking his head.

"I don't want your wife to be ninety years old, leaning on a walker, still visiting you in prison."

Judge Banner smiled in response, then murmured, "I'll think about it, but for right now that key is all I can offer you. I've always thought that you and Ms. Farrow were two of the brightest lawyers to ever walk into my courtroom. You'll figure it out."

"Once we do, your time is up," George warned.

The judge nodded in response, then walked toward his

parked car. George watched the man for a few seconds, noticing that the once-proud man's shoulders slumped. George placed the key in his pocket, then sat in his car again. Judge Banner was right about one thing. He wouldn't be able to understand the significance of the key without Amelia's help. Or, at least, that's the lie he told himself.

Chapter 16

"Ms. Farrow."

Amelia flinched at the sound of Jenkins's voice. She had been holed up in her den staring so hard at the wedding pictures of Heather and Nicolas that she hadn't heard him enter. She had stared at their happy, smiling faces in the pictures and had tried to see any sign that Nicolas was not happy. There was nothing. Maybe there were no signs. Maybe Heather was right. Everyone had to take their chances and just pray that their love stood the test of time.

"I'm sorry to disturb you, but Mr. Austell is at the door," Jenkins said.

She smiled at him, then set aside the pictures and uncurled from her chair. She followed Jenkins into the living room and smiled when she saw Brian standing in the foyer, looking as uncomfortable as he had when he'd asked her to marry him. He occasionally glanced at Morse, who sat at the dining room table still cleaning guns. When Brian saw Amelia, he grinned nervously.

"I never thought that I'd miss George," he said with a light laugh.

She smiled in return, then motioned him toward the kitchen.

"My father sent you to make certain that I came straight home after work, didn't he?" she asked as she opened the refrigerator and pulled out numerous containers. She had forgotten to ask Jenkins and Morse what type of foods they ate, so she decided to heat one of Constance's pasta dishes. Most people ate pasta.

Brian heavily sighed, like a long-suffering martyr, then said, "Why is everything I do met with your suspicion?"

"I don't know, Brian. What would give me any reason to doubt your word?" she asked dryly.

He didn't attempt to pretend not to understand her. "I just wanted to see you, make certain that you were all right."

"I'm all right."

Brian frowned and said, "You shouldn't be cooking, Amelia. You've been through too much. Let me take you out to dinner. We'll go to Stanley's. I know you can't resist Stanley's. Lasagna, tiramisu, a nice bottle of red wine. It could be like old times."

She had to admit to herself that she was tempted. She loved the Italian restaurant. But she would have to sit at the table across from Brian for that length of time. And while she had missed him, she wasn't ready to spend two hours talking to him in a restaurant.

"As tempting as that is, I have a lot of work to finish tonight."

"Ms. Farrow," Jenkins said from the door frame of the

kitchen, "if you need anything, I'll be outside."

He sent Brian a warning stare, then walked out the kitchen door toward the driveway.

"What does he think you'll need with me in the house?" Brian asked while watching Jenkins through the kitchen window.

She decided not to answer that question because she didn't want to hurt Brian's feelings. She began to chop parsley at the counter, wincing at the slight pull on the stitches in her hand. She had taken the bandage off before she went to court that morning. Her hand hurt and the stitches pulled on the skin, but the huge white bandage had been a constant reminder of what had happened to her and she no longer wanted to wear it.

"At least, allow me to call my cook over here and fix you dinner," Brian said, frustration evident in his tone.

"I'm just adding parsley. Constance did all the cooking," she cheerfully told him.

"Constance is still trying out new recipes on you?"

"Yes, and I don't want to disappoint her by not trying it."

"You've always been so stubborn," he muttered as he ran his hands down his face.

"I'll take that as a compliment," she said, not allowing his sour attitude to affect her. She was determined to be happy, regardless of the fact that the man she had made love to in a restaurant last night had not bothered to call, and she had been too proud and too scared to call him.

"I hate this, Amie," Brian abruptly declared while pounding a closed hand on the counter. "I hate the fact that you have bodyguards roaming around your house with weapons, that you have those awful-looking stitches in your hand, and that you and I . . . that we're not together anymore."

At his pronouncement Amelia's eyes widened and she accidentally dropped the dripping wet parsley on the floor. She quickly scooped up the parsley.

"I don't know what to say," she finally stuttered. When he sent her a hopeful look, she took a deep breath, then said, "Actually, for the first time since I walked into that room and saw you with Stella Brooks, I do know what to say. We are too compatible, Brian."

Confusion crossed his features. "That's a good thing, Amie. Remember?"

"No, it's not. We're so compatible, so perfect, that we'd get bored with each other. You'd find someone else or I would. And then we wouldn't even be friends."

"Is this about that . . . that defense attorney?"

"No," she answered truthfully.

"You're involved with him, though, aren't you?"

Flashes of George's hands on her skin, his mouth against her neck, the feel of him inside of her, raced across her mind. She swallowed, then said, "Yes."

Brian silently nodded, then stared at a spot above her right shoulder. If she didn't know better, she would have thought that he was actually hurt.

"We would have been good together, Amie."

"We would have been perfect," she agreed, but didn't add that perfection was not necessarily a good thing when it came to love.

He hesitated, then said, "I've always been curious. Why didn't you tell your father the reason why you canceled the wedding?"

"He loves you like a son. I knew that if he found out that you slept with another woman the night before our wedding he would have ended that relationship. Not because he would never want to see you again, but because he would feel that he would have to end all contact with you out of some strange show of loyalty to me. I couldn't do that to him, not over . . . not over a marriage that never should have gotten that close to the altar in the first place." She smiled, then patted his shoulder and asked, "So are you staying for dinner?"

The corner of his mouth lifted. "Am I invited to stay for dinner?"

"I think there's enough food for one ex-fiancé."

The intercom mounted on the kitchen wall buzzed, gratefully providing an interruption to the awkward scene. She could envision herself easily falling into a relationship with Brian. Being with him was so easy. They had the same history, the same interests, practically the same family. Except her body didn't sing and her heart didn't pound when she thought of Brian.

"Ms. Farrow, this is Jenkins," came the deep voice of the bodyguard over the speaker. "The man from the courthouse, George Gibson, is here to see you."

She was surprised by the strength of emotions that slammed into her.

"Send him in," she responded. She depressed the intercom button, then rested her forehead against the wall to collect her thoughts. When she turned to face Brian, she found him studying her with an inscrutable expression.

"George is here," she told him, attempting to keep the tremor out of her voice.

"That my invitation to leave?"

"You don't have to leave. I doubt that George is staying. I don't know why he's here—"

"I do. He's not as big a fool as he looks."

She heard the knock on the front door. She tried not to look as anxious as she felt, but she darted a nervous glance toward the door. Brian sighed, then wrapped his arms around her in the type of brotherly hug that she had missed.

"I miss you, Amie. Don't let him get off too easy." He briefly caressed her face, then walked out the kitchen door.

She stared at his retreating figure through the window and she smiled to herself, because it would be good having her childhood friend back. There was another knock on the front door and her heart jumped again. She rushed through the house and hesitated when her hand touched the knob. She met George's eyes through the pane of glass next to the door. Neither smiled. She took a deep breath, then opened the door.

She hungrily drank in the sight of him, the bruises that still marred his beautiful milky brown skin, and the dark circles around his eyes. The rumpled suit and the askew tie made her smile and ball her hands into fists to resist reaching for him. She stared at his hands that hung by his sides. The hands that could make her lose all self-control.

"May I come in?" he asked hesitantly, not sounding like his usual cocky self, and she realized that she missed his usual cocky self.

She opened the door wider and George walked in, his scent drifting past her. She closed the door, then watched him amble into her living room. She crossed her arms over her chest to protect herself from his intense gaze; then she walked into the living room, making certain to stand as far across the room from him as possible.

A tense silence stretched between them. When she remained motionless he said with a resigned sigh, "I guess that means I'll start. We need to talk."

Her voice was calm, emotionless, as she responded, "There is nothing to talk about."

"I think making love on a desk in a restaurant, then leaving without exchanging more than two sentences warrants a talk."

"It was nothing, right, George? Just a one-night stand," she said, not able to keep the bitterness from her voice.

He stalked across the room. "Don't start that Ice Princess routine with me!" he abruptly shouted. "If you're angry with me, just tell me that you're angry. Don't give me snide remarks or . . . or this debutante put-down crap where I can't tell if I've just been insulted or not."

She battled down the anger that made her want to scream. She clenched her hands into fists but kept her tone cool as she said, "If you're going to scream at me, you can leave right now."

"If you can't handle an adult conversation, maybe I will," he retorted, then turned on his heel toward the door.

She sucked in her breath as if he had hit her. It made her angrier that he actually would leave. She said quickly before he could take one step, "At least, I don't revel in my flaws."

He was still for a moment; then he turned to face her.

His expression was hard. "What the hell are you talking about?"

"What am I talking about?" she repeated in a strained voice. "I'm talking about you. Everything is a joke to you."

"What's wrong with that? I'd rather laugh first, before anyone else tries to laugh at me."

"People wouldn't laugh, George, if you wouldn't make yourself a joke. You make a joke about your clients, your practice, yourself. I once asked you why you don't work at a big downtown firm or join one of the white-collar defense firms. I know why. Because you're scared. Your biggest fear in life is that no one will take you seriously. How is anyone supposed to take you seriously when you don't even take yourself seriously?"

"You don't know anything about me, Amelia," he said through clenched teeth.

"I've stood across from you in court almost every week for the last year! I know that the only one your apathetic attitude impresses is you!"

"At least, I'm not a fake, Pollyanna spoiled princess living in a castle—"

"I can't change who I am, George," she angrily told him. She felt the tears fill her eyes, but she battled them back. "I can't change who my father is, what my last name is. I can't change that I have money. If you don't like it, if you can't accept it, then . . . then why are you here?"

"I don't care about your money, Amelia."

"Yes, you do. You're obsessed with it."

"Since you've never gone to sleep with only fifty cents left in your pocket and rent due the next day, you can't comment about my obsession with money."

"I will not allow you to make me feel bad about who I am."

"But you can pass judgments on me?"

"I have never judged you," she said defensively.

"You believe every bad thing you ever heard about me. You never gave me a chance to defend myself. Only the great Amelia Farrow could care about rooting out corrupt judges and cops. George Gibson was obviously in it just for the money. Right, Amelia? You said it yourself."

"That is not true, George," she protested. "You wanted me to believe that, but once I got past all of the bullshit you spout, I saw the truth. You care too much."

"Now you see the truth about me?" he asked in disbelief. "Or it is that now you're making up your version of the truth, so you can accept your attraction to me? Otherwise, you'd have to accept that you slept with someone like me."

She bit her bottom lip to bite off her protest and stared into his sincere dark eyes. He thought she was too good for him? He was the only good thing to happen to her since she passed the Bar. She instantly saw the regret cross his face when he realized what he had revealed. There was no cockiness now or even anger. He just looked uncomfortable and prepared to escape.

She moved across the room to stand in front of him. At first he wouldn't meet her eyes; then she touched his stubble-roughened face and she saw the desire flare in his eyes as he looked at her.

"I work at the DA's office because I can't think of another way I want to spend my day," she whispered. "I kissed you, I made love to you, because I like doing that, too. I like you because you're a kind, decent, and caring man. You're the most caring man I've ever met in my life, whether you want me to know it or not. Any other questions?"

He stared at her, his expression indecipherable. Then he took a deep breath. "I laugh because that was the only defense I had as a kid. If I made people laugh, if I made people think that I didn't care, then no one had the power to hurt me. I guess I feel the same philosophy applies as an adult, because, frankly, I've been hurt enough to last a lifetime."

For the first time, she saw the raw pain in his eyes at the memory of his childhood. He lowered his gaze and stuffed his hands into his pants pockets and her heart broke at that moment. For George Gibson. For the little boy that he had been.

"I'm sorry, George."

"I spent my entire childhood scraping and fighting for everything I ever had. The only way I survived was to keep my head down, to mind my own business, to not take sides. You and I are so different."

"Not that different," she whispered. And she realized that she truly meant it. No matter how much she had in common with Brian, George was the only man who felt like he was a part of her soul.

"I guess not," he murmured, his hand reaching across the space between them to link her fingers with his.

His dark gaze met hers again and she rightfully should have melted from the intensity. His other hand touched her neck and she almost gasped from the heat that flashed through her.

George grinned in response, then pulled her to him so quickly that she slammed against his body with an open-mouthed gasp. His tongue immediately plunged into her mouth. At the explosion of feelings, she wrapped her arms around his neck and moved closer into the circle he created with his arms and powerful legs.

She had never wanted anyone as much as she wanted this one man. Not just his kisses and his touches, not just him pulsating inside of her, but she wanted his laughs and his thoughts. She even wanted his tears. She didn't allow him to control the kiss. He didn't allow her to control the kiss. Their tongues battled, warred, and eventually settled into an ancient mating ritual that caused her body to ache in places that she had forgotten about in her drive to wait for her image of the perfect man.

His hands searched her body for some hidden treasure until one hand rested on her right breast. He sighed into her mouth and she smiled in the kiss, his tongue gliding over her tongue and teeth as a result. She felt the hot hand on her breast down to the depths of her center, to her curling toes. She ended the kiss to catch her breath, but George immediately attacked her mouth again, his tongue sweeping through her mouth, draining every part of her, giving every part of him. Her entire body flowed as she felt every part of his body against hers, hard and unyielding. Everywhere he was hard, and she wanted to feel every part of it.

"The bedroom," she whispered against his lips.

"You have one?" he asked, sounding as if he was in a fog.

She laughed against his mouth, then said, "Yes, George, I have a bedroom. You've been there, remember?"

He grinned for a moment; then he pressed his hungry mouth against hers again. She laughed because he was eager. She trembled because she was, too.

Chapter 17

Somehow, they made it to the bedroom with most of their clothes still on. George's shirt hung halfway off his chest, his pants were partially unbuttoned, but his shoes and socks had been lost on the stairway. Her sleeveless blouse had been stretched out of shape. Her bra and underwear were missing, but she still wore her skirt. She felt like a mountain of clay as his hands molded her and caressed her into a liquid pool of heat and desire. The two fell onto the bed in a heap of entwined arms and legs.

His kisses were hard and wet, but his hands were soft and gentle. She had stared at his hands in court, wondering how they would feel. Now, she knew. They felt like clouds caressing her body, as close to heaven as she could imagine. His mouth finally moved from hers and she felt his tongue blaze a slick, wet trail down her neck to her nipple. She gasped his name and, of their own accord, her legs fell open. He immediately shifted his weight to lie in the middle of the juncture of her thighs.

She gasped again when she felt the hard bulge in his pants pressing against her.

His tongue circled around one nipple, driving her head to fall back in pure ecstasy; then he moved to the other breast to give it the same treatment. She ran her hands over his back and realized that he still wore his shirt. She immediately dragged it down his arms and threw it off the bed onto the floor. She felt his grin against her delicate skin before he gently nipped her right nipple, then planted wet, open mouthed kisses down her stomach until he reached the waistband of her skirt.

He glanced up at her again, a question in his eyes. She wanted to tell him that she wouldn't stop him. Not even Donaldson himself standing in the doorway could stop her. His tongue dipped even lower and she lost whatever control over her reactions that she thought she would have.

"George?"

"Ssh, baby, let me love you."

His hands skimmed and caressed every part of her body. His dark eyes visually touched every part of her body. He whispered her name and touched her as if she were the most expensive item he had ever been allowed near. Her body hummed, her arms felt too lax to move, and all she could do was lie in the cocoon of sensual pleasure and bite her lower lip against the onslaught of powerful emotions that his hands and tongue released.

George nipped her bottom lip, enough to make it sting; then he dragged his tongue across her lower lip to make her sigh. He hovered above her once more and she met his gaze. She wanted to ask him what he saw, but he abruptly leaned off the bed and reached for his pants on the floor. She tried to speak when she saw the small square package he pulled out of a pocket, but she could only move enough to wrap her arms around him and bring him to her mouth again. Her eyes slid closed as she felt his tongue claim her mouth once more, as only he was capable of doing. She wondered if she would ever get the need for the taste of his kisses out of her body now. She honestly didn't know if she wanted to.

She gasped in surprise and pleasure when he abruptly surged into her, the hard length of him filling her to the point where she could only squeeze shut her eyes and hold in the pleasure. He instantly stopped moving and stared at her with a concerned expression on his face. Under the moonlight that shone through the curtains, sweat glistened on his forehead, chest, and arms from the strain, but he waited and loomed over her.

His voice was thick and deep as he pressed, "Did I hurt you?"

She wordlessly shook her head in response, since she couldn't form words to save her life; then she grabbed the short, silky curls on his head to bring his addictive lips to her mouth again. He moved inside her as their lips grazed over each other and their tongues laced. Amelia shut her eyes to block out anything that distracted from the feelings he caused in her. This time the waves were more intense, the feelings in her body more powerful and concentrated.

She heard his moans of pleasure and then he whispered her name, with such awe and reverence that it was too much. The kisses, the feeling of him inside of her, loving her, and then his low, warm voice were enough to send her into that flurry of stars that caused her to soundlessly gasp his name. Not seconds later, George shuddered above her.

He collapsed onto the bed next to her and took several deep breaths before he turned to her. He wiped sweat-dampened strands of hair from her face; then his eyes scanned her face. He seemed satisfied and placed a soft kiss on her forehead before he returned to his side of the bed.

"Shit," he muttered as he lay back on the mounds of pillows and stared at the shadows on the dark bedroom ceiling. He knew that he should have found a better word to describe . . . paradise . . . but he couldn't. He was just a man. No man would have known what to say after an experience like that.

"My sentiments exactly," she murmured from her position next to him on the bed.

He turned on his side to look at her. When she continued to stare at the ceiling, he trailed a finger down her shoulder, loving the incredibly soft feel of skin beneath his hand. He shivered, not from lust or even desire but from the knowledge that he could touch her.

"A woman who uses *shit* to sum up what we just did . . . you're going to have a problem getting rid of me, lady."

She laughed in response, and he silently sighed in relief that she hadn't recoiled in disgust. He felt relaxed and content, even though he had a feeling that he had lost something in the last hour. Namely, his freedom. With a woman like Amelia Farrow in his blood, he didn't think that he would ever be able to think of or touch another woman again.

He rubbed a hand over his sweaty face, then looked at her again. He saw the sweat beaded on her face and her chest to where she had brought up the sheets to cover herself. He saw the darkness of her breasts beneath the pale covers and he forgot all about sweat. He suddenly realized that what he had thought in half-jest was the truth. If she didn't notice, he could envision spending the rest of his life with her.

The once-comfortable silence between them grew heavy as his thoughts turned to forever. The most frightening aspect was that he could picture forever with her and it wasn't a bad picture. It was a wonderful image. As if she could read minds and she didn't like what she was reading, Amelia suddenly shifted from him in the bed.

"Do you want anything to drink?" she asked in a strained voice.

"I'll get it," he quickly volunteered.

"I can—"

"No, I'll do it."

Before she could protest again, he got up from the bed. He grabbed his pants off the floor, then dashed into the open door of the bathroom inside the bedroom. He cleaned up as quickly as he could and pulled on his pants. He avoided his reflection in the mirror because he couldn't look at himself after purposely leading himself toward heartbreak. He cursed, then opened the door and pasted a smile on his face. She still lay on the bed in the same position as when he'd left. He forced a smile in her general direction, then practically ran out of the room.

He reached the kitchen and leaned against the counter, resisting the urge to vomit in the sink. He didn't know how other men responded when they finally realized that they had found a woman to spend the rest of their lives with, but it made him mildly nauseous. Especially when the woman would laugh in his face at the idea.

He cursed, then quickly filled two glasses with water. He took a deep breath, then returned to the bedroom, feeling as if every step were the march toward a firing squad. He almost dropped the glasses when he returned to the bed room with the scent of their loving lingering in the air. She had turned on the bedside lamp and opened a window to allow in the Los Angeles early-spring coolness. She stiffly lay in the bed, with the sheets pulled tight underneath her armpits.

He handed her a glass, then walked around the bed and set down his own. Feeling suddenly self-conscious, he sat on the bed, then squirmed out of his pants. He tried not to look at her as he crawled under the covers and took several sips of water from his glass.

"George . . ." she began haltingly.

When she didn't continue, he looked at her. She met his gaze and as if his hands had their own mind, he touched her face. His fingers traced the moist sweetness of her lips and then the raven black arched eyebrows. He touched a soft kiss to her mouth, and with her response he closed his eyes at her taste. He would remember that taste for the rest of his life. It was like the song had claimed: she was a girl and she tasted like "sugar, spice, and everything nice." It suddenly didn't matter what her last name was, who she worked for, or all the other reasons that a relationship between them wouldn't work.

His lips clung to hers for a second longer, trying to memorize the shape and taste of her lips, before he forced a smile and asked, "Are you sleepy?"

Her expression was somber as she said, "No."

He took the glass from her hands and set it on the night table next to his. He turned to her and she was waiting with open arms. Their lips met and, in unison, they lay down with Amelia on top of him. He placed his hands on her bare waist underneath the sheet tangled around them. Her skin felt like flower petals. Flower petals dipped in golden honey.

He stroked a hand over her skin and she smiled and snuggled against his chest. Her face glistened with a sheen of sweat that made her shine for him. His hands traveled from her waist to knead her behind. He decided that he hadn't paid nearly enough attention to her behind. She gasped his name against his ear, and her nipples pressing into his chest began to call for his attention.

She raised her head to smile at him before she placed a long, wet kiss on his mouth. Her tongue swept through his mouth, tangling with his tongue, making his hands involuntarily dig into her body. Her soft, bare skin rubbed against his, creating a sexual tension as she writhed against his body in slow, predatory moves that he never would have thought she was capable of. She took the matter into her own hands and placed him inside of her with such torturous slowness that he could only watch her and whisper her name. He forgot all about his doubts and vulnerabilities because Amelia Farrow was making him crazy.

After only a few hours, Amelia felt the emptiness in the bed from George's disappearance. Her hand smoothed over the empty cotton sheets still warmed by his body.

He was gone. She wondered if she could pretend to be unfeeling about this. She opened her eyes and her breath caught in her throat when she saw George standing by the window, with his back to her. He wore only his pants, and she bit her bottom lip at the slowly rising sun's ability to caress his bare chest when she was too nervous to make that move.

He suddenly turned and, as if he had been caught, he froze. In the dawn light he sent her a fake smile, then sat on the window seat, as far from her as he could be and remain in the bedroom.

"Did I wake you?" he softly asked.

"No. . . . Are you OK?"

He didn't answer her question but instead said, "I should leave. I have an early-morning appointment and I need to go home and shower and . . . and do other stuff."

She swallowed the sudden lump in her throat, then murmured, "OK."

Despite his words, he remained where he stood. "Judge Banner approached me last night."

"Judge Banner . . ." Her voice trailed off as she sat up and clutched the sheet to her breasts. "I thought he was refusing to cooperate with the police."

"I'm not the police."

"What did he say?"

"He gave me a key." He pulled the key out of his pocket and held it up to the light for her to see.

"When did you see Judge Banner? In court?"

"A few hours before I came over here."

The sudden realization that he had only come over to talk about Judge Banner almost knocked her back into the bed. She pulled the sheet tighter around her body, feeling like a giant fool. George had wanted to talk about Judge Banner and she had thrown herself at him. Embarrassment flashed through her face and anger made her jaw clench. She was angry at him for not saying something sooner and at herself for once more allowing emotions to make her lose her normal iron-tight control.

George continued, apparently oblivious to the new direction of her thoughts. "He wouldn't tell me what the key was for. He thought that you and I could figure it out. He's scared, Amelia. I'm pretty certain that Donaldson threatened to hurt his wife."

She tried to block her thoughts of betrayal and instead concentrate on Donaldson. She wrapped the sheet around her body, then stood from the bed, ignoring George's eyes. She walked across the room to grab her robe off the back of a chair and wrapped it around herself and the sheet.

"Why is Banner still protecting Donaldson?"

"Maybe Banner knows that Donaldson's tentacles in the police department go too deep for him to be truly protected." He paused, then said softly, "He didn't have to help us at all, Amelia."

"A useless key . . . that's a lot of help," she responded dryly.

She crossed the room and took the key from his hands, careful not to touch any part of him. She didn't trust herself to touch him. She wanted to scream at him that he should have told her about Banner. He should have called instead of coming to the door. He had probably laughed to himself when he realized how easy it had been to get her into bed. For the second time in two days. For the first time, she regretted it all. Even the amazing feelings he caused in her. It had all been a game to him. And she had fallen for the whole thing. Tears filled her eyes and she viciously swiped at them. Each time she'd trusted him, and each time she'd paid for it.

"He just needs time to think," George said, defending Judge Banner. "I bet we'll get a phone call from him either today or tomorrow. He's too smart not to know that helping us catch Donaldson is better for him."

"Are you his attorney now?" she asked coldly, glaring at him. "Is that why I'm suddenly subjected to this passionate plea for Judge Banner? If it is, you're wasting your time with me, George. I'm too close to the case. There's no way Grayson would assign me as prosecuting attorney. Looks like you just wasted a night."

She wanted to applaud his acting skills when she saw the confusion cross his face. "Wasted a night . . . ? Banner is not my client."

She lowered her gaze to the key, trying to see through the sudden haze of tears. She wished that she could believe George. She wanted to believe him, but he'd always told her that all he wanted was the money. Maybe he considered getting her in bed a side benefit, not that she had provided much resistance.

"I can send this to the lab tomorrow and see if they can identify what type of key this is for. One of the techs owes me a favor. He'll keep it quiet—"

Her statement was interrupted when George grabbed her shoulders. "What is going on here, Amelia?"

"You tell me," she angrily shot back.

"Banner is not my client," he repeated, through clenched teeth.

"Of course not." She snorted in disbelief. "Nothing,

George, absolutely nothing is going on." She moved out of his reach and said, "Weren't you about to leave?"

Once more, he remained glued to his spot. "Don't shut me out, Amelia. Not now," he said quietly.

She knew that he wasn't talking about Donaldson. He was talking about them, about what had happened between them, but she refused to acknowledge his softly spoken words. She wanted to tell him that making love to him was a mistake, that it never should have happened. But she couldn't force out the lie.

The silence in the bedroom was broken by the ringing cellular telephone in his suit coat pocket on the floor. Their gazes held for another second; then he cursed and reached for the phone. When his eyes finally left her, she released the breath that she didn't know she held and walked into the bathroom, closing the door behind her. She had never run out of a room before, but she couldn't face him. She buried her face in her hands and took several deep breaths. She wanted him out of her bedroom. She wanted him out of her house. But she knew that even when he left her house, it would take a longer time for the memory of him to leave her body.

She flinched when she heard a soft knock on the other side of the bathroom door. "I have to leave now. An emergency with a client. He was arrested tonight, he's in jail, and his wife is in labor with their first child."

Amelia took a deep breath. "Fine."

"Call me once you know the results of the tests for the key."

Tears clogged her throat as she shook her head in disbelief. The whole night had been a lie. He didn't care about her. He wanted to protect his new client and make more money. She had thought that Brian's betrayal had hurt, but it was nothing compared to what George Gibson had done to her.

"Are you all right?" came George's concerned voice.

"I'm fine. I'll call you about the key."

She waited until she heard his footsteps recede and then she opened the bathroom door. She hadn't cried herself to sleep in a long time, since childhood, but she would allow herself this one time. And then she would become angry. Very angry.

Chapter 18

Amelia walked into Richard Grayson's office later that morning with Jenkins and Morse close behind.

"Dionne said that you wanted to see me," she said without pretense of a morning greeting.

Grayson's blank expression remained the same as his eyes drifted to her bodyguards. "Will you two gentlemen leave us alone?"

"I don't—"

"There's one way in and one way out. No one can get in here to hurt her. I understand that you men have a job to do, but so do we," Grayson told the protesting Jenkins. At Jenkins's glance in her direction, she nodded in agreement.

Jenkins shrugged reluctantly nodded, then motioned to Morse. The two men walked out of the office and closed the door behind them.

"Does the other one ever talk?" Grayson asked with a bemused expression. When she didn't answer, his smile disappeared and he motioned to the leather sofa in the corner of the large office. "Let's sit down over there."

"I'd rather not—"

"Sit down, Amelia," he not-so-gently ordered.

She bit her bottom lip, then walked across the room and sat on the sofa. He joined her. She noticed the manila envelope in his hands. "I understand that this is a very vulnerable period for you, and if you need to take a leave of absence to digest all that's happening, then I would be happy to grant you one."

"I told you before, I don't want a leave of absence, Richard. I need to work."

"Then understand that I cannot treat you any differently than I would any of my other ADAs." She nodded in confusion at his grave expression. She didn't know what Grayson was dancing around, but the sinking sensation in her stomach told her that she would not like what was coming next. "How many cases against George Gibson do you have pending?"

"Excuse me?"

"I'm warning you because I like you. When you first joined this office, I swore I would treat you like any other ADA, but over the years you've become one of my best attorneys. I don't want you to be sidetracked . . . by anyone."

She didn't try to sound sweet or deferential as she normally would have done. "Who I spend my time with off-duty is none of this office's concern as long as I continue to adequately do my job."

"It becomes this office's business when the person you choose to spend your time with is buddies with the main suspect of a major investigation that you initiated. If the

Bar heard about this, Amelia, you could be in trouble. Big trouble."

"What are you talking about . . . ?" Her voice trailed off when Grayson opened the envelope and handed her several black-and-white pictures. The vantage point was from a distance and the miniblinds on the building's windows partially distorted the view, but it clearly showed George talking to Maurice Donaldson. The two men were laughing as if George had told one of his jokes. He didn't look scared or angry that he faced the man who had tried to kill her. She stared at the pictures speechless for several seconds. Tears blurred her vision but thankfully didn't spill. She finally looked at Grayson. "Where did you get these?"

"That's not important—"

"Are you spying on me, Richard?"

He heavily sighed, then said, "Your behavior these last few days has been out of character. I was concerned. I know Gibson's type, what a man like that is after. I called your father." She covered her gasp with one hand as she tossed the pictures onto the table, as if touching them would poison her.

"And he hired someone to follow George and to take these pictures," Amelia finished for him. She shook her head—not certain whether to feel pain at George's betrayal or the betrayal from her boss. Since her feelings concerning George were too complex and raw to unravel, she focused on Richard. "How could you?"

"He's your father, Amelia. He had a right to know." When she didn't respond, he continued. "It's a good thing or we never would have known that Gibson's involved with Donaldson. He's been playing us from the start. No wonder it always seemed that Donaldson was a step ahead of us. He knew everything that we knew from Gibson."

"No, it can't be true," she said softly. "If George is working for Donaldson, why did he save Judge Banner?"

"You never did tell me why you happened to be at the judge's house that night. Whose idea was it to go to Banner's house that night? I'm betting that it wasn't Gibson's idea."

She hesitated, then said, "It was mine."

"He had to save him since you were standing there, Amelia. He didn't want you to know the truth. At least, not yet."

"If he didn't want anyone to know about their relationship, why would he have Donaldson meet him in his office? He would have picked a more discreet location—"

"He didn't know that he was being followed. Who would have thought that Gibson was involved in this? He's been playing us all. He obviously has been feeding his client the direction of this investigation." Grayson laid his thick hand over hers and whispered, "I'm sorry, Amelia."

She nodded and jumped to her feet. She didn't think she could hold back her tears anymore. "I have to prepare for my morning hearings."

"Amelia, don't be angry with yourself. You have a good heart and this is what happens when good people like you believe in bad people like Gibson. When we pick up Donaldson, Gibson is going down, too."

"On what charges? The last time I checked, talking to a client was not a crime." She cringed at her automatic need to defend him, but she didn't withdraw the question.

"I'll create new ones for him if I have to. He hurt you, he's made a joke out of this office, and he will not get away with that," Grayson said fiercely.

She didn't say another word and walked out of the office. She didn't halt her stride as she saw Jenkins waiting for her at the double doors, but said tightly, "We're going to the federal courthouse."

Ten minutes later, Jenkins parked his custom-designed SUV in front of the intimidating building. Amelia didn't wait for either man to open her door as she had been instructed to. She jumped from the car and practically ran toward the entrance. The ride to the courthouse, the time she'd spent in Grayson's office, had driven her anger to the point of no return.

She didn't wait for Jenkins and Morse when they were held back by the screaming metal detectors at the entrance of the courthouse. She didn't wait for the elevators. Instead, she ran up the two flights of stairs that circled above the lobby to the various courtrooms, ignoring Jenkins's calling her name. By the time she reached her father's courtroom, her anger had turned into a full-blown rage. She burst into the room, throwing the double doors open with a loud bang.

Everyone in the courtroom turned at her entrance. Behind the bench her father's eyebrows rose in surprise while the two attorneys who stood before him in a conference glanced at each other, then at her. The eleven people in the jury box and the defendant all turned to see what had drawn the judge's attention. There was another loud crash as Jenkins and Morse burst into the room seconds later. All eyes shifted to the two men, but Amelia kept her gaze on her father as her chest rose and fell for air and calm.

Without one word from her, Kenneth pounded his gavel on the desk and said, "Twenty-minute recess."

He motioned to Amelia, then disappeared behind the door that led to his private chambers. Ignoring everyone's speculative gazes, she straightened her suit jacket, then walked through the courtroom and the same door. When she entered his spacious office, her father was unzipping his black robe. Neither spoke while Amelia closed the door behind her and he settled behind his desk.

"Grayson told you," Kenneth finally said, holding her gaze.

"You had no right!" she erupted, crossing the office to glare at him over the desk. "You had no right to pry into my private life like that or to tell my boss!"

"You're hysterical, Amelia. If you calm down, we can discuss this like two rational adults."

"I will not calm down! I've been calm for twenty-nine years and what has it gotten me? Nothing!" She didn't stop the tears this time as they rolled down her face. "Did it ever occur to you that maybe I didn't want to know the truth?"

"No one makes a fool of my daughter."

"Why, Dad? Because it will reflect on you?" she said. "George may have used me and played me for a fool, but it was me. Not you. I've spent my whole life watching you and Mother make fools of each other. I finally realized that it wasn't about me; it's about you two and your sick need to punish each other. Just like your marriage is none of my business, my relationship—or whatever it is—with George is none of your business."

"You are my daughter, and I'm going to do whatever I have to in order to protect you," he insisted stubbornly.

"You should have done that twenty years ago when I wanted nothing more than for my daddy to ride in and rescue me. There were so many nights that I cried myself to sleep wishing, hoping, that just once you would stop in my bedroom to talk or just to tell me that you loved me like daddies did on TV. And it never happened. Not once!" she cried. "Now it's too late. You can't play daddy when I'm twenty-nine years old. I don't need you anymore."

His face paled and she wondered if she had finally broken the unwritten Farrow rules, whatever they were.

"I wanted to help," he said, his voice strained.

"You didn't help," she told him, feeling too drained to scream anymore. "You hurt me. You've managed to talk to half of Los Angeles County about my problems, but not me. It hurts, Dad. It hurts a lot."

"I am sorry, Amelia. I never would have done it if I thought that you would react this way, but now you know the truth about that Gibson character."

"The truth that you didn't even have the courage to tell me yourself. I had to hear from my boss that the man I love is using me." More tears rained down her cheeks as the truth finally dawned on her. She loved George Gibson. More than she had ever loved anyone. Even though she knew the truth about him, she still loved him. And that hurt more than her father's betrayal.

"You love him?" he asked, shocked. "He works for the man who tried to kill you."

She was calm as she told him, "Maybe he does. To be honest, I don't know who disgusts me more—you or him."

"I didn't . . ." Uncharacteristically, Kenneth was at a loss for words. He stared at his clasped hands on his desk.

"I can't stand the sight of you right now," she said through clenched teeth.

She wiped away her tears, then turned to walk to the door. It hadn't been a Hallmark moment, but she had finally told him how she felt, and for that she felt good.

"Wait, let me call the driver. He'll take you back to your office."

She didn't slow her stride as she tossed over her shoulder, "I'll walk."

Amelia held up her chin as she walked through the courtroom and out the double doors, ignoring the stares from the still-stunned attorneys who waited in the court-room. Once she pushed out of the double doors, it was as if a switch had been flipped and she lost all of her steam, all of her anger. She only felt the sadness. She slid down a nearby wall until she plopped on the floor in an unladylike heap that would have horrified her on any other day.

She was too numb to cry, too numb to even feel any-more. Everything her father had said about George was true. He only cared about money. He only cared about winning. She meant nothing to him. More important, it was her fault for allowing herself to even think that he did care. She should have seen the truth from the first kiss. Even now, her body remembered and longed for his touch. Even after discovering that he had used her, she wanted to run to him and have him hold her.

Chapter 19

George walked into his apartment and quickly locked the door behind him. He placed his briefcase on the table near the door and hung his coat in the hall closet. It had been a long day. He tried to blame it on the long delays in court and his more irate than usual clients, but actually that was a typical day. The truth was it had been a long day because he hadn't spoken to Amelia or seen her. He had called her office, her cell phone, more than once, and she hadn't answered or returned any of his phone calls. He was the king of the brush-off, and he knew when he was being given one.

He cursed to himself and walked into the kitchen. He stared blankly into his refrigerator, without taking stock of the contents, then slammed the door. He barely resisted the urge to kick over the kitchen table. He should be used to the rejection. It hadn't bothered him in a long time before Amelia, but mostly that was because he rejected anyone first before she had the chance to reject him. Who knew that less than a week would have been the time limit with Amelia? He would have at least waited a week before he would have thought about getting out of Dodge.

Over the course of the day, he realized it was for the worse that he had made love to her, because now his memories would be haunted by her. For the rest of his life, he would have to attempt to forget the taste of her and the feel of her skin underneath his palms, what being inside of her made him feel like. That was enough to drive a man insane.

There was a sudden brisk knock on the door. He quickly unlocked the door and opened it. He tried not to appear too surprised that Amelia stood on the other side. She looked beautiful, as usual, and . . . and not quite like his Amelia. There was something missing from her eyes. George couldn't describe it, but he could tell that someone or something had hurt her. He had wanted to protect her, not only from everyone else, but also from himself. Judging from her expression, he was beginning to realize that she protected herself from him just fine on her own.

"Are you all right?" he asked anxiously, grabbing her arms and practically dragging her into the apartment. He kicked the door closed with his foot, then turned to anxiously search her face for any signs of hurt.

"I'm fine," she said with a wobbly smile that told him she was anything but fine. She regretted having spent the night with him. It was obvious. He shouldn't have been hurt; he had been planning to tell her that he thought it was a mistake. A mistake that he would dream about for the rest of his life.

"Where are your bodyguards?"

"I didn't want them around this evening. I told them

I was going to the bathroom at work and then I left through the back entrance."

"Amelia, it's too dangerous—" At her warning look he instead said, "I've been calling you all day."

Her voice was dull as she said, "I just got one message an hour ago." He didn't tell her that he had only left one message the fourth or fifth time he called. She didn't appear to notice his hesitation and continued. "I had a busy day in court. I stopped by to tell you that I have the results from the lab about the key—"

"Forget the key," George said abruptly. He linked his hands with hers, trying to ignore the hesitation he felt in her grip that hadn't been there before. He took a deep breath and said, "Normally, I dread hearing these four words, but . . . we need to talk."

"About?" she asked blankly.

"About . . . about last night. About us. About everything."

"There's nothing to talk about," she said with another fake smile that almost made him angry as she pulled her hands from his.

He tried for patience. "Yes, there is. Obviously, you're still upset—"

"I'm not upset."

"Yes, you are," he insisted.

"It was a mistake," she said simply.

"A mistake?"

"The two of us . . . we both want to see Donaldson get what he deserves. My weakness made it more than that," she said in that flat voice.

George was momentarily speechless as he stared at

her closed expression. She didn't sound like herself. She sounded too angry and hurt. She took the opportunity to avoid his gaze and glance around the apartment. His shoulders straightened as he tried to imagine what his impression would be of the small, almost barracklike apartment if he lived in a spacious *Better Homes & Gardens* house in one of the most prestigious areas of the city, like she did. Not good. He rubbed a hand over his eyes and shook his head.

He didn't have much to brag about in his fourth-floor apartment, but it was clean and the few pieces of furniture that he did have were handcrafted and unique. There wasn't much light allowed into the apartment by the two windows in the living room, but he didn't need the view of the rooftops of the scores of nearby restaurants and minimalls.

"George, what is this about?" she finally said in a small voice, causing him to turn to her in surprise. He had never heard her sound so lonely. "Before this whole situation arose, you never paid attention to me outside of court except to make fun of me."

Then he recognized the suspicion in her narrowed eyes. Anger and disappointment curled inside his stomach, as her behavior since last night became clear. She didn't trust him. He had thought that last night they'd moved past the distrust and suspicion, but he could see it in her expression. He winced because it hurt. A lot.

"What are you talking about?"

"I just find it suspicious that I'm attacked and you're not, even though we both witnessed the same event—"

"You told and I didn't," he said through clenched teeth.

"I also didn't get an office visit from Maurice Donaldson."

Her words hung in the air like a balloon before they hit him as if a ball of lead had swung into his stomach. "How did you find out about that?"

"Does it matter?" she said. Suddenly, with a hard expression on her face, she stalked across the room toward him while unbuttoning her blouse.

Normally her movements would have spurred George into some kind of action, into fulfilling one of the millions of fantasies that he'd had about her in the last few hours, but now he could only watch. And curse himself. Because if he were her, he wouldn't trust him, either.

"This is what you want, isn't it, George?" she asked in an ice-cold voice while she stripped off her blouse. Even the sight of honey and blue lace did not prompt him to act. "You want to sleep with me so you can tell the boys about the time you made Amelia Farrow scream, how you made her believe that you cared, while all the time you were playing her like a complete fool—"

"Stop it," he ordered, grabbing her hands as she reached for the clasp at the waistband of her skirt.

"May as well get your last lay, George," she said in a silky voice that conveyed her anger, hatred, and hurt all at once.

"Damn it, Amelia, stop it."

She tore her hands from his and crossed her arms over her chest to cover herself. Anger still lay across her features as she said, almost desperately, "Then deny it. You gave me the key when you didn't have to. I never would have known. Tell me the truth, George. Tell me you threw Donaldson out on his ass. Tell me that this is not about you setting clients free and making me look like a fool."

"You spied on me," he whispered, surprised that she had fooled him. He had actually thought he could have something with Amelia, and he had allowed her to hurt him. He didn't think anyone had the power to do that anymore. And he suddenly became angry. Maybe he wasn't worthy of anyone's automatic trust, but just once he wished that he didn't have to fight so damn hard to earn it.

"Are you working for Donaldson?" she demanded.

His hard tone matched hers as he answered, "If I said no would you believe me?"

She didn't answer but picked her blouse off the ground. She quickly slipped her arms through the sleeves and buttoned it. She walked across the room to her briefcase that she had dropped near the door.

"That's what I thought," he muttered. He could make love to her, he could make her sigh his name, he could maybe even make her love him if he was real lucky, but she would never trust him. He tried to convince himself that he didn't care.

She softly said, "The tech at the lab told me that the key belonged to a Honda Accord. On a hunch, I checked the courthouse records to see what type of car Nathan Finnegan drove. He drives a Honda Accord."

"Why are you telling me this now?"

"Because I keep my word," she answered stiffly, holding his gaze. "I told you that I would give you the test results and I have."

"And now you think you're leaving?" he asked in disbelief as she turned to the door. She once more faced him. If anyone saw her now, the truth would be out. Amelia Farrow was no Mary Poppins. She was a fierce warrior who hated his guts, and there were dangerous men looking for her and her information. No matter how much George tried to tell himself that someone who didn't trust him was not worth his trust, he also knew that he could not let Amelia do this by herself. If anything happened to her, he would never be able to live with himself. He said through clenched teeth, "I don't care what you think about me right now, but I gave you that key and whatever it leads to belongs to me."

She took a step toward him, the renewed anger screaming across her face. "Without me, you wouldn't even know what the key was for."

"I could have figured it out."

"If you think that we're still going to work together, then you must truly believe I'm the biggest idiot on the face of this earth."

He nonchalantly shrugged, just to anger her further. "You said it, not me."

"Go to hell, George," she said through clenched teeth, then turned to the door.

He grabbed her arm before she could leave. She whirled around to face him, and the hatred in her eyes caused him to involuntarily drop her arm. No one had ever looked at him with such distaste and anger . . . and hurt.

He forced himself to hide his emotions and said tonelessly, "We can do this together or you can give me back the key. It's your choice."

"What type of choice is that? You'll just give the key—and whatever evidence it leads to—to Donaldson."

He closed the distance between them, causing her to take several steps back until she bumped into the door. He didn't stop until he towered over her and she was forced to crane her neck to look at him.

"If I really wanted to, don't you think I could take that key right now?" he asked in a silky voice that threatened with its softness. Only because he saw a flash of fear through the anger in her expression did he walk away from her to grab his jacket from the sofa. "I'm assuming that Finnegan's car is still at the impound lot? We'll search his car and, hopefully, find out what he died for."

He didn't wait for her answer but walked past her and out the door. He only released the air trapped in his lungs when he heard his apartment door close and the click of her heels on the hallway floor behind him.

Amelia sat in the passenger seat of George's dark car and concentrated on the dim light of the guard's station in the expansive darkness of the police impound lot as she sipped the remains of her soda through the straw. She could only see the faint outline of one man through the windows of the small building. The lot wasn't that large, but it was filled to capacity with the cars of victims, criminals, and police undercover vehicles, and all of it was enclosed by a very high wire fence.

"If we do find something, what are we going to do with it?" George asked, breaking the heavy silence in the car.

They were the first words he'd spoken since they had left his apartment. She was glad to hear his voice, to think of something besides the disappointed and angry looks he kept giving her. He didn't even come inside her house when she'd snuck inside to change clothes. She should have been resentful of him, resentful of his looks, especially since she kept reminding herself that she didn't trust him. But a small part of her, the realistic part, called her a liar.

"If it's what I think it is, the evidence Finnegan has to bring down Donaldson's entire operation, I'll take it to Grayson."

"What if I want to keep the evidence and take it to Grayson myself?" he asked in a strange tone, then looked at her. The headlights of a passing car briefly shone in his eyes. They were flat and cold. Amelia wrapped her arms around herself. She wasn't scared of him. She was scared of what she would do for him.

"That's not going to happen, George," she finally said.

He laughed bitterly and said, "You never trusted me—"

"Unfortunately for us both, I did."

He stared at her for a few seconds and she saw the thousands of unspoken words in his eyes. He finally sighed, then said, "Come on. The guards are changing shifts." He reached for the door handle, then visibly hesitated and turned to her and said, "We don't have to do this. In fact, we probably shouldn't do this. Both of us don't have to go. Why don't you wait in the car and I'll—"

She almost thought that he was concerned for her safety; then she shook her head and said, "I was going to do this without you. Don't get in my way."

"If we find something and remove it, we'll never be able to authenticate it."

"This isn't a court of law. We can worry about that when the time comes."

"You sound like me," he muttered.

She put her own ski mask in place and ran across the street. She heard his footsteps pounding on the pavement after her. They reached the chain-link fence that encircled the cars. He pulled a pair of wire cutters from the black satchel he carried and created a small, unnoticeable opening for them to squirm through, since the top of the fence was looped with barbed wire. Sweat began to roll down her face underneath the scratchy mask as they carefully and silently made their way among the cars.

The only illumination in the lot came from dim overhead lights that provided enough visibility to tell her that she had almost kicked over a table of machine parts. She moved closer to George. She craned her neck to keep an eye on the slowly revolving camera. At the last minute, she tugged his shirt and the two crouched to the ground against a large car as the camera aimed in their direction. She tried not to, but she trembled from the wait as George held up his fingers counting until the camera changed direction as he had noted while they watched in his car across the street.

Finally, he motioned for her to stand and she willed her legs to cooperate. It was too quiet, too dark. She was an attorney, not a thief or whatever she was pretending to be while she paraded around the darkness in all black and a ski mask. She kept her eyes trained on George's back and tried not to allow her doubts to plague her. He moved with such confidence and grace that she did feel a little better. He also moved like a man who had done this before. Many times before. Standing across from him in his apartment, even as she accused him of working for Donaldson, proved to her that she would love this man until the day she died. Nothing would change that.

They finally reached Nathan Finnegan's car. From his crouched position George placed the key in the lock and turned. All of the locks automatically opened. He slid into the front passenger seat while Amelia climbed into the backseat. It was too dark for her to see if there was anything on the seats, but she felt around the leather and found nothing. The floors were clean to the touch as well. She lay on the backseat and felt under the seats.

"I feel something," she whispered excitedly, then grunted and tugged at the envelope.

"Stay down! The camera's turning this way," he harshly whispered.

She lowered herself as close to the floor as possible. She found her face mashed into the carpet and her legs scrunched against one door.

He once more sounded like the cold stranger he had become as he said, "The camera's gone. We have to get out of here."

She tugged harder and the envelope was free from the bottom of the seat. In the dim light she saw it was a large manila envelope. She quickly opened it, and a compact disc fell into her hands.

"This has to be it," she told him.

"Are you sure?"

"A compact disc."

"I haven't found anything up here. That has to be it. Now I'm really worried about authentication issues," he muttered.

The two slid from the car and softly closed the car doors. She matched his long stride as they sprinted across the lot toward the gate. She heard his heavy breathing that matched hers. All of a sudden night turned into day. Every light inside the impound lot was turned on. Searchlights focused on them and she heard several men's deep voices shouting at them.

"Keep going," George ordered, tugging on her hand.

She looked over her shoulder and saw the outline of two men with high-beam flashlights and guns running toward them. When they reached the gate, George kicked open the hole he had cut. He practically pushed Amelia through the opening; then he crawled after her.

"Open the damn gate!" one of the men shouted as he hopped into a patrol car.

The locked gate on the impound lot gave Amelia and George time to run to his car. They jumped inside, and before the men could unlock the gate, the tires on the Chevy loudly screeched and George sped the car down the street. Trying to catch her breath and stop the fear stomping in her heart, she looked over her shoulder. She sighed, relieved, and leaned against the seat when she saw no car headlights or police sirens behind them. She slid off her mask as George ripped his off and threw it on the backseat of the car.

She looked across the car at him. He was grinning from ear to ear. "Now, that was a piece of cake."

She just stared at him, then closed her eyes and prayed that the police wouldn't knock on her door that night. She would prefer to be taken to jail in the morning.

Chapter 20

George and Amelia sat in silence in the darkened study of her house. He nodded at her and she directed the mouse to scroll through the document on the computer screen. He heard Amelia's amazed sigh as the list of names and numbers grew longer and longer. She rapidly moved through the list, but George saw several names he recognized and knew that he was looking at a list of all the corrupt judges and cops on Donaldson's payroll.

George gulped down a sip of the bottle of water near him on the desk, then offered it to her. She shook her head in response, her eyes still trained on the screen.

"Finnegan stole Donaldson's files," Amelia said softly.

"We can bring down Donaldson, Parker, and the whole gang," George murmured. Neither one of them smiled.

"Judge Driscoll," she murmured, shaking her head. "I never would have thought that he would accept a bribe. He and my father went to law school together. . . . Judge

Langston. . . . Donaldson even listed the amounts he gave each person and the specific items he gave as gifts."

"This is going to destroy a lot of careers," George said.

She turned from the screen to glare at him. And he saw the prosecutor that she was in her blood. "For accepting bribes and tainting the justice system, these men and women deserve to have their careers destroyed. What about Thomas Chin? Donaldson learned that man's name and address from Nathan Finnegan or Judge Banner, who presided over the case. You break the law, you pay the price."

"We've broken the law . . . a lot," he reminded her.

"That was different," she instantly responded.

"Maybe some of the people on this list feel the same way." He pointed to a name on the screen and said, "This guy right here . . . Officer Frederick Johnson works in the same precinct as Wayne. His daughter has leukemia and he doesn't have the money to pay for her medical bills. He accepted five hundred dollars from Donaldson, according to this list, probably to fix a traffic ticket. Are you going to condemn him, too?"

She was silent for a moment, but he noticed the anger immediately left her eyes at the mention of a child, just as she had been galvanized by the mention of Thomas Chin's children no longer having a father. She would make a good mother. George never thought about his future children because he'd never thought he would have any, but the idea of a little girl wearing a headband cuddling next to him as he read her a bedtime story seemed right. He instantly wiped the image from his mind because it would never happen for him, especially not with Amelia.

She sent him a small smile, then said, "We now see

why I'm an assistant district attorney and why you're a criminal defense attorney."

She didn't add the rest—what they both thought. She would never trust him, exactly because of those differences.

"I'm going home. I'll meet you at your office tomorrow morning at nine o'clock to take the evidence to Grayson." He grabbed his jacket off the back of the chair, then stood. He waited for her to stop him, to ask him to stay, but she didn't.

He stared down at her and resisted the urge to touch her one last time. She met his gaze and there was nothing that needed to be said. It was apparent in her eyes. He could have sworn until next year that he didn't work for Donaldson and she would not have believed him. He bent down and placed a kiss on her forehead.

"Good-bye, Amelia."

He didn't wait for her response but turned and walked out of the house. George practically ran to his car and slammed the door. He screeched down the hill and cursed. The first woman he could admit to loving and she didn't trust him.

He wanted to tell her. He wanted to say those three words, but he had never said those words in his life. He was thirty-one years old and he had never said, "I love you," to another human being. The realization took his breath away. And he realized that if he didn't say them to Amelia, he would never say them. He'd never believed in true loves and all that magic movie love, but he had found it. And he realized that he was at a crossroads. Without her, he could continue his life—breakfast with Wayne, his penniless and probably guilty clients, his occasional meaningless dates. With Amelia, he could have her and whatever the future brought, which he knew would include laughter and arguments and more good times than he'd know what to do with. George felt like a coward, but he didn't turn the car around. When a man thought about changing his life so drastically, he needed to think about it for more than a few minutes.

Thirty minutes later, George walked into his dark apartment. He switched on the light and jumped in surprise when he saw Wayne. He wore his police uniform and sat like a wooden statue on George's sofa.

"You scared the hell out of me," George muttered. "Why are you sitting in the dark?"

Wayne's expression never changed as he said, "Where did you and Amelia disappear to tonight?"

George fell onto the easy chair and sighed tiredly. He had left this apartment that morning with such hopes, such expectations of how his life would change, loving Amelia. He laughed bitterly at the outcome of the day.

"What are you talking about?" George finally asked Wayne.

"I've been following you two for the past few days—"

George opened his eyes and stared at Wayne. "You've been following us?"

"Donaldson wants the list, George," Wayne said simply.

George stared at Wayne in disbelief and shock. "You work for Donaldson," he said, barely able to force the words out.

Wayne smiled, a sad smile, and said, "What did you expect? A man flashes ten thousand dollars in front of your face, what would you do?"

"Say no," George said from between clenched teeth.

"Damn it, that's what you do, Wayne. How could you? All of those talks about truth, justice, and the American way. It was all bull, wasn't it?"

Wayne stood and slowly pulled his gun from his holster and pointed it at George. George dryly laughed at the scene, then muttered, "A perfect end to a perfect day."

"It doesn't have to end this way. Just tell me where Finnegan hid the list."

"What list?"

"Don't play hero, George; it doesn't suit you."

"You would shoot me, Wayne?" George asked in disbelief. "We've known each other since we were six years old. We're the only family—"

"I don't want to shoot you, but I will if you don't tell me where the list is."

"Let's just beat it out of him," came another voice from behind George.

George whirled around to see Kevin Parker standing in the door frame. George's entire body tensed as he pointed one finger at Kevin. "You and me need to have a little talk, man."

Kevin sent George a nasty smile, then pulled out his own gun. "The only talking we're going to do is you telling me where the list is. I can't guarantee that you'll like what I have to say back."

George looked from Kevin to Wayne. He would have never thought Wayne could turn. He would have never thought that he could love Amelia. And at the thought of Amelia, he calmed. Whatever he did, he didn't want her involved. He almost laughed. It was a fine time for him to turn selfless, with two guns pointed at his head, but he figured now was as good a time as any.

"Amelia and I went to Finnegan's apartment tonight, but we didn't find anything. Our next stop was his storage locker in Santa Fe Springs."

"Storage locker," Wayne repeated in disbelief.

"He's lying," Kevin said simply.

"I'm not lying," George said calmly. "I found a monthly bill at his apartment for a storage locker in Santa Fe Springs. That has to be where he hid the list."

"I thought you didn't know what list I was talking about," Wayne said, smirking.

"Amelia has the list, doesn't she?" Wayne guessed, looking at George thoughtfully. "You two found the list and she didn't trust you with it." He glared at Kevin and said, "I told you she wouldn't give something that important to him."

"Let's go get her," Kevin said simply.

George almost lunged at the large man at the thought of him anywhere near Amelia, but Wayne held up a hand to Kevin. "She has those bodyguards, remember? It won't be as easy to waltz into her house, like you did last time, with two ex-marines staying there."

"What are we going to do?" Kevin asked George's question for him.

"I don't know."

"Maybe that's why Maurice wanted us to bring this loser back to the office," Kevin said, grabbing George's arm and twisting it behind his back, sending a sharp jab of pain through him. "Once we tell your woman we have you, she'll bring us the list."

George actually laughed, then said, "You may want to figure out another plan, Wayne."

"He's right, Parker," Wayne said, shaking his head.

"She won't bring the list to us to save him. She thinks he works with us."

It took several seconds for Kevin to understand. "It'll work. I've watched these two together. She'll come. And we'll have to make certain that she comes alone."

George tried to sound unconcerned as he said, "Let me talk to her alone. I can get the list from her and bring it to you guys. Wayne can go with me and see the whole transaction take place. We don't have to involve her in this."

"No way, lover boy," Kevin snapped.

Wayne rolled his eyes, then walked out the door. Kevin hustled George out the door of his apartment and toward the car waiting on the street.

Amelia lay on her bed and stared at the television in the far corner of the room. She didn't know what the program was about and she had been watching it for two hours. She stared at the envelope next to her on the bed. The disc held the key to her career advancement, Donaldson's downfall, her attacker's identity, and justice for Chin and Finnegan. She should have been ecstatic. She had won. But tears filled her eyes.

It sounded trite, but without George the victory meant nothing. She rightfully should have hated him. He'd used her. He worked for the enemy, except a small part of her wondered, if George truly worked for Donaldson, he should have taken the disc from her. She hadn't hidden it. He could have driven her straight to Donaldson's office and there would have been nothing she could have done. But he didn't. He had driven her home and he had looked at her with such heartbreak in his eyes, such disappointment, it had broken her heart.

But her father would have been proud. She had stood strong against any weakness. Against love. She had a reasonable doubt, and George was guilty until proven innocent. She had done what was right for the state of California and for the Farrow name, but neither notion would warm her now or hold her in his arms.

The telephone on her nightstand rang and she debated answering it. She could not talk to Heather or her mother, who still fussed about going to New York but somehow had been at Amelia's house earlier that night, and she especially could not talk to her father. She just wanted to wallow in self-pity. At least for tonight, because she had finally accepted that she had found the most imperfect perfect man and she had lost him. She swiped at her eyes as she pressed the volume down on the television with the remote control.

"Hello," she greeted into the receiver, trying not to sound as if she had spent the last two hours crying.

"Amelia, it's Wayne Phillips. Remember me? George's friend."

She froze at the mention of George's name, then remembered to breathe. She clutched the telephone, then said, "Of course I remember you, Wayne. How are you?"

"Not good," he said, sounding more amused than upset. "George and I have gotten ourselves into a little situation. Donaldson has us at gunpoint."

"Are you hurt? Is George hurt?" she asked immediately as her stomach dropped to her feet. A man didn't hold his employee hostage, did he . . . unless it was for her benefit.

"We're fine, for now. They have George in another room. I'm scared about what they might do to him."

"No!" she cried, placing one hand over her mouth.

"They know you found the list in Finnegan's car. They want it or they'll kill us. Bring it to the Rinaldi Building. Do you know where that is?"

Amelia was silent as the more rational part of her actually hesitated. Wayne and George had known each other since they were children. If George worked for Donaldson, then Wayne did, too. She could be walking into a trap. She could be sacrificing the key to proving Donaldson was a criminal; she could be sacrificing her life. The only thing that spurred her to stand up and search for her clothes was the possibility that Wayne could be telling the truth. George could be held at gunpoint, he might not work for Donaldson, and she would never forgive herself if something happened to him. For once, a Farrow would do what was right for that Farrow. Screw the justice system.

"I can be there in twenty minutes," she told Wayne.

"No bodyguards, Amelia, and no police."

She shivered at the note of finality in his voice. "What's to stop them from killing us once I give them the disc?"

"I don't know," Wayne said with a tired sigh. "You don't have to come, Amelia."

She thought of George and shook her head. He would come for her. Regardless of where his allegiance lay, she knew that he would.

"I'll be there, Wayne. I promise."

"Once you give them the list this will all be over. Come quick, Amelia. Understand?"

"Yes," she said, the tears in her eyes interfering with

her attempts to button her pants. "Where's George? I want to talk to him."

"I think—"

The line went silent and all she heard was the dial tone. She cursed, then slammed the receiver down. She pulled on a sweater, then slipped into her boots. She grabbed the envelope containing the damaging list, then stared at her bedroom window, then at her closed bedroom door. She could have asked Jenkins and Morse for help, to call the police, to follow her at a safe distance. But she didn't. If there was a chance that George could be hurt because of her, she didn't want to risk it. Of course, she wasn't a complete fool, so she wrote down what had happened and taped the note to her bedroom window. Wayne said no one could follow her, but that didn't mean they couldn't come on their own. She just needed enough time to convince Donaldson that she had come alone.

She opened her bedroom window and stared at the large tree next to her house. She tucked the envelope in the back of her jeans with the thin retractable baton that Jenkins had given to her with a stern warning "not to press this button," when he first started working for her, then climbed onto the ledge. She held on to the window frame with one hand and reached for the tree limb closest to her. She grimaced at the strain. The limb was just beyond her fingertips.

She stared at the ground again. She said a quick prayer, then leaped for the limb. The rough contact of the scratchy bark against her face caused her to curse even as she smiled in relief. She quickly climbed down the tree, then ran toward the garage. She searched through the darkness of the garage for the spare set of keys she kept in the tool drawer. She found them, then climbed into her car. She couldn't avoid the noise as she started the engine.

She reversed out the garage as Jenkins and Morse ran out of the house. She sent them both an apologetic wave, then sped down the street and prayed that she wasn't too late.

It was too dark and too cold as Amelia rode in the empty elevator toward the roof of the twenty-floor Rinaldi Building. She hadn't known whether to be relieved or scared when she found the office building door open and was able to walk into the empty lobby. She clutched the envelope in her clammy hands as the elevator continued. She realized at that moment that she didn't care about the contents. She just wanted George safe in her arms. She loved him. It was a hell of a time to realize it, but she loved a defense attorney.

The elevator doors slid open. She no longer hesitated but walked toward the open door that showed a slice of the night sky. The wind whipped her hair around her face as she stepped onto the roof. Maurice Donaldson and the man from her nightmares stood on the other side of the roof. She had thought she could handle this, but when she stared into Kevin Parker's eyes, she gasped and would have run to the elevator if she could move. He was taller than she remembered, bigger, and his wide mouth shaped into a permanent scowl as he studied her. A visible gash stood on the side of his neck—exactly where she remembered burying the piece of glass in her attacker.

"It is a pleasure to finally meet you, Ms. Farrow, or may I call you Amelia?" Donaldson graciously asked as he walked across the roof to stand across from her.

She tore her eyes from Kevin Parker to stare at Donaldson. She regained her nerves and told herself to pretend that she was in court. She had faced men tougher than Kevin Parker and Maurice Donaldson in court too many times to count. And she had sent each one to prison. Of course that had been in court with a deputy standing next to her. On the roof of a twenty-story building at midnight was another thing entirely.

She remembered that she was a Farrow and said, "Your attempt at displaying some form of manners doesn't fool me or scare me; it only irritates me."

There was a tense moment of silence; then Donaldson began to laugh. He glanced over her shoulder and said, "I guess you were right about her, Kevin. She is a handful."

She tried to hide her shudder of fear when she once more glanced at Kevin. Judging from Donaldson's knowing smile, she didn't hide it well.

"You remember Kevin, don't you?" Donaldson said pleasantly. "He remembers you."

She forced herself to ignore Parker and asked through clenched teeth, "Where is George?"

"Right here, Amelia," Wayne said from behind her. She whirled around to see Wayne and George walk through the door and onto the roof.

There were no guns pointed at the men, no risk of life. Tears filled her eyes as she stared at George's empty expression. She had been right. She had been hurt before, but never to this extent. She thought the pain in her chest would explode into tears.

George told her in a hard tone, "Give them the disc, Amelia, then get out of here."

"You two work for him?" she whispered through her tears.

"I'm a wonderful employer, Ms. Farrow," Donaldson said. "I've been thinking of adding an ADA to my staff. But I probably couldn't afford you."

She ignored him and continued to stare at George, praying that her eyes deceived her. "George?"

"Give them the disc and get out of here," he repeated, this time not meeting her eyes.

"This is what you want," she said to Donaldson, holding up the envelope. "You think I'm stupid? I didn't bring you everything. You won't get the other half of the list until I return to my house." For once, being known as squeaky clean helped her, because no one on the roof could tell that she lied. She wished she had thought of that safety precaution before she was halfway to the building.

"You wouldn't dare!" Kevin roared, starting toward her.

Donaldson held up his hand and Kevin stopped, but he glared at her. Amelia released her breath of fear, then realized that George stood next to her. She hadn't seen him move across the roof. She quickly took a step from him. As far as she was concerned, he was just as dangerous as Kevin Parker and Maurice Donaldson.

"What are you talking about, Ms. Farrow? You didn't make this transaction more difficult, did you?" Donaldson asked with a sigh of disappointment.

She saw the doubt in his eyes and she smiled, a smile that made witnesses tremble in their seats in courtrooms, as she coolly said, "Do you really think that the judges on your payroll are going to soil their soft manicured hands in prison to protect you? You don't pay them enough. They'll turn on you so fast that it will make your head spin. I've seen it before. As soon as the first judge or cop sees the inside of a jail cell or interrogation room from the other side of the table, we won't be able to shut him up. We'll know everything about your operation. And you won't have to say one word."

Donaldson's smile disappeared and he ordered, "Tell me where the rest of the list is."

"Not until I'm safely at home."

Donaldson only smiled in response, then shook his head. He glanced at Kevin and said, "What do you think?"

"We're wasting our time with her," Kevin said.

"I don't understand who you're protecting, Ms. Farrow," Donaldson said, looking truly confused. "My activities don't hurt anyone. I deal with the people who come to me, I don't take my business to civilians."

"You've heard my conditions," she said, trying to sound brave, though she figured that her heart was slamming against her chest loud enough for Donaldson to hear.

"Wayne, kill George," Donaldson said simply.

Wayne pulled out his gun and Amelia screamed, turning to George. He didn't move to defend himself, to run; he only stared at her. She looked from Wayne to George, then back again.

"What's going on?" she demanded, staring at George for an answer.

He didn't speak; he just shook his head and stared at the ground. For once, no smart remarks, no smirks, nothing. Just a sadness and a regret that made her want to cry for different reasons. She knew at that moment that George had never worked for Donaldson. He never would because working for a man like Donaldson would go against everything in his life that he had worked for. And he had worked for so much and accomplished so much, Amelia realized at that moment. She not only loved him, but she respected him. And she was going to lose him because she had waited too long to see what had been obvious since he'd first walked into a courtroom.

"Why did you come, Amelia?" George whispered while shaking his head in regret.

"It should be obvious by now, Ms. Farrow," Donaldson said with an unconcerned laugh. "George doesn't work for me. I propositioned him, but he kicked me out of his office. I never thought he would work for me, but I had to try. It looks like you had less faith in him than I did, and I didn't even sleep with him.

"I don't blame you, though. He's been trained to think only about himself, just like I was. He should rightfully care more about his own skin than a few people he's never met before. Why should he risk his life to turn in a few dirty cops and judges when all he has to do is turn over the information to me and receive one million dollars in return? But there's something about George I know that you couldn't believe. He's a decent man. The last decent man left in Los Angeles, and he's going to be killed by his girlfriend."

"No!" she cried, tears in her eyes. "I'll tell you—"

"Don't tell them anything," George said through clenched teeth. "The location of the rest of the list is the only bargaining chip you have to get out of here alive."

She met his gaze and she wanted to touch him, to tell him that she had believed in him. Deep in her heart. Instead, she shook her head. "I can't let them kill you."

"He's lying," George suddenly said, and she heard the

desperation in his voice. "I work for him. He's trying to trick you again."

"I don't believe you," she said softly, then turned to Donaldson. Her mind moved in a million different directions. She had only one weapon—her mouth—to get her and George out alive, and judging from the look in his eyes, he wasn't going to help her.

"How'd you know who to pick, Donaldson?" she asked. "How'd you know who was weak enough to accept your bribes?"

"Whether you want to accept it or not, Ms. Farrow, Mr. Gibson and I are more alike than you think," Donaldson answered mildly. "We both grew up in environments where we had to study and learn human behavior just to survive. I know who needs a few threats to do what I want, I know who only needs the scent of money, and I know who's desperate enough to accept the first crumb I throw their way."

"And Nathan Finnegan? Which category did he fit?" Amelia asked.

"He was just greedy," Donaldson dismissed. "I knew he was preparing to leave town, but I didn't know that he was planning to blackmail me until we found the files missing, but, of course, it was too late then. He was already dead."

Amelia pressed, "So you had Parker kill him and you paid your stooges in the courthouse and police lab to look the other way?"

"Money does make the world go round, as you well know, Ms. Farrow."

"And Thomas Chin? Did you have something to do with his death?" George asked, and Amelia almost sighed in relief. He hadn't completely disappeared on her.

"Chin is not the innocent that you think," Donaldson answered. "He accepted the money to be the dissenting vote in a case against one of my employees, but at the last minute he had conscience pangs. Good conscience, bad timing." Donaldson shook his head as he looked at George and mused, "Kind of like you, George. Your conscience took the wrong time to suddenly become active. You could have a mansion in Bel Air, cars, no more bill collectors, any woman in LA County who you want. The offer is still open. I can use your services."

George held Amelia's gaze as Donaldson spoke. She liked to think that she didn't feel doubt, and when she stared into his familiar and honest brown eyes, she realized that she didn't.

He paused for only a moment before he said, "I said no before, and the answer is still no."

"Is it her?" Donaldson asked, surprised, while motioning toward Amelia.

"You were wrong about me. I've never been like you, Donaldson."

"That's too bad," he murmured, then abruptly smiled while he looked from Amelia to George. "Ms. Farrow, tell me where the other half of my list is or I will blow off every one of Mr. Gibson's limbs, and while he's choking on his own blood, I'll start on you."

Parker pulled a gun from his jacket and pointed it at George.

George saw the fear on her face. He would have given anything if she weren't in the middle of this. He had thought she would throw the disc on the ground and storm away when she saw him supposedly on Donaldson's team. Either she loved him or she was more stubborn than he thought. He liked to think it was love.

George's satisfaction at the prospect of her love was short-lived when he heard Amelia scream. He whirled around to see Wayne turn his gun on her. Donaldson smiled and waved his hand in confirmation for the first shot.

"No, Wayne!" George pleaded, prepared to launch himself at his best friend.

"Everyone stand where they are and drop the weapons," Wayne ordered, sounding suspiciously like a cop again. Everyone on the roof froze, more from surprise than from Wayne's orders. "This place is surrounded. Maurice Donaldson and Kevin Parker, you're both under arrest for the murder of Nathan Finnegan and for a bunch of other damn stuff that I'll think of before the arraignment."

"Wayne, what are you doing?" George asked, confused.

Wayne had the nerve to wink at him as he said, "I told you that one day you'd need a cop."

"This place isn't surrounded," Donaldson said confidently. "I'd know if it was. You're bluffing."

"Drop your weapons now," Wayne demanded.

"If the cops were here, they'd already be upstairs by now. You're flying solo tonight, aren't you, Wayne? You'd have to be or else I'd know," Donaldson said, sounding unconcerned.

"Your control in the department isn't as deep as you think it is," Wayne coldly told him. "We've known about you and your dirty cops for months. Now, tell Kevin to drop the damn gun before I blow out your brains."

"Then where's the cavalry?" Donaldson asked. With a wide grin he looked toward the door. George hopefully followed his gaze. Several seconds ticked by, but there was no mass of cops racing through the door. Donaldson smugly smiled, then said, "I thought so. Now, it looks like we have a tricky situation."

"I can't let you do this, Maurice," Wayne said through clenched teeth.

"Watch out!" Amelia suddenly screamed, pointing behind Wayne and George.

The escapee Milton Tucker flew around the air vents and launched himself at Wayne. The two men tumbled to the ground, each grappling for the gun in Wayne's hand. Donaldson reached for the disc in Amelia's hand. In one continuous motion Amelia clicked open the small, thin metal baton and slammed it onto his arm, knocking the gun from his hand. George noticed Parker taking aim at Wayne, instantly propelled himself across the roof, and slammed into the solid wall of Kevin Parker.

The two men fell to the hard ground with a force strong enough to make George think he had knocked some teeth loose. Parker's gun clattered across the roof to harmlessly land out of reach. Parker was the first to recover and slammed his fist into George's face. He registered the flash of pain at the same time he tasted the blood in his mouth. He was momentarily stunned from the pain, but he managed to avoid Parker's second fist and scramble to his feet.

He cursed again as the pain raged in his mouth. He saw Amelia swinging the baton like a major-league baseball player, but Donaldson barely managed to avoid each swing by wildly contorting his body and screaming in fear. George turned toward Parker again to duck another fist. The man had hands the size of hamhocks. If he had to take another punch from Parker, he would probably pass out, and neither Amelia nor Wayne would ever let him live that down, if they all survived this.

George avoided another fist and this time swung one of his own. Even though Parker stumbled slightly from the impact, George had a feeling the white heat flashing through his probably broken hand hurt more than Parker's face did. Parker continued to advance toward him and George almost stumbled over the window washer's equipment. In one move he kicked up an empty bucket, then kicked it toward Parker's face. Parker barely managed to avoid it and George used the distraction to punch the man in the face again, then the stomach, and finally landed a fist on Parker's chin that contained all of his anger and revenge for Parker hurting Amelia.

Blood squirted in one direction as Parker's face swung in the other. Like a pile of cement, Parker dropped to the floor, unconscious. George recovered Parker's gun that was too close to the unconscious man, and tucked it in his pants waistband.

The door to the roof suddenly blew off the hinges and a gang of uniformed police officers, followed by Jenkins and Morse, began to run onto the roof, their guns drawn. George wondered if Parker had knocked loose a few of his brain cells, because he found himself glad to see the cops, until he heard a sound that would haunt him for the rest of his life. Amelia screamed, a bloodcurdling cry that turned his blood cold.

George turned in time to see Donaldson and Amelia

teetering on the ledge of the building, Donaldson's hand on her sweater the only thing that separated her from a very long fall. She struggled with him, but Donaldson pushed her farther over the ledge. George began to move even as he heard the police shouting orders at Donaldson to release Amelia. Gravity became George's enemy, not because of what it might do to Amelia but because it slowed him down.

With a bloody smile of feigned regret in George's direction, Donaldson released her sweater. She disappeared over the edge of the building.

Without hesitating in his sprint across the roof, George grabbed the black rope coiled at the end of the window washer's platform and continued as fast as his legs could carry him toward the edge that she had disappeared over. From the corner of his eye he saw the mass of police officers race through the door toward him, trying to stop him.

"Wayne!" George screamed, hoping, praying, that his friend would get the message that he didn't have time to explain; then he dived head-first over the edge of the building.

Amelia realized that she stared at the night sky as she plummeted toward the sidewalk. It was true what people said about perception before impending death. Flashes of her life played before her eyes. She saw her unhappy mother, her frustrated father, and the fact that, despite their numerous shortcomings, they loved her. She saw her time with Brian and how he had loved her as best he could. Her friends. Her colleagues. And there was George. Always George.

One second she was staring at the dark, star-covered sky reliving her life; the next she stared at a man in the shape of a human bullet speeding toward her. The human bullet spread out his arms and legs to slow the momentum and swung toward her, like a slightly less graceful version of Spiderman. She didn't realize it was George until his familiar arms wrapped around her waist and slammed her against his body. She grunted at the hard impact and the painful grip of his arms around her waist, but she didn't protest and clung to his neck.

"Hang on!" George screamed over the wind whipping around them as they continued to plunge toward the earth.

She grabbed the cord above their heads with both hands. He suddenly lurched to one side and she felt the arc of the rope swing toward the building. Instead of screaming over the rapidly approaching ground, she screamed as she and George hurtled toward the building at a speed that hinted at a very painful impact.

Just when she thought that they would slam into the building, George pulled a gun from his waistband and began to shoot at the glass wall. The loud explosions rang in her ears and drowned out her need to scream. The glass splintered and as the two approached it, George kicked out his legs. The glass crashed thousands of tiny fragments as George and Amelia crashed into the building with a spectacular sound.

The two released the rope at the same time and in a cloud of raining glass they plowed onto the wooden desk inside an office. The air was momentarily knocked from her lungs as she hit the hard desk with a thud that sent the desk crashing to the floor in numerous pieces. Her momentum sent her skidding across the room and into a chair that crumbled around her. George crashed onto the floor next to her, his feet kicking over the other chair and the computer that had survived the first hit.

Several seconds passed and neither George nor Amelia moved. The only sound in the room was the still-cracking glass. Stiff pain registered in every portion of her body. Pain and shock. She should have been dead. She didn't know if she could truly grasp that she wasn't. It was only then that she realized that George had willingly jumped off a building for her. If she didn't love him before, then she had to love him now.

She forced her head to turn to the side and she saw George on his back, staring at the ceiling, as his chest rapidly moved up and down. He slowly turned his head to stare at her, a wince of pain on his face. He managed to sit up and he dusted the glass and debris off his body. He crawled across the room and helped her to sit up.

"Are you all right?" he asked, concern etched on his face as his hands moved across her eyes and mouth, then neck, as if reassuring himself that she was alive.

She ignored the pain and slid her arms around him, then whispered in awe, "You saved my life."

"I know," he said, sounding more surprised than she had felt when she saw him in the sky.

She moved from his arms to stare into his beautiful eyes that she thought she would never see again. "You could have been killed, George. Don't ever do anything like that again. Don't ever scare me like that again. I love you too much to lose you now."

He leaned his forehead against hers. "You came, Amelia," he whispered. "Even though you believed I worked for Donaldson, you came. No one has ever believed in me. For giving me that, I owe you my life."

She waited for him to continue, to tell her that he loved her, but he didn't. He ran his fingers down her face, but there was no proclamation of love. She told herself that being alive was all the proof she needed, but a small part of her still wondered.

One second she was in a sea of glass; the next there was a unit of uniformed police officers crashing into the room through the door. The men swept Amelia into one ambulance and George into a different one.

Chapter 21

"You could have told me," George said to Wayne while glaring at him across the hospital room.

The paramedics had taken George to the hospital, where the doctor had pronounced George "lucky" to only have a broken arm, which he had set in a cast that hurt more than the bone itself. Amelia had ridden in a different ambulance that had been followed by her father's limousine, Grayson's limousine, and her mother's limousine.

He loved Amelia Farrow. And it scared the hell out of him. He could face Donaldson and his gang for her. He could jump off a building for her. But it seemed too horrifying to say those three words out loud to her. Loving Amelia would mean expectations and responsibilities. It would mean home. For a man who never had that, it was almost too overwhelming to comprehend all at once. Not to mention the fact that Amelia may not love him in return. That thought alone seemed more frightening than anything else that he could imagine.

"I couldn't tell you, George," Wayne patiently said, watching George pull on his T-shirt, or attempt to do so. The pain seared the side of his chest, where his ribs had been injured by the crash into the building, as well as Kevin's well-placed iron fists. George finally managed to pull the shirt with a cut-wide sleeve to accommodate his cast over his head. His loud gasps of air from the effort didn't subtract from his feelings of mild triumph.

"I thought you were one of them. You lied to me," George finally accused Wayne. "You pointed a gun at me! Don't think I'm going to forget that part."

Wayne actually appeared wounded as he said, "I can't believe you thought that I would accept money from someone like Donaldson. After everything we saw as kids because of men like Donaldson, you really thought that I would work for him? You should have had a little more faith in me than that."

George glared at Wayne for a full second before he said, "If I didn't think it would hurt my sore hand, I would hit you right now."

"What's wrong?" Wayne asked innocently.

"What's wrong?" George repeated in disbelief. "The woman I love had a gun pointed to her head and you couldn't clue me in to the fact that you were working undercover."

"What could I have done?"

"You could have winked or . . . or done that secret hand thing we did when we were kids and we didn't want anyone to know we talked."

"What secret hand thing?"

George momentarily paused as he tried to remember the "secret hand thing." Finally, he impatiently snapped,

"You should have done something to tell me. I thought you were going to kill her."

"I was never going to kill her . . . or you, for that matter."

"I know that now," he groaned.

"I'm sorry, for what it's worth," Wayne said, sincerity in his eyes. "I wanted to tell you, especially when you got mixed up in all of this, but I couldn't. And after you two got involved, my bosses told me to watch how everything played out. I always had your back, George. I had people tailing you the whole time."

"The whole time?" George repeated, thinking of some of his less legal activities over the last few days.

"They did lose you a few times . . . around the same time that someone broke into Finnegan's apartment and car. You're not going to tell me that was you, right, George? I know that a well-respected attorney would never do anything as illegal as robbery."

"Robbery is larceny when the defendant uses force. I never used force to borrow any of the items that I needed. And if I really want to nitpick, I never technically committed larceny because I never intended to keep the items that I borrowed—"

Wayne sighed loudly. "You win, George; you win. No one is going to know about your not-robbery, not-larceny."

George laughed, then grinned when he thought of Wayne playing a rogue cop. "I don't think I ever really believed that you were a part of Donaldson's gang. It was . . . too weird."

"Someone had to infiltrate his gang, and my bosses picked me."

"What happened to Nathan Finnegan's body?"

"He's not dead. Parker shot him, but discovered him still alive—barely. When Parker smuggled him out of the courthouse, I took him to the hospital. He's in police custody. He'll be testifying against Donaldson."

"That means Amelia was targeted for nothing."

"We never would have found out about Thomas Chin if it weren't for you and Amelia. I thought that Donaldson had him killed, but I had no proof. Besides, Donaldson would have found the file in the car if it weren't for you two. I couldn't chance going to the car to get it. Thanks to you, Parker is resting uncomfortably in the prison hospital. And thanks to me, Donaldson is going to spend the rest of his natural life in jail."

"You could have clued us in, Wayne." George sighed heavily, then ran his hands over his face. He was in so much pain, so tired, and had loved a woman who he still wasn't sure completely trusted him. Not that it mattered, because he would never be able to tell her that he loved her, because he was a coward. "This is just weird," he muttered, thinking about himself more than any other part of the night.

Wayne laughed, then said, "The weird part was watching you plunge over a twenty-story building head-first. If I hadn't been pummeling Tucker's face in, I probably would have thought that I was dreaming."

"If I had thought about it, I wouldn't have done it," George assured him while trying not to laugh because that would have hurt too much. "It was just a . . . reflex."

"Reflex?" Wayne repeated in disbelief. "How can you call jumping off a building reflex? That is not reflex, George, that's insanity."

"I had to do something."

"But jumping off a building . . . If the SWAT team hadn't grabbed the rope, you would have been a dead insane man."

"Get over it, Wayne," George commanded.

Wayne sat on the examination bed and studied George as he tried to pull on his sweater. He gave up on the effort and tossed the sweater to Wayne.

"Do you realize what you just did?" Wayne asked in amazement. "You jumped off a twenty-story building for a woman."

"I had forgotten about that between then and now. Thanks for reminding me," George muttered dryly, then laughed. His laughter ended in a spasm of pain and he winced.

"I can't explain why I did it, except that I couldn't *not* do it," George said finally.

"I know why you did it, George," Wayne said quietly. "You love her. The woman you love was going to die and you couldn't allow that to happen. You're a hero, and heroes always save their women in the most spectacular way they can."

"If I could have created the scenario, it would not have involved a twenty-story building," he muttered reluctantly.

Wayne's laughter faded when George looked at him and asked desperately, "What can I possibly offer her?"

"Just yourself, George," Wayne assured him, then added with a grin, "That's a pretty damn good offer. And since I think Amelia is a smart lady, she'll recognize that and realize she's getting a good bargain."

"I can offer her my penniless and probably guilty clients and an only slightly successful law practice . . . in a good week," George muttered. "A guy like Brian can offer her everything that I can't—"

"Brian?! That guy in the suit who came to the hospital a few hours ago?!" Wayne snorted in disbelief. "You have nothing to worry about from that walking Brooks Brothers ad. In fact, you don't have to worry about any competition . . . ever! You could leave dirty underwear on the floor, never wash a dish or put down the toilet lid, and there's absolutely nothing that she could say. You jumped off a building for her, for God's sake. Do you know how much you can get away with now?"

George laughed, then said, "You and I see it that way, but knowing Amelia . . . she won't see it that way." He cleared his throat, then asked, "What about Judge Banner? What do you think will happen to him?"

"He's singing like a canary, even as we speak. Finnegan supports Banner's story that Banner set up the meeting to warn him that Donaldson was becoming irritated. It's highly unlikely that Banner will serve any jail time. He probably will be removed from the bench, but considering the jail time he could have faced, he should be feeling pretty lucky right now."

"I wonder how Amelia will feel about that when she hears."

"She's the one who recommended to Grayson that Banner receive probation," Wayne said, then smiled as he said, "Maybe you're rubbing off on her, too."

"I hope so," he murmured with a grin.

Wayne abruptly sobered, then said quietly, "I know you and I have this unspoken pact not to talk about the past, the bad times at the different foster homes and the orphanages—"

"Wayne," George said while shaking his head. He didn't like to talk about it. He didn't like to think about it. There had been a lot of good people in the foster care system, but there had been some bad ones. The bad ones still caused George to wake up in chills some nights.

"Let me finish," Wayne said quietly. "I want you to know, in case you ever decide to jump off a building to save Amelia again and I'm not around to save your ass, that without you, my childhood . . . it would have been unbearable. What happened to us as kids . . . no kid should have to live through it, but we did, and somehow you still managed to keep whatever makes you George Gibson—the reluctant defender of the poor, guilty, and just plain stupid. You care about people, you always have, and no Mr. Ashford or anyone else can take that from you. They may have suppressed it for a while, but they could never take it away, which is why you became a lawyer and you represent those people and you'll never get paid. But without that part of you, I wouldn't be here, either. Thanks for being there, George, for being my family."

George cleared his throat over the clog of emotions there. He had always thought he had no one or nothing, but he had Wayne. And he had Amelia, too. And that was better than some people would ever have who were surrounded by family and friends. He didn't trust himself to speak but instead used his good hand to squeeze Wayne's shoulder.

The door suddenly opened and George stared in surprise as Kenneth and Alice Farrow walked into the hospital room. He had never met the older man, but with one look at the man's firmly set mouth and dark eyes, George knew that every attorney horror story he had heard from his courtroom was true. Kenneth took no prisoners in dispensing justice. Standing next to him, Alice looked more delicate and beautiful. She also looked like she had been through hell during the past few hours as she stood by her daughter's bedside.

George tried to jump off the examination table, but at the jab of pain he was forced to move more slowly. "Hi," he said awkwardly, then glanced at Wayne for help. "You must be Judge Kenneth Farrow—"

"Oh, George, thank you," Alice gasped as she threw herself into his arms. George grimaced, but he returned the woman's painful embrace. She wiped the tears from her eyes as she looked at him. "If anything had happened to my Amie, I don't know what I would have done. . . ."

George wordlessly nodded, accepting Alice's embrace, because he didn't know what to say. He couldn't exactly tell Amelia's parents that he had no other choice but to do something because living without Amelia was not an option.

Alice smiled through her tears and squeezed his hand. "We're taking Amelia home now. The doctors said that she was fine besides a few cuts and bruises, but we'll take that over her being . . . Thank you, George."

Alice turned to the door, then tugged on Kenneth's sleeve as he stared at George. Kenneth cleared his throat, then said in a deep voice, "When I'm wrong, I say I'm wrong. I was wrong about you, Gibson."

"I was wrong about you, too, sir."

Kenneth hesitated and George hoped that the older man wouldn't ask him what that meant, because he didn't think Amelia would appreciate him telling her father what he had previously thought.

Kenneth cleared his throat, then said gruffly, "My daughter loves you. I hope you're worth it."

"I hope so, too."

The older man abruptly nodded, then turned and walked from the room.

George hadn't imagined the tears in the older man's eyes. Alice gratefully smiled at George once more, then followed her husband out of the room.

"The future in-laws?" Wayne asked with a low whistle of either amazement or empathy. "Good luck."

George grinned in response, because the idea of Kenneth Farrow as his father-in-law only sent his heart into mild palpitations and not the heart attack that he should have suffered.

"What am I going to do with you?" Heather demanded as she once more gave Amelia a hug that literally cut off her oxygen supply.

Amelia finally managed to tear herself from Heather's arms and stood up from the hospital examination table. She was not hurt besides tiny cuts from the glass and bruises on her back and thighs from crashing through a window, but her parents had not listened. Once more she had been bundled into an ambulance and driven to the hospital, but this time lying in the hospital bed had been a lot different from only a few days before when she had felt scared and alone. Now, whether George knew it or not, she was not alone. She looked at Heather and thought of her parents, and even Brian, and she realized she had never been alone. Her life had not been how she had envisioned it, with feuding parents who couldn't ask her a question but instead learned the answers from her friends, and an ex-fiancé, and loving a defense attorney, but she loved her life and she wouldn't change it for the world.

"Maybe your mother is right and you should spend the night in the hospital," Heather said as she watched Amelia with worried eyes.

"No more Hotel Hospital," Amelia firmly said. "As long as I can walk out of here on my own two feet, that's what I'm doing."

"I can't believe everything that's happened the last few days. You should have told me what was going on."

"So I could put you in danger, too?"

"You should have called the police before you went riding to George's rescue like the Lone Ranger," Heather admonished.

"I wasn't thinking," Amelia admitted, avoiding Heather's gaze. "All I could think about was seeing him, making certain that he was safe."

"You love him, Amie," she softly whispered.

Amelia grinned, then said, "I do."

Heather sighed in contentment, then squeezed Amelia in another hug. "I'm happy for you. It's time that even Amelia Farrow had a little happiness."

Amelia's smile faded when she saw the sadness on the edges of Heather's smile. This time, she squeezed her friend's hand and asked, "How have you been?"

A forced, faltering smile spread across Heather's face, but she nodded more firmly as she said, "I'm going to be all right. I promise." Her faltering grin turned into a real one as she said, "Now I think it's time that you see that man you risked life and limb to save."

A flit of nerves washed through Amelia's stomach,

more powerful than when she'd stared Donaldson in the face. She didn't know why she was nervous. George obviously loved her. He had risked his life to save her. Then her thoughts came to an abrupt stop, because he had also risked his life to save Judge Banner. He had stayed at her house, on an uncomfortable chair, before he loved her. He represented clients who couldn't afford him and would never pay their entire fee.

She suddenly realized that despite his loud and numerous protests to the contrary, George Gibson was inherently a hero. He needed to make people feel better; he needed to help them. Maybe jumping off a roof was extreme, but not for a true hero, one who always thought about others first. She didn't know how she could ever believe that a man like him could work for Donaldson or use her. He may not love her, but he would never purposely hurt her or any other person—unless that person sat on the witness stand trying to put one of his clients in jail; then all bets were off. She suddenly felt very nervous, because she remembered that while she had been professing her love, wondering at its marvel, George had been silent

"What's wrong?" Heather asked, apparently noticing her worry.

"I love him, but I don't know if he loves me," Amelia whispered, shaking her head.

Heather laughed, then said, "He jumped off a building with nothing but a rope, Amie. Of course he loves you."

"You don't know him. You don't know how he thinks. He can't stand to see people hurt or in pain. He likes to think he's this apathetic, 'doesn't-concern-me' rebel, but he's not. He's the most caring man I know." Amelia buried her face in her hands as the horror of her accusations sank into her. "I can't believe I didn't understand this from the beginning. He talked about helping me because of the possibility of attorney fees, but he just needed that excuse so that he could help his clients, help the courts, even help Nathan Finnegan."

"I don't understand," her friend said, confused.

Amelia looked at her and whispered, "George doesn't love me."

"Of course he does."

"I told him, after we crashed into the window, and he never said anything."

"He had just fought a man twice his size and had a sheet of glass embedded in his body; maybe he didn't have time to write a lyrical poem on the virtues of his love for you," Heather dryly responded.

"Then why hasn't he come to see me?"

"Does he have to do everything, Amie?" Heather abruptly grabbed Amelia's shoulders and squeezed. Hard. "Life isn't always about the big Hollywood proclamation of love. You told him that you love him; he didn't run away. That's a start. And take it from someone who knows: I'd rather have a man think about it and only say it when he means it, than to hear it on the first date and every day we spend together for three years except for the one day he doesn't say it and that's when he tells you that he's leaving you for a woman named after a car."

Amelia felt the sting of her friend's words but also nodded in understanding. She squeezed Heather's hand, then straightened her shoulders and walked out of the examination room, with Heather behind her. Her parents rushed toward her from their chairs in the lounge at the end of the hall at the same time that another examination room door opened.

She held her breath when she saw Wayne walk out of the room. George followed behind him, his arm in a white cast, a pinch of pain in his expression. She was the only one who saw him, since her parents and Heather were focused on her. Amelia's attention was momentarily distracted as her parents both hugged her in a strange family hug where the two almost went into contortions to avoid touching each other. Amelia tried to disengage from their hug as she once more glanced in George's direction. He watched her. There was a strange expression on his face that wasn't quite a smile or a frown. It was a strange in-between expression that almost hinted at regret.

Before she could smile or wave at him, he lowered his head and walked away. He left.

Chapter 22

Amelia cautiously walked down the stairs of her house as she heard the voices in the kitchen. It was almost eight o'clock in the morning. She had overslept. It was probably allowable, considering the night before, but life continued. She had hearings that morning and pleadings due in court, and . . . and she had George. Or she hoped that she had George. He had walked away without a second glance in the hospital. She could have seen that as proof that he'd never wanted her, that it was all about proving the corruption, but she knew better now. George was scared: Scared of succeeding, scared of winning, but he didn't know her that well if he thought she would give up that easily. When Amelia Farrow decided to win, she didn't play fair. At least, when it came to him.

But if she wanted to battle with George, first she had to get past the dragons guarding the castle, otherwise known as her parents. Alice and Kenneth had unofficially moved into her house. They had driven her home from the hospital and spent the night, probably the first time that they had slept under the same roof in years. It also meant that they had been in each other's presence for more consecutive hours than Amelia could remember since she was a child. Naturally, her parents were on the verge of killing each other.

She entered the kitchen and whatever the two had been arguing about instantly disappeared as they both faced her with equally fake smiles. She tried hard not to laugh, but the sight of the two pretending to get along was almost enough to send her into hysterics. Maybe she was more tired than she thought. She choked back another laugh when she smelled the burnt toast.

"We fixed breakfast," Alice said with forced cheerfulness.

"We burned breakfast," Kenneth corrected with a disgusted expression. "We tried to get Lupe to come over here and cook, but she absolutely refused. She says she's scared to work here. I have no idea what she's scared of. It's not as if you're attacked every week."

"The eggs are more crispy than burnt," Alice tried again.

"Thanks. . . . Honestly, I appreciate the thought, but I don't have time," Amelia told her parents. "I'll just grab something at the courthouse cafeteria."

"You're going to work today?" Kenneth asked, amazed, taking in her suit and briefcase. "Grayson would understand if you took the day off."

"I'm not taking today off. I've already spoken to Richard this morning. Last night, the police made arrests throughout Donaldson's organization. For all of his big talk, Donaldson apparently confessed everything last night to make a deal. The DA's office has a long road ahead of it, getting the pleas and confessions of all of these people."

"Won't you be scared?" Alice whispered while clutching Amelia's hands.

"The only time I'm not scared is when I'm in a court-house."

"Some things never change," Alice said.

Amelia watched in amazement as her parents shared an almost secret smile.

"When you were a baby, sometimes I would take you with me to the courthouse to work at nights," Kenneth explained, his voice surprisingly soft.

Amelia closely examined her father, surprised by his unkempt appearance. She had never seen the top button on his shirt undone. . . . Actually, she had never seen him without a tie. Not only did he not have on a tie, but his shirt was partially unbuttoned, his pants were wrinkled, and it looked like he needed a shave. And her mother. Her mother had actually touched her father earlier at the hospital when the doctor gave Amelia the all-clear. On purpose. Alice wore not a trace of makeup, her dress was at least two seasons old, and her glorious world-famous hair was tied back in a bun. In other words, Amelia wanted to know what aliens inhabited her parents' bodies.

"It was the one place that would quiet you down," Alice continued the memories of Amelia's childhood. "Some kids fall asleep in cars or in rocking chairs, but all you needed was the smell of dirty law books and a deserted courtroom and you were out like a light."

"I don't remember," Amelia said quietly.

"You were just a baby," Kenneth mumbled, sounding almost regretful. "I would read opposing counsel's briefs to you. When you thought an argument was weak, you would cry."

"Oh, Kenneth," Alice laughed while shaking her head. "Your father insisted that you would be a legal genius before you could speak. He was right, though. You've done good for yourself, darling. We're so proud."

"I liked reading to you," Kenneth said. "I should have done more of it. Your mother and I both should have done more of a lot of things." Alice nodded, for once agreeing with her husband.

At twenty-nine years old, Amelia suddenly realized something. She didn't have perfect parents, but then again, she wasn't the perfect daughter. Still, they were her parents. And how boring it would have been to have Cliff and Claire Huxtable when she had an international supermodel for a mother and a feared federal judge for a father.

"You did good, both of you did good," she said simply. She ignored their stunned expressions and picked up her briefcase. "I have to go or I'll be late."

"What about dinner? Tonight? Just the three of us?" Alice asked, then darted a nervous glance at Kenneth and corrected herself, "Amie and I tonight and Amie and you tomorrow night?"

"Sounds good to me," Kenneth said with a nod of obvious relief that he wouldn't have to spend more time with his wife. They both stared at Amelia as her father asked, "What do you say?"

Her parents were reaching out to her. She could have pushed their efforts aside, not out of cruelty but out of the regret and the loss it would necessarily uncover from the past. But she didn't.

"I'd love to."

Kenneth cleared his throat, then grumbled, "You can invite George if you want."

"I will," she said instead of throwing her arms around him like she wanted, because even with the almost heart-to-heart talk, they were still the Farrows.

She smiled at both of her parents, then walked out of the kitchen. She heard their arguing resume before she started the car, and for some reason it made her smile at how reassuring the sound was. It was good to know that some things never changed.

George closed the file he was reading as the scent of lavender floated around him, replacing the stale and institutional odor of Judge Stants's courtroom. Along with the judge, the bailiff, the court reporter, and his client, he turned as Amelia walked into the courtroom. As she set her briefcase on the table and found whatever she looked for, George closely examined her and was satisfied that she looked healthy and well rested. He sighed in relief and even smiled when he saw the head-band holding back the soft strands of hair, because it meant things were back to normal. And normal meant that he and Amelia were on opposite sides.

"I apologize for my tardiness, Your Honor," she said.

"Considering what you've been through since I last saw you, the fact that you got yourself here is all I could ask for," Judge Stants said with a nod of acknowledgment.

"Thank you, Your Honor," she said.

"I told you two to come up with a plea in this case for our next meeting. Am I to assume that because of the circumstances of this past week, you two never had that chance?"

"That's correct, Your Honor," Amelia said, still not bothering to look at George.

It was going to happen, he realized. They would finish this case, she would give him a polite smile, and he would never see her *sans* headband, and a lot of other things, again. As his heart constricted, George realized he could not live his life like that. He had one chance to have the happiness, the family he had always dreamed about— even though he never admitted he dreamed about it.

He wanted the kids, whom he would never leave and whom he would hug at least twice a day, even when they were teenagers and wouldn't want him to. He wanted the house where he could grumble as he mowed the lawn— although he remembered Amelia's expansive lawn and he dismissed that fantasy. He even wanted his own damn dog, whom he would name Spot just for the hell of it. But most of all he wanted Amelia; he wanted to see her kiss their children good night and shove equally ridiculous headbands on their daughters' heads. And even if it all never happened, George was for once getting involved and risking it.

"In that case—"

"Your Honor, if I may address the court," George interrupted the judge. Like a good two-day Boy Scout, George had prepared himself for the scenario, but he hadn't known he would go through with it until he saw her. He glanced at Amelia and, for the first time, he saw her hands shaking. He had never seen her act nervous in a courtroom. It helped him to control his own shaking hands.

He cleared his throat, then glanced at his client, who

nodded in consent, before he said, "I've already discussed this case with Rudy Harris, and he is prepared to continue trial tomorrow morning. I believe that Your Honor knows Mr. Harris and what a fine attorney he is. My client has consented to the substitution and has signed an affidavit. I request to withdraw from this matter, effective immediately. Here is my withdrawal and substitution of counsel along with Mr. Harris's—"

Daniel O'Connor stood and interrupted George with a clearly rehearsed, "I fully support this, Your Honor." He immediately sat back down.

George hid his grin behind a cough. He had told Daniel that he may be questioned on his response to the withdrawal, but he hadn't meant that Daniel should answer the question before it was asked.

The judge looked at Daniel as if he had suddenly appeared from another planet. He appeared on the verge of speaking to Daniel, then turned to George and stuttered, "What are the reasons for your withdrawal? Is this because of this past weekend? Do you need more time to prepare for trial?"

"I . . . I'm no longer objective where Ms. Farrow is concerned, Your Honor. I feel that this lack of objectivity would interfere with my ability to adequately defend my client. In other words, it's hard to argue against a woman I care about as much as I do Ms. Farrow."

His announcement exploded like a bomb in the room. The judge sputtered, the court reporter grinned, and Amelia dropped her papers.

"What?" Amelia gasped in disbelief.

George forced himself to look at Amelia and found her staring at him. She wasn't smiling or grinning; she just stared at him. He wasn't sure if that was a good sign or a bad sign. He decided to look at the judge instead. At least, his emotions were clear. He was irritated.

"This is great," Judge Stants muttered, sounding annoyed, while the female bailiff loudly sighed in longing from the corner of the courtroom. "Off the record, Deirdre." The court reporter immediately stopped typing, then sent George an encouraging smile. He grinned in return. He needed all the encouragement he could get, since none came from Amelia. "Mr. Gibson, are you certain about this?"

"Absolutely, Your Honor. My client will not suffer. Rudy Harris is a competent attorney. He will defend Mr. O'Connor to the best of his ability, and considering that he hasn't done anything wrong, it shouldn't be a hard job—"

"Objection, Your Honor," Amelia said, coming to life. When Judge Stants looked at her, she quickly added, "To the last part about the defendant not having done anything wrong. The state contends running a truck into someone's home is very wrong." George grinned because he loved the woman, even if she did object in the middle of his proclamation of love.

Judge Stants demanded, "Am I to assume that you have no objections to the withdrawal of counsel, Ms. Farrow?"

George held his breath until he heard Amelia answer, "I have no objections."

The court reporter resumed typing and Judge Stants said while shaking his head, "Counsel's motion to withdraw is granted. We will resume tomorrow morning at nine o'clock, with the jury, and Rudy Harris representing the defendant." He glanced from George to Amelia, then muttered, "Call me a romantic, but I'll even give Mr. Harris two extra days to prepare."

He slowly rose from the bench and lumbered toward his chambers. George was surprised when his client began to shake his hand.

"We haven't won yet. You're still in trial," George told him.

"I know, but . . . good luck with her," Daniel O'Connor said with a nod in Amelia's direction. "I'm in this mess because of a woman. I don't know if she'll ever forgive me. . . . I don't know why she wouldn't, it's not like I aimed to hit Tanner, but my Molly is worth it. And even though she's trying to put me in jail, I have a feeling that your woman is, too."

Daniel patted George on the shoulder, then walked out of the courtroom. George stared across the room at Amelia as the others filed out of the courtroom, leaving them completely alone. Now that they stood alone, George wondered what he would say. From the hesitant look on Amelia's face, she wondered the same thing.

"How are you?" she asked, glancing at his cast.

"Alive," he said, with a grin he couldn't control.

She grinned, then pulled him into her arms and stood on her tiptoes to place a kiss on his neck.

She whispered against his ear, "I love you, George."

She felt his muscles tense under her hands and she looked at him. He looked frightened. More frightened than when he had walked onto the roof and faced Donaldson. She tried to move from his arms to ask what was wrong, but his arms tightened around her waist and he pulled her against him.

"I know," he said quietly. "You never would have come last night if you didn't."

"I'm sorry that I didn't believe you," she said quietly, not ashamed by the tears that filled her eyes. "This whole time, all you did was help me and protect me and make me feel safe. You got involved when you didn't have to . . . You risked your life for me, and I threw it back in your face every chance I got."

"No, you didn't. You came to that building with the disc to save my life, even though you had doubts—"

"I'm apologizing here, Gibson. It's something a Farrow doesn't have to do often, so let me finish," she said firmly. She smiled at his grave expression, then promised, "And if you give me the chance, I'll spend the rest of my life making it up to you."

He didn't smile back. Instead, he repeated uncertainly, "The rest of your life . . . That's a long time."

"That's the idea." Her smile became forced when she saw the hesitation written across his face.

"For the rest of your life?" His expression sobered as he placed a small distance between them again. "We're just so different, Amelia. You said so in the beginning. I learned from my childhood that it's best not to know what paradise is, rather than to have it, be able to touch it for a little while, and then have it ripped away."

"I'm not going anywhere, George. I promise," she said calmly.

She reached for his hand, but he actually moved out of her reach. She saw from the clench of his jaw in pain how much the quick movement cost him and she hid her smile, because no matter how hard he tried not to be, George Gibson was an honorable, admirable man. She would love spending the rest of her life telling him that.

"I don't think you understand who I really am," he tried again. "I started chasing Donaldson with you for the money it would bring me. Remember? I'm every bad thing you think of in a criminal defense attorney."

"No, you didn't. You did it for your clients, Nathan Finnegan, Anna Chin . . . I bet you even did it for Maddie and her sons."

"But our backgrounds—"

"None of that matters to me."

"It matters to me."

"Why? Is it the money, my job—"

"It's not the money. It's not that you're a district attorney."

"Then what, George? Are you scared? I'm scared, too."

"Maybe I am scared," he said with a long-suffering sigh. "Maybe all of this time, all of the jokes and laughs have been because I am scared."

She took his hand and this time he didn't pull away. He stared at her. "You don't have to be scared of me. You don't have to be scared of how happy we're going to be," she assured him.

"I trust you, Amelia," he said, a strange look settling on his face as he pulled her against his chest.

She smiled, then closed her eyes. For a man like George Gibson, trusting her was the same as loving her, because she realized something that George didn't—he only trusted those people whom he loved. She forced herself to move from his arms or risk standing in the courtroom all day with him. She tried to gather her belongings, but he wouldn't release her.

He suddenly grinned, then asked in a low voice that

made her wonder why she thought spending the whole day in the courtroom with him was a bad thing, "How exactly are you planning to make it up to me? You were pretty mean, hurt my feelings and all, accused me of working for Donaldson, accused me of wanting to tell—"

She instantly shut him up when she leaned toward him and whispered, "Anything you want, anywhere you want it, for the rest of my life."

"I think I could handle those terms," he murmured, grinning.

She smiled in return, then kissed the warm palm of his large hand. "You drive a hard bargain, Gibson."

He laughed, then said, "Amelia?"

"Yes?"

"I love you." It was a simple phrase—three words— but never had anything sounded so right, so good to her ears, as those words coming from his mouth.

Her soul rejoiced and she couldn't control the wide grin that covered her face when she saw the relief and sincerity gleaming in his eyes.

"I know," she lightly responded. "I never enter a bargaining situation unless I know the outcome."

"Me neither," he said, grinning.

"You know that I would have beat you on the O'Connor case."

"In your dreams, counselor."

"You can sit in the gallery and watch me beat Rudy, though."

She thought he would proclaim his ex-client's innocence again, but instead he said, "I just might do that."

She couldn't prevent her open smile, and he grinned in return. She knew eventually they would argue. Their lives would be a huge mess, arguing about money, his practice, her job, and his clients. Heather liked him, but Amelia didn't know if her other friends would. Her mother liked him, but she didn't know if her father would. She could feel a growing headache thinking about all the potential problems.

Then she sighed in contentment and planted a kiss on his waiting lips. She looked forward to each and every moment of it.

Turn the page for an excerpt from
Tamara Sneed's upcoming romance

All the Man I Need

Coming soon from St. Martin's Paperbacks

Lana Hargrove had spent half of her life running from men. Men who either wanted more than she was willing to give—like a second date, or a returned phone call or e-mail—or men who wanted to give her too much—like the key to their house or a kidney. But after spending five months in a self-defense class that she had initially taken because the instructor looked like a shorter, darker version of Boris Kodjoe, she had vowed never to run from a man in fear. Not that she ever had before, because Lana Hargrove was scared of no man, but she didn't want there to be a first time either, which was exactly why Lana decided to confront the man who had been following her for the last half hour on the crowded streets of the Georgetown shopping district.

Lana turned down a quiet, tree-lined street that branched off from Wisconsin, the main street in the heart of Georgetown. She hurried on her tiptoes—so that her three-inch stiletto heels didn't make noise against the pavement—to the opening of the alley. She set her three shopping bags on the ground, then waited. Sure enough, she heard the steady rhythm of footsteps on the sidewalk. It had to be the pervert.

Lana balled her right hand into a fist and patiently waited, remembering to breathe evenly and deeply. She was following her training perfectly, except for the part where she had planned this confrontation. Her self-defense instructor, Raj, who later turned out to be married with two kids and, more important, had a personality as exciting as a package of tofu, had always taught the other smitten and subsequently disappointed women in his class to avoid confrontation and to only engage "the enemy" when forced to. Lana had never liked avoiding anything.

She tensed as the footsteps grew nearer, then as she was about to jump out and attack, a short white man walked past her, yelling into his cell phone. Lana stared past the man, confused. There was no one else on the sidewalk. Where was the tall black man in the baseball cap and sunglasses? Lana had been certain that there had been a tall black man, with impossibly broad shoulders, following her. Men usually followed her because she was an attractive black woman in Washington, D.C., where black men followed any black woman as if she held the Holy Grail. The following thing didn't bother her. It was the fact that the man never made his move. He just followed her. The lurking stalkers she didn't like, the open and obvious stalkers she could deal with.

Lana was so preoccupied with her disappointment that she wouldn't be able to kick some pervert's butt today, that she didn't notice the man with the baseball cap and sunglasses until he stood almost in her face. Her instincts took over. She grabbed his hand and tugged and pulled with a warrior yell that would have made Raj proud. The man flipped over like a Hollywood stuntman and landed in the middle of the sidewalk with a loud groan that made Lana smile in satisfaction.

She placed one thin heel squarely in the middle of his chest and stared down at him, feeling mildly triumphant, even though common sense told her to just run. Unfortunately, a lack of common sense was one of the traits she would actually admit that she had inherited from her father.

"Why are you following me?" Lana asked coolly, as if she had all the time in the world.

Then she noticed his face, which was fully visible since his cap and glasses had flown off during the fall. The majority of his face was chocolate-brown perfection, a perfect nose and full lips, almond-shaped eyes, and eyebrows as dark as midnight and silky smooth. But then there was the left side of his face, which was very far from perfection. It was as if one half of his face had melted and the tangled, scarred tissue had frozen to preserve the injustice of it in comparison to the majority of his dark, unblemished skin. Only a small portion of his face was horribly scarred, but it was enough to draw her attention and enough horror and sympathy flowed through her body to make her take her foot off his chest.

The man took the opportunity that her obvious shock provided and pushed her off him and scrambled to his feet. She almost lost her balance but remained on her feet just in time for him to grab her shoulders and slam her into the brick wall behind her, hard enough for her to wince in pain and berate herself for feeling sympathy for him. His hands were hard on her shoulders as he pinned her to the wall. It was a strange time to notice, but she saw how dark and intense his eyes were. If his hands hadn't been digging into her shoulders at that moment, she would have thought that he was as easily manipulated as most men she had met.

"Are you scared, Lana?" he demanded in a husky voice, as his mouth hovered inches from hers.